Song for Katya

Song for Katya

Kevin Stevens

W F HOWES LTD

This large print edition published in 2006 by
W F Howes Ltd
Unit 4, Rearsby Business Park, Gaddesby Lane,
Rearsby, Leicester LE7 4YH

1 3 5 7 9 10 8 6 4 2

First published in 2005
by Pocket Books

A CIP catalogue record for this book is available
from the British Library

X000 000 020 5640

ISBN 1 84505 928 X

Typeset by Palimpsest Book Production Limited,
Polmont, Stirlingshire
Printed and bound in Great Britain
by Antony Rowe Ltd, Chippenham, Wilts.

For Janice, Christian, Alice and Andrew

ACKNOWLEDGEMENTS

My thanks to the following, who read this novel at various stages of its life and offered invaluable advice and encouragement: Janice Stevens, Treasa Coady, Mary Kate Halpin, Jason Sommer, Michael Tallon, Penny Harris and Hazel Orme.

'I have always preferred playing without an audience', Bill Evans

DETOUR AHEAD

CHAPTER 1

A month or so before his eighteenth birthday, Drew Fisher threw a change of clothes and a scuffed folder of piano transcriptions into his duffel bag and hitchhiked from Boston to New York City. He had been east less than a week, out from Montana for a final look at the New England Conservatory, where his parents hoped he would land a full-ride scholarship for the fall. It was mid-June, hot, humid and windless. Kennedy had just returned from Vienna, shaken by Khrushchev's bullying and threats of tanks rolling into Berlin.

In Boston Drew stayed with his grandmother, in the sprawling Queen Anne house his mother had grown up in and still spoke of with affection. He found it dark and stilted, with pre-Raphaelite prints on the walls and crocheted antimacassars on the faded furniture. An out-of-tune Knabe grand sat in the parlour, with plaster-of-paris busts of the great composers lined up along the lid. Each morning Drew played jazz for an hour while his grandmother was at mass, which only reminded him of the true purpose of his odyssey. The day after the Conservatory interview, he packed his bag, left his grandma a note, and headed for the turnpike.

For a buck and a half a night, he took a room in a flop-house on Seventh Avenue South, the kind of place Welfare sent the tough cases. Daytimes, he wandered into midtown to admire the Steinways at the Klavierhaus or escape the heat with a movie at Times Square. He ate on the cheap in Broadway luncheonettes. By five each evening he was back in his cell-like digs, smoking a Kool in his undershirt and studying his smudged transcriptions, spread like war plans across the lumpy mattress. At the foot of the bed a tiny barred window revealed why the cramped, stuffy room was more valuable to him than a suite at the Plaza. Across Seventh, wedged between Rivoli's Pizza and a beauty salon offering a manicure-pedicure combo for five bucks, was his Mecca: the brick façade and red marquee of the Village Vanguard.

There were a lot of great jazz clubs in Greenwich Village in 1961, but that June only one was featuring Bill Evans. Drew spent all three nights he could afford in the dark basement of the Vanguard, listening reverently to the man whose playing had convinced him that jazz could be as delicately expressive as Chopin. Two years earlier, when he'd first heard the haunting chords of 'Blue in Green', Drew had known he must play jazz piano. The man had that kind of effect. Since then he'd collected every Bill Evans recording he could find. He'd tracked his tours and residencies, transcribed the piano solos from *Kind of Blue*, and saved every penny he could from summer jobs and dance gigs as he had moved towards this week when, in the best club in the jazz capital of the world, he would see his hero playing live. Heady stuff for a kid from the sticks who wasn't even old enough to buy a beer.

Armed with a fake ID, Drew was first in line for tickets each day, and sat at the table closest to the band on Friday and Saturday nights, nursing a Coke and hanging on every note. Evans started a number upright, shoulders lifted, cigarette between his lips, his face gaunt and pale in the low house-lights. As the tune progressed, he hunched into the keyboard, as if drawn by the delicate intensity of its tone. By the end of the piece his face nearly touched his hands and the slick curve of his dark hair moved in and out of the light as his fingers caressed the keys or let those famous silences resonate. The sound lifted Drew's spirit to an almost sacred ecstasy.

Evans enhanced the mystique with his demeanour. He never spoke, either to his bandmates or the audience. After a tune, he lit a cigarette and wiped his brow with a white handkerchief, staring through black horn-rims at the red velvet curtains behind the stage. The drummer and bassist, dressed like their leader in dark suits and thin black ties, played without reference to sheet music or visual cues. Tunes were not even counted off. Yet the band, in a way Drew had only ever imagined, played with a single voice. Between sets, Evans rose slowly from the forty-year-old Steinway and disappeared backstage without a nod or a smile. Workmanlike and aloof on the surface, but what passion beneath! Each evening Drew went back to his room in a fever, the sloping sidewalks and rough brick of the Village swirling around him, all light, shade and shimmer like an Evans ballad.

On Sunday night Drew was asked to share his table with engineers from Riverside Records, who set up their microphones and two-track recorder directly in front of the bandstand. They captured the musicians in superior form, as well as Drew's shouts of appreciation and prolonged applause. He was closer to the mikes than the musicians were. And when these recordings were released the following year, Drew bought the LPs, played them constantly in the years that followed, and swore to anyone who would listen that he could hear his own voice in the background, above the tinkle of glasses. It was, he liked to say, his first recording.

Twenty years later, as he sat in the curtained rear seat of a black Volga sedan, slooping along the salted, snow-packed highway from the new airport at Sheremetyevo to the frozen heart of Moscow, phrases from those Vanguard sets were in his mind. It was many years since he had played the records, but he could no more forget the tunes than he could his parents' voices. As the Russian winter blurred past the frosted window, he listened in his head to the opening notes of 'My Foolish Heart' and marvelled once more at the *naïveté* of that seventeen-year-old, with his pack of Kools and glass of Coca-Cola, breathless with admiration but without an inkling of the darkness behind the notes. As if the hollow cheeks and backstage visits were simply part of the hip image. As if the yearning in those phrases was nothing more than God-given talent, without reference to circumstance.

When the chance to visit Russia had come along, Drew jumped at it. It had been a bad year: problems he'd thought solved had resurfaced. Getting away from the States would be good for him, he could sense it. Of Russian descent, Evans himself had tried twice to visit Moscow and both times was denied a visa because of his drug addiction. Now, like others Drew had loved, he was gone. Two months ago Drew had stood at his grave in Baton Rouge and promised a requiem. He would come to Russia and find a song for Evans and others he had lost. And for himself.

The day was overcast and dusky. The white birches beckoned from the side of the road like lonely girls. Behind them firs were laden with crusted snow. Steam rose from twisted pipes, and amber streetlights, already lit in early afternoon, gave the snow a subterranean glow. Here were depths of cold he had not known since boyhood Montana. Cold that hurt your face and froze your spit before it reached the ground. Walking from the arrivals terminal to the parking lot, loading the instruments into the Dodge van laid on by the embassy, he'd had plenty of time to be reminded. Salim, wearing nothing but a cloth coat over his *dashiki*, couldn't believe it – there was nothing like this in Oakland. But something else was lurking beneath the chill, something Drew hadn't known in Montana: a density, a graininess, a film of dust and despair.

Salim sat beside him, his wide nostrils taking in the stale air of the car heater and the reek of diesel fumes. 'Some shit, boys. Some *cold* shit. Yoshi, my man, you get this deep freeze in Tokyo?'

Yoshi, sitting shotgun, shook his head. The heater roared and the wipers scraped dry snow from the windshield. Maxim, their chauffeur, whistled between his teeth and eyed Salim's broad face suspiciously in the rear-view mirror. The Volga swept through the resin glow of the highway, hugging the treacherous road impressively. They passed within the city limits and crossed the Moscow river, dotted with ice-fishing huts. Ahead Drew could see the distinctive square tail-lights of the embassy's Lincoln. As bandleader, Marshall got the luxury vehicle. The instrument-laden Dodge completed the caravanserai.

As they approached the city centre, traffic slowed. The temperature display at the central post office flashed minus thirty – Celsius, Yoshi reminded them. The sky was low and colourless. Then, as if in a dream, the Kremlin rose up, solid, baroque, pristine, its towers topped by bright red stars that glowed in the frigid air. Beside it the onion domes of St Basil's, swirling, multi-coloured and lit from beneath. They slid to a stop. 'Hotel,' Maxim said, with a jerk of his thumb, and they piled out. Salim and Yoshi streaked up the steps, but Drew paused, eyes fixed on the marvels across the square. After the drab ride from the airport, the domes and spires had an incandescence that seemed unreal.

Maxim backed the Volga, tyres spinning, into a parking bay. Drew wiped his nose and rubbed his cheeks. He had imagined this moment. He had expected, with uncharacteristic ingenuousness, something like the swelling excitement of his first visit to New York – a burst of Rachmaninov, echoes of history. But there was no spark, nothing but the deadening cold of the Russian winter.

Without fanfare another Evans melody flowed into his mind: the soft, falling opening of 'Some Other Time'. Two chords, repeated by piano and bass, carrying across two decades. It was a simple song, resonant with heartache and uncertainty. Five thousand miles from last night's bed, Drew felt familiar ghosts gathering in the darkness: temptation, loneliness, death. Evans dead four months to the day. His mother a year ago in February. And Jessie.

He made his way up the frozen hotel steps, asking himself why he could never have what he truly wished for, and what he did get he was bound to lose.

CHAPTER 2

Katya held the red silk dress, still on its hanger, against herself. 'This one?'

Cross-legged on the sofa in her pyjamas, Anna frowned.

'Or this?' Katya said, holding aloft a chocolate-coloured poplin gown that she knew was too tight across her hips.

Her daughter pretended to weigh the choices. They both knew that the red dress was right for the party, but the ritual of analysis was too enjoyable to abandon just yet. 'Try it on,' she said.

'Which?'

'The red.' Twelve last November, Anna had lately exchanged the chatter of childhood for longish periods of reflection. She had grown more discriminating and attentive. Although her son was a year older, Katya turned to Anna for adult conversation.

She sashayed across the room. 'Yes?'

'Yes.' Anna laughed. 'I think so.'

'With the black shoes?'

'And your long necklace!'

Katya stopped in front of the bay window and looked outside for Sasha, who was walking the dogs. Fresh snowfall covered the broad stretch of lawn between the building and the birch-lined private road. For the first time in her life she had space: a five-room flat, with a living room that did not double as a bedroom, and a garden. Security and comfort for her children and her grandmother. She had been remarried for six months and continued to adjust, but she did not have to look far to see what her new husband – cosmonaut, Red Army colonel, Hero of the Soviet Union – had brought to her life.

'What time does the party start, Mama?'

'Eight o'clock.'

Anna stretched her legs and stood up. She came over and put her head on her mother's shoulder, her arms round her waist. 'And do we have to . . . ?'

'Anna, please. We have already agreed.'

'She's a witch.'

'Anna!'

'Ask Sasha. It's true.'

Tonight her children were to stay with her mother-in-law, Ariadne, who lived on the opposite side of the Star City complex. They didn't like her and Katya couldn't blame them. But they had to go. Her husband was in Kazakhstan, and Katya's grandmother herself, frail and nearly blind, needed looking after.

'Last week,' Anna said, clutching her mother,

'she told us we were spoiled because we wouldn't eat her *kasha*.'

'*I* wouldn't eat her *kasha*.'

'See, Mama? You *do* agree. She *is* a witch. An ugly one.'

'I don't agree with *that*. And, besides, there is no discussion. I have work to do and you have to stay with Ariadne – tonight, next Wednesday, and the week I am away. It is all arranged.'

Anna pushed her away, petulant. 'Work? Is that what you call going to a party in your fancy dress and high heels?'

The front door opened and the sound of barking filled the flat. Katya stepped into the hallway. 'Sasha,' she hissed, 'keep the animals quiet. Your grandmother is sleeping.'

The dogs slid and scrabbled on the parquet floor as Sasha herded them into his bedroom. Katya checked the hall clock. Ten a.m. Her grandmother would emerge soon from the back room, tetchy, expecting tea and yogurt.

Sasha padded into the living room in his socks. His cheeks were flushed after the walk and his hair unruly. Katya patted down a few stray strands and he pushed away her hand.

'Is it still cold?' she asked him.

'Yes, but no wind. And the roads, Mama, all snowploughed and salted.'

In Star City the usual Soviet inefficiencies were diminished: hot water was always available; grounds were maintained; no potholes marred the roads. The perks made Katya uneasy, but the kids marvelled at the new world their mother's marriage had opened up for them.

Anna was still sulking. 'Why are you abandoning us?'

'She's not abandoning us,' Sasha said. 'She's working.'

'Thank you, Sasha.'

'Working with the enemy.'

'Excuse me! With American musicians, who are our guests.'

Sasha's eyes sparkled. 'Actually, it is Ariadne who is the enemy.' He puffed out his cheeks and made horns on his head with his forefingers.

Anna cackled. She put her hands under her pyjama top and bunched her fists to conjure up Ariadne's ponderous bosom. Then she stuck out her lower lip and lurched across the room, hips swaying. It was a faultless impression and Sasha laughed so hard that the dogs started barking again.

'Anna, Sasha, please. That's enough!' But Katya could not suppress a smile, and soon all three were on the sofa, leaning into each other with laughter. Her children were her friends, soulmates, confidants, she thought. She would do anything for them.

She had done much already. Marrying Ilya had not been an easy decision. He was nearly fifty-one, seventeen years her senior, and had brought with him a meddling mother and an intense commitment to his job. There was as much pressure as privilege in being a cosmonaut. He was on the Soyuz T-4 back-up crew, launch date 13 March, a Friday. Their bedroom had a queen-sized bed, flown in from West Germany, but most nights Katya slept alone while Ilya tossed in a cramped bunk in a barracks in Kazakhstan. She saw him for twenty-four hours every other week. If he made the flight, he would spin in space for several months, doing repair work and preventive maintenance on the Salyut-6 space station while she watched ballet on the new Sony and took his neutered Dalmatians for long walks in the snow.

It was a secure life for Katya and her family. But some mornings when she woke she had forgotten where she was, what name she had assumed. Timoshenko: the name was as solid as a Ukrainian peasant. Decent, like Ilya, the star-gazer who remained earthbound and offered little in the way of passion. A man married to his mission. A man her former colleagues at the institute would have lampooned: the barrel chest slightly puffed, the medals gleaming, the set of his cap and line of his jaw evoking patriotism and loyalty. And why not, with all that they had brought him in status, exclusivity, imported luxury and the hand of an intelligent and accomplished woman?

'Sasha, get the ironing-board for me. And, Anna, please get dressed. Babushka will be up soon.'

Anna left the room while Sasha did as she had asked and flashed his mother one of his charming,

14

bright-eyed smiles. She and Anna might have their spats but he was always good-natured.

And he seemed to like his stepfather. They talked about rockets: Proton 4s, Cosmos B1s, R7 Vostocks, fuselage diameters and total thrust. The race against the Americans. Sasha was a science buff and loved examining the souvenirs of Ilya's career. From above the television his official cosmonaut photograph surveyed the room with Soviet gravitas, his decorations and Red Army citations ranged alongside it. A framed letter from Brezhnev congratulated him on his bravery during his Soyuz-18 command in 1975, for which he had received the Order of Lenin.

His image gazed down on Katya now as she ironed the silk dress. Sasha liked him, but he hardly knew him. Neither did Katya: in six months of marriage they had spent no more than a dozen nights together. Ilya's photograph was more familiar to her than he was.

Sasha listened to the radio. Anna tidied her room. Their Saturday-morning routine continued, enlivened for Katya by the prospect of the party tonight at the Moscow Hotel and the knowledge that she was working again.

For reasons of protocol and internal security, marrying Ilya had obliged her to give up her lectureship at the Institute of International Relations. Suddenly she had nothing to do. The summer had been all right – during the school holidays she and the children had had the new world of cosmonaut privilege to explore: the splendid *dacha* at Zhukovka, the special shops with Italian shoes and English toys, the new black Chaika with the chauffeur to ferry them between Star City, Moscow and the country. But once Anna and Sasha were back at school Katya grew bored. She missed the buzz that had surrounded her old home in Leninsky Street. She missed teaching. And she missed company. Apart from her grandmother and her mother-in-law, she knew no one in the complex and had nothing to do but rattle about in the spacious flat, shop for food and visit the badly stocked library.

Then, in December, Leonid Petrosian, chairman of the Soviet-American Cultural Exchange, had telephoned. In recent years frosty relations between the superpowers had curtailed the organisation's activities, and Leonid had let go most of his staff. But a visit by a New York jazz band had been approved for January and he needed help. Jazz was a special interest of his. Would Katya help him run the three-week tour? Many years ago, after the break-up with her first husband, she had managed several such visits for the Exchange during the summer. Her English and administrative skills were excellent. Leonid, she knew, could be unpleasantly lecherous, but she could manage him – and the opportunity was too good to refuse. It was a chance to be busy and productive, if only for three weeks. And though Ilya wasn't happy about it, he couldn't complain – he was never around.

She heard her grandmother shuffle into the kitchen and attempt to light the stove. She folded the ironing-board and followed her in. '*Babushka, shto delaesh?*'

A simple Polish gas stove – was that too much to ask for instead of this German monstrosity, with its confusing dials and unnecessary features? Her grandmother's eyes were weary: why, at her age, after all she had suffered, must she relearn how to boil water?

'I'll do it.' Katya filled the kettle and lit the ring. Her grandmother had moved to Star City from Katya's parents' *dacha* at the end of the summer, when they returned to their diplomatic station in Ethiopia. She'd had four months to adjust, but it wasn't enough.

'The dogs were yapping. All night they were yapping, and the snow ploughs made an awful rumble.'

'It is quieter than Leninsky, Babushka. And the dogs are well behaved.'

'Did you buy my yogurt?'

'This morning.'

Babushka peered into the oversized Zanussi refrigerator as if it was a crypt. 'Half a litre?'

'I'll get more.'

'Send Sasha.'

'He's busy.'

'Listening to the radio is busy?'

Katya returned to the living room. Her grand-mother followed and stood at the door. Sasha got up and kissed his great-grandmother. 'Good morning, Babushka.'

She was looking past him, at the dress draped over the back of the sofa. Even though her eyesight was failing, she could see clearly when she wanted to. 'You're going out?' she asked Katya.

'Sasha, go and make your bed.'

'But, Mama—'

'Take the radio with you.'

Katya lifted the dress off the chair and hung it from the curtain rail. The snow outside was so bright that the silk glowed red against the living-room wall. When Sasha had gone, she said, 'I'm going out tonight, Babushka. As I told you.'

'With the Americans.'

'It is work. My work.'

'A red silk dress for work?'

'Our national colour,' Katya said flatly.

Her grandmother was slow and shrivelled, but she exuded an unmistakable authority. Her son, Katya's father, had moved in its shadow all his life. 'This is not a good time to be associating with Americans,' she said.

'Has it ever been?'

The old woman slid into the room. 'If it goes well, there is no benefit. No one wishes to draw attention to good relations with a country that boycotts our people. And if it goes poorly . . .' She shrugged. It was a scathing reminder of wintry Russian realities.

'This tour is not political,' Katya said.

Her grandmother's eyes wavered, but her voice was sharp. 'Everything is political.'

How could Katya argue with a woman who had waited three years for news of her husband, turning up at the gates of the Lubyanka each month with a ten-kilogram parcel, only to be arrested herself in 1939 and sent to Karaganda for twenty-eight months? She had been the wife of an enemy of the people. Her fourteen-year-old son was left in Moscow to fend for himself. A musician and dancer, *protégée* of Anna Pavlova, she had stood in a cattle car for three days and nights, marched twenty-five miles to the camp complex, leaned against barbed wire in freezing rain for five hours while camp officers drank vodka and watched patriotic films. Released without explanation on the eve of Operation Barbarossa, she had returned to Moscow and her son in time for the privations of war and the tragic discovery that her husband had been shot dead on the night of his arrest in 1936.

'I've made soup,' Katya said.

'The stove.'

'It's borscht – you can eat it cold.'

'I'll have the yogurt.'

'Eat the soup. Please, you need it.'

'I need you to look after me. No – that's not right. I need to know you're not doing anything foolish.'

The kettle whistled. Katya went into the kitchen and prepared a pot of English breakfast tea. Babushka trailed behind her.

'Tanya will be here tonight,' Katya said, 'and on Wednesday. I will be home early.' Tanya was a local woman who occasionally kept Babushka company when Katya was not around.

'Tanya is a buffoon.'

Katya poured the tea and did not reply.

'Next week?' Babushka persisted.

Next week Katya would be travelling with the Cultural Exchange to Leningrad. She had not mentioned it yet, had avoided thinking about it in case it did not happen. Babushka had her hands round the teacup. The skin was like paper, the nails ridged and purple.

This time it was Katya who shrugged. 'Next week is next week.'

CHAPTER 3

'*W*here?'

As always, a baritone flourish, a flash of irony.

'Russia.'

Silence at the other end of the line. Drew's father would be standing in the draughty, raftered hall, stooped and swaying.

'We've been invited by—'

'The Soviet Union. You mean you're going to the Soviet Union.'

'Well, yeah.'

'They're allowing you?'

'Like I said, they invited us.'

'Not the *Russians*. The State Department.'

'This isn't the fifties, Dad.'

'No, it's the eighties. It's worse. Reagan's going to make the McCarthy hearings look like a kangaroo court. And don't forget whose son you are.'

As if he could.

His dad's voice hissed in the receiver, picking up sibilance on its lonely journey across the Great Plains; 'I thought you said *Montana* was too cold. And too far.'

'It is.'

His dad snorted. 'Fine, Drew. You can fly behind the Iron Curtain but you can't visit your old man.'

An old weariness descended. Drew examined the torn edges of his fingernails and thought about the escape forbidden him. How good it would be to get high. 'When I'm back, maybe I'll . . . maybe . . .'

But there was no point in continuing. His father had retreated into the silence that was his hallmark. After thirty years of isolation, he cultivated his grudges like he drank his Scotch – copiously, recklessly. His wife was dead, his reputation had been restored too late to matter, and his only child was at a distance in every sense.

'I'll call you when I'm back, Dad.'

'I'm not going anywhere.'

The line had clicked dead, and Drew saw him sloping into the kitchen, opening the scratched pine cabinet and taking out the bottle of Ballantine's. Another betrayal, another drink.

Although his father's words had been spoken many weeks ago, they lay fresh in Drew's ear now. John Fisher defined himself not just by what he had done but by what history had denied him. China had been his – the whole of Asia, even. Russia was what might have been. On his first morning outside the United States in twenty-five years Drew recalled his family's last days overseas, his father's rage and his mother's tears.

He had slept poorly in his overheated hotel

room. This morning the temperature was twenty-five below and the Volga's heater wasn't working properly, so the band had arrived at the embassy on Novinsky Boulevard stiff and cold. A Marine military policeman led them inside. Marshall was irritable. Well groomed, as always, but the effects of jet-lag were evident in the hint of weariness beneath his eyes and his repeated throat-clearing. Salim, hulking and impassive, was glancing around suspiciously.

Yoshi, thin as bamboo, slapped his cold arms against his sides and grimaced. 'Good to be back home,' he said. It was a twist on a standard Yoshi joke about Japanese restaurants. Nobody laughed, but he was right. After the gloomy hotel and the tumbledown streets, the place was disconcertingly familiar. Drew took it all in with his father's eyes: the ash panelling, the government-issue furniture, the grey carpets and strip lighting. The wide bright ties and short-sleeved polyester shirts. The vending machines spangled with brand names. Every detail exact and yet weirdly out of context. Everything clean in an American way: not scrubbed and polished, just not allowed to grow old. There was always more where that came from in the country where everything was disposable. Including people.

'Here you are, gentlemen. This'll take the chill off.' The MP handed them Styrofoam cups of hot coffee. He was a handsome, long-boned kid with almond eyes and an easy smile. He moved, in his

23

full-dress uniform, with the over-precision of a man who had chaos in his background. Sure enough, he turned out to be from the same East Oakland neighbourhood as Salim.

'One week to go,' Salim said brightly.

'You got that.'

'Men in black gonna kick those sorry Eagle asses or what?'

'Most *definitely*.'

Beneath the buckles and brass the kid got loose-limbed and down-home as the two men savoured the prospects for their hometown team.

Drew waited for Marshall's pronouncement: tiredness tended to emphasize his arrogance and raise his opinions.

'The Raiders are good,' Marshall said, 'but wild-card teams don't win the Super Bowl.'

'As a rule, I'd have to agree with you,' Salim said, 'but this is a team that *breaks* the rules. Am I right, Sergeant, or am I right?'

The MP smiled uneasily. He wasn't a sergeant, and he wasn't used to contradicting men in authority. And Marshall, alert, controlled, imposing, with a military-style moustache, crescents of grey round his ears, and a tailored camel-hair overcoat, was clearly in charge here. He also had a musician's command of silence, and used it now to bend the tone of the moment in his direction. He sipped his coffee and set a big hand on the MP's shoulder. 'I believe we have an appointment, son.'

The kid all but saluted as he left the room.

Salim raised his eyebrows but said nothing.

Marshall was not in a good mood: he did not like being here. Opening their tour at the embassy was one thing – a gig was a gig, and he saw himself as an ambassador of jazz – but being hauled in by bureaucrats for a pep talk rankled, no matter how much he pretended it did not. He sniffed, nostrils flaring, then coughed into his hand.

This tour was important to him. In 1971 illness had caused him to miss a visit to Moscow with the Duke Ellington Orchestra, which had since been a talking-point among the musicians who had gone. It, too, had been arranged by the Soviet-American Cultural Exchange, and a couple of years ago he had struck up a cordial correspondence with Leonid Petrosian. An invitation looked certain until politics interfered – Afghanistan and Iran – and cultural visits dried up in both directions. Then, out of the blue last November, Petrosian had cabled: 'You must come in January.' It appeared that he had a patron in the Politburo, but the window of opportunity was narrow.

Marshall had applied to the Soviet consulate for visas and notified the State Department. A week later State was in touch, happy to 'support' the tour, but the band must play its first engagement at the US Embassy and conclude with a concert at Spaso House, the residence of the American ambassador. There would also be a mandatory briefing by political officers. That, as Drew had explained to Salim on the way over, meant the CIA. His upbringing had taught him a few things.

The MP returned and led them to an office at the rear of the building. Two men, one black, one white, both with cropped hair and pin-striped suits, welcomed them coolly. As they hung up their coats Salim whispered to Drew: 'Check it out: black Brad and white Brad.'

An old feeling settled on Drew: as if he had crank in his pocket and a cop was nearby.

They all sat. The white officer led the spiel. 'Welcome, gentlemen. My name's Mike Ahern and this is Rick Washington. We're very pleased you can join us here. And we want you to have a safe and successful stay in the Soviet Union. What we do is, with all visitors, take you through a type of orientation, a brief overview, so to speak, of issues that, as American citizens, you should be aware of.'

Ahern had a drained Irish complexion, hair prematurely grey, and wide, muscular shoulders. A guy who worked out daily in the compound gym, benching his body weight as he plotted escapades essential to the national interest. He had a sandy moustache and pink hands. When his eyes weren't straying to Drew, he looked at Marshall, who sat back in a plastic swivel chair, legs crossed.

'We've encouraged jazz groups to visit here in the past. It's a unique American art form.' The sentence hung in the air like a fluffed note.

'The new administration appreciates jazz.' Washington took over. 'I'm sure you know that the Woody Herman Orchestra is playing this week in Washington at the inaugural ball.'

'That a fact?' Salim said, hunching forward, sucking his teeth. Washington looked him over. He, too, was muscular, stuffed into pinstripes and oxfords. Slow gestures, casual gait, but a body like iron. His eyes were softer than his colleague's.

Ahern shifted gear. 'Of course, this isn't the best time for a visit. We don't have to tell you about current tensions.' The bullshit over, he now spoke as if he was addressing an audience at the back of the room, or beyond. 'The war in Afghanistan. The Olympic boycott. The hostages in Iran. Thank God our folks are coming home this week.'

Marshall sat up, let his elbows rest on his knees. 'What do the hostages in Iran have to do with our visit?'

'Sir,' Washington said, 'we're not here to talk politics.'

'What *are* we talking about then?'

'All we're saying is that this is not like visiting Western Europe or Japan' – he nodded at Yoshi – 'or even a place like Hungary. There are special conditions, and it's important for us all to act with caution. We have guidelines.'

Salim grimaced and shook his head. 'Ah, the rules, man. I could smell the rules coming!'

'Salim,' Marshall said quietly, 'are you going to let these men do their job?'

'Hey. All ears.'

Washington had the Rhodes scholar look: intelligent, athletic, and self-important. Proud to serve, but only as one of the best. Everyone said so. 'Outside of this building,' he said, 'you'll be followed everywhere. Watched twenty-four hours a day.'

'Didn't know you guys were so vigilant,' Salim said.

'Don't get me wrong. We'd like to be. But we don't have the budget. The KGB does, though, and they'll be at your elbow every second. At your performances. On the streets. When you sightsee. In your beds.'

Ahern had spooked Drew from the moment they walked in, but Washington, he sensed, was a reasonable guy who understood that he was not talking to a bunch of tourists from Iowa. The problem was, he was the kind of black man Salim hated: establishment, suburban, deracinated, as Salim would see it. They were polar opposites, and the air between them bristled with hostility.

'We mandate sticking closely to your schedules and routines,' Ahern said, 'avoiding unnecessary contact with anyone not officially designated to assist you, keeping in close touch with the embassy at all times.'

'Are you worried they're going to recruit us?' Marshall said. It was more a statement than a question.

Ahern pondered the comment. 'You're missing

28

the point here, Mr Powell. It's not them we're concerned about. It's *you*. It's our duty to protect you.'

'I've been protecting myself pretty well for sixty-six years, Mr Ahern. As for surveillance and attempts at controlling my behaviour, I really don't think there's anything they could do to us here that I didn't experience playing barn-dances in Oklahoma in 1934. Or serving with my regiment – my all-black regiment – in the South Pacific. I've only been in this country a day, but so far we've encountered nothing but graciousness.' Marshall stood up and pulled at his cuffs.

Ahern also got to his feet. 'All the same, sir, we recommend keeping in regular contact with the consulate and strongly advise that you do not fraternize with Russians.'

Marshall smiled. 'We're their guests,' he said.

'There will be those within the group you're dealing with who may attempt an entrapment of some sort. In whose interest it would be to create a scandal.'

Marshall looked puzzled. 'How so?'

'There might be offers of sex,' Ahern said. 'Or drugs.'

A shiver of apprehension flowed through Drew. Now he saw. This guy had *files*. On his dad, on him. How could it be otherwise? His chest felt tight and a prickling heat spread across his face.

Salim glanced at him, then returned his attention to Ahern. 'What kind of shit is this?' he said.

Marshall took his coat from the rack. 'There's no drug use in this band.'

'Any Russian you talk to would deny it,' Ahern said, 'but there's a big drug problem here. Soldiers mostly. They get hooked in Afghanistan and bring the habit home with them.'

'And they're going to tie us down and shoot us up?' Salim said. He turned to Marshall. 'We have to listen to this jive?'

Ahern cleared his throat. He had zeroed in on Drew. I'm after you, his eyes said. You may get away from me now, but I'm after you. Drew began to sweat beneath the fluorescent lights.

But he was no match for Marshall. 'Gentlemen,' he said to the officers, 'we are guests of the Soviet-American Cultural Exchange. We do not need and do not want your supervision. We know how to conduct ourselves. There will be no drug use or inappropriate sexual behaviour by my band members, no matter what is on offer. Is that clear? We are representatives of the United States of America and we are here to spread the gospel of jazz. That is what we do.' He raised a hand. 'Come and listen,' he said. 'Listen and learn.' Silence for two beats, a concluding sweep of his hand. Performance over. He left the room and the other musicians followed. Ahern watched Drew all the way out.

Salim paced Drew's hotel room like a jaguar. Ten storeys below, black limousines sped across Red

Square through fresh snow. Drew leaned against the window, allowed the glass to cool his forehead.

'He knows.'

'Who?'

'Ahern.'

'He don't know shit.'

'Salim, this is a world I'm familiar with, believe me. Guys like him are paid to turn over every stone.'

Salim stuck a finger in his face. 'Welcome to the street. His trip is control, dig? So he knows. Nothing he'd like better than to see you back on the needle because stoned is safe. From his perspective. It gives *him* the power.'

'What are you saying?'

'Saying stick with the programme and you cool. Got nothing to worry about.'

Nothing to worry about. When he was high Drew had never worried – about his father's anger, his mother's pain or Jessie's suffering.

Salim resumed his pacing. 'Just another brother in lockdown,' he said.

'Ahern?'

'Black Brad.'

'You're worrying about the wrong man, Salim. Washington is OK. He's doing his job but he's not looking to string somebody up.'

'Bullshit. They bring him along to us so we don't think it's a race thing. But it *is*. He's one these brothers looking to *e*-rase. Doin' his thing all Ivy League and network television – you know what I'm talking about?'

'You always think it's a race thing.'

'Always is, my man. Where you been living? Ask Yoshi. They see him, they see yes-yes-ah-so, or slit-eyed and super-pissed. Jap Uncle Tom or screaming kamikaze. Like in California, during the war? They round up decent American citizens and stick their sorry asses in a concentration camp. Why? Yellow skin and slanty eyes, don't you doubt it. Don't ever hear about no German-Americans bein' rounded up back then.'

'Plenty of white people were discriminated against.'

Salim snorted. 'They round up Germans, they have to close down Cincinnati. Watts they close down. Hiroshima they close down. They don't close down no *Cincinnati*.'

Salim argued liked he drummed: fierce, in your face. Too much sound for some, too much hiss and slur, but fast, full and driving. Rolls and rimshots that careened and urged. Plenty of hi-hat round the beat. Drew encouraged those ranting analyses. They swung. They entertained. Most of all, they helped him distance his despair. Their exchanges had developed between sessions, after hours, during long afternoons on the road, and paralleled an onstage closeness. Yoshi, though his English wasn't that great, was allowed in. It was a rhythm-section thing, a rank-and-file gig. When the leader was around they kept the conversation neutral and low-key.

But this time Salim was missing the signals. He

32

was too hung up on black politics to see the obvious. Ahern *knew*. And knew that Drew knew he knew. Locked down, in Salim's phrase, by politics and attitude but in control of prisons for those he didn't trust. And he didn't trust Drew. Ahern would infect Drew with his paranoia.

Salim put a hand on his shoulder. 'Hey,' he said. 'Be cool. We got a party to go to.'

The tour's opening reception was at the Moscow Hotel that evening, just across Red Square. Embassy personnel, Marshall had assured them, were not invited.

'I could use a drink,' Drew said. He stepped away from the window. 'God, it looks cold out there.'

'Weatherman says it's warming up.'

'How do you know? You speak Russian?'

Salim grinned. 'Maybe I do, my man. Maybe I do.'

CHAPTER 4

What would they be like?

Leonid had cautioned her. 'These are jazzmen, Katya. A breed apart.'

'Americans are a breed apart.'

His dark eyes smiled. 'Within America they are different. Jazz is its own country.'

He had lent her the band's records. The music was strident and rhythmic and, it seemed, out of tune. Only the piano made sense to her ear, and then only on the slower songs. The fast-tempo pieces made her nervous.

'You may find their language as strange as their music,' Leonid said. 'Much slang. On occasion, vulgarity.'

'You forget I lived in the United States, Leonid.'

'Not where these men lived, I think.'

Both she and Leonid came from diplomatic families who, at different periods, had been stationed in Washington. In the late fifties, the peak of the Khrushchev thaw, she had had the rare privilege of attending an American school in Arlington, Virginia. For three years she had learned American history and English grammar;

she was excused civics, morning prayer, and the Pledge of Allegiance.

Since then her English had served her well. While she had been at the University of Moscow, she had worked as an Intourist guide for American visitors, and during Nixon's visits in the seventies she had had the plum job of official interpreter, which got her into parts of the Kremlin that even her father hadn't seen. At her postgraduate institute she had studied, then taught, American foreign policy. A specialist. *Spetsialist.* She savoured the Russian word, with its élitist overtones.

'Well,' she said, 'let them say what they will. I am not the official translator this time. I have only to ensure that the events are properly arranged, our guests looked after.'

She took the Chaika to the party, dropping off the kids at Ariadne's flat on the way. Although the bitter cold had lifted, her driver, Volodya, wouldn't allow them into the car until he had let it run for fifteen minutes, heater turned up full. By the time they got in, the leather seats were warm to the touch. Anna was sulking but Sasha was exuberant: machines had that effect on him. 'Volodya.'

'Yes, Sasha.'

'How many horsepower does it have?'

'The Chaika?'

'Yes.'

Volodya's eyes, dark-ringed, appeared in the rear-view mirror. 'Two hundred and twenty.'

'Ah. Eight cylinders?'

'Of course. Also disc brakes, ball-joint wheel suspension, electromagnetic interlocking system.' Volodya smiled. He encouraged Sasha's interest in trucks, cars and motorcycles.

'Brezhnev owns a Chaika, yes?' Sasha asked.

'Several. He drives like a madman.'

This time Katya met Volodya's eye. She straightened Anna's plaits. 'Remember to thank Ariadne for having you. Ask her if there is anything you can do to help. Remind her that tomorrow the piano teacher comes at twelve.'

Anna didn't answer. She was writing her name in the condensation on the window.

'Anna!'

'Yes, Mama,' she said, with a long sigh.

It took less than ten minutes to reach Ariadne's house, and Katya felt a surge of excitement at the night ahead, mixed with annoyance that she and her daughter would part on bad terms.

'Gorky Automobile Plant,' Sasha said.

'Yes. Started production of the GAZ-14 in 1977.' Volodya thumped the steering-wheel. 'We're riding in one of the first ever made.'

'Superior to the Zil.'

'So some believe.'

'Anna,' Katya whispered, 'I will see you in the morning. First thing.'

'Ye-es, Mama.'

As Volodya drove out of Star City the duty guard stepped from his post and touched his cap. Katya had never known such deference, thanks to the limousine and its official number plates. As a diplomat's daughter, she had always been privileged, but marriage to Ilya had lifted her to a new level.

At once the road worsened: the lighting lapsed and potholes rattled the car. Its ball-joint suspension would be put to the test. Katya peered out at the starless sky. It was six o'clock and it had been pitch black for hours. But she did not have to see the passing landscape to feel its bleakness. The headlights caught the edges of dilapidation: broken pipes, scattered rubble, refuse heaped beneath the snow. Even the birches seemed tainted. They were on the Moscow ring road, which combined the worst of urban and rural. Factory waste and derelict buildings. Poor roads. Half-finished construction projects rusting away from inefficiency or lack of funds. Moscow was in bad shape. Cockroaches and mice overran even the newest apartments. Services were haphazard. *Stagnation* – the word was on everyone's mind and no one's lips. Katya despaired of her city – and her country. And whenever she encountered the desolation that her marriage had allowed her to escape, she was brought back to the morning when Ilya had proposed to her and the evening, a month later, when she accepted him.

She had agonized over it with her boss at the institute, then in Leningrad with Elena, her closest friend. She had spent hours on the phone with her mother, who had been unambiguous: 'Think of the children,' she had said. 'Think of what they have missed. Of what you have suffered.'

'I would have to leave my job, Mama.'

'Who needs a job? Look at his position.'

'And what of love?' Katya had asked.

In answer, her mother had misquoted Chekhov: ' "When you marry, there will be no time left for love." ' So like her to refer to a classic and, so spectacularly, miss its meaning. 'Besides,' she had continued, 'look where love took you the first time.'

That barb had found its mark. But Katya refused to make the facile link between passion and the abuse she and the children had suffered from her first husband, a womanizing, low-level diplomat with a liking for Armenian brandy and Russian rhetoric.

What was simple was her love for her children. That, in the end, had tipped the balance. They would have protection, opportunity, access to the essentials of a civilized life. Katya would have the satisfaction of knowing she had provided for herself and for them – indirectly, perhaps, but in the only way available to a Soviet woman.

Her mood improved as they entered the city. Its crumbling grandeur and layered history never failed to raise her spirits. The icons of her youth were visible everywhere: the Gothic reach of the wedding-cake buildings, the untended façades and domes of the churches, the pillared porticoes of library and institute, the glowing stars of the

Kremlin. The streetlights glittered in the frosty air, and the trolleybuses crawled along the wide boulevards. The Soviet capital was decrepit, perhaps, but still imperial. The city lights seemed to bring clarity to her thoughts, and her mind settled on the tasks ahead.

'What time is it, Volodya?'

'Six thirty.'

'The Exchange offices first. And hurry, please. I'm late.'

He lifted his hand, implying that he would not break the law to get her there on time – even if it had been his insistence on heating the car that had delayed them.

'I have the agendas to copy,' she said. 'Leonid did not confirm our travel arrangements until this afternoon.'

'Yes, ma'am.'

With some affection she looked at the back of his neck, and the torn collar of his jacket. He was so tall that his head grazed the ceiling of the spacious limousine. 'Volodya, you can go home after leaving me at the hotel.'

'I'll wait for you.'

'No. I stay in the city tonight. It's arranged.'

'Are you sure you don't want me to wait?'

'Yes.'

He nodded, and again their eyes met in the rear-view mirror. If she had to have someone working for her, Volodya was a good choice: he was alert, unflappable, competent. He made only supportive comments, he was easygoing and patient. And he liked her son.

'Go out and enjoy yourself, Volodya. It's Saturday night.'

He made another familiar gesture. I am enjoying myself already, it suggested.

Not for the first time, it occurred to her that she was more at ease with him than she was with her husband.

Her first marriage had been like a swan dive. With Ilya, she had waded in holding her breath. She could never have suspected that a deep insecurity lay beneath his assured demeanour and starched uniform. He worried that all he possessed would be taken away. At night, even on their Paris honeymoon, anxiety ballooned into nightmare. He was a servant of the state who wanted nothing so much as to be hurled into the heavens atop a Proton rocket on Friday the thirteenth, yet his night sweats came not from visions of a fiery death but from the fear that, like the bovine masses, he would have to queue one day for bread, barter for services, and abandon his spacious flat with its Western appliances.

In his eyes his heroism was insufficient. The Soyuz-18 mission, for which he had received the Order of Lenin, had been aborted two hundred kilometres into space when third-stage rocket separation had failed. Ilya and his co-pilot had returned to earth at more than twenty Gs. Re-entry and landing had severely injured his partner, and Ilya had nursed him in the cold for eight hours before they were rescued. The accident had stalled the space programme for more than two years, and initially Ilya was denied his space-flight bonus. He had had to appeal all the way to the General Secretary before he was paid.

It was a measure of his tenacity and fear that, at over fifty, he had returned from the disaster to win a back-up assignment on another major mission. It was also a measure of his sense of self. What he wanted more than anything, Katya had learned, was flight time. Not love, family life, or a lifelong partner. Flight time! His colleagues had accumulated days of it. To his shame, his current log was twenty-one minutes and twenty-seven seconds. A record like that could make a man dispensable. When active duty ceased, past achievement would be his only currency, and he knew the Party would not reward with continued privileges a man whose only mission had been a failure – letter from Brezhnev or not. He had stood at the window of their Paris hotel and peered at the sky. Woke his new wife in the middle of the night with shouts of terror.

For security she had married the most insecure of men. And what she had thought during their courtship was a dignified, courteous silence had been mute, tortured anxiety. He had feared she would say no. Yet when she accepted he did not fall into her arms. Her commitment secured, the ring on her finger, he installed her in lacklustre

41

domesticity in Star City and turned back to his real goal. Flight time. She had become, she reflected, in darker moments, another decoration for his wall.

Volodya stopped the car in front of the Exchange, clicked on the hazard lights and turned in his seat. 'Would you like me to come in?'

'No. I won't be long.' But she didn't move.

He had a cigarette in his hand and was waiting for her to get out before he lit it. 'You are late, yes?'

'Yes, Volodya.' She was looking at Anna's name, still visible on the window. 'My daughter is unhappy tonight. She doesn't have Sasha's interest in disc brakes.'

He laughed. 'I have a daughter myself,' he said. 'Fifteen years of age.'

'I know.'

'Do you know how girls learn to be women?'

'Tell me.'

'By making their parents suffer.'

'You are too cynical, Volodya.'

He stuck the unlit cigarette between his lips. 'Maybe so. But it is true.'

'I'll let you have your smoke,' she said, and stepped out into the night.

CHAPTER 5

The musicians were escorted to the party by their translator, a small man with thick glasses, dancing hands and a Trotsky beard. He spoke heavily accented English, with Oxonian diction, perfect grammar and a lisp, keeping his head perfectly still, as if he wore a neck-brace. That afternoon he had led them on a tour of the old city. They liked him. He looked elfin inside his oversized parka, and his eyes were friendly. His odd, light voice delivered conventional Soviet accounts of the sites, but a lively intelligence swelled beneath his words. His name, to Salim's delight, was Reef.

'Reef, my man, that is a hip moniker. They call you Reefer? You dig herb? Got to have a reet-a-voutee riff rippling on that reef thing, right?'

Even Marshall had laughed.

Reef smiled and rocked on his heels as he faced the low winter sun. He might not have understood it, but he seemed to enjoy the humour. 'It is a rare name, yes, even in the Soviet Union.'

'Like Fish here has a funny name.'

'Your name is Fish?' he said to Drew.

'Fisher.'

'Ah! Like Bobby Fischer. Perhaps you are related?' He raised a gloved hand above his head and pointed upwards, as if the immensity of the sky was the only way to measure the chess champion's stature.

'Different spelling.'

'Such a master, this Bobby Fischer. The greatest ever, I think. His play so brilliant, so simple. And almost a decade now since he trounced our Spassky. Perhaps long enough to allow me to express appreciation for the only American capable of beating the Soviet best. What has become of this genius?'

'Last I heard,' Marshall said, 'he was living in some basement in Pasadena writing racist pamphlets.'

A second official, Oleg, had accompanied them on the walkabout. A compact, balding man in his mid-thirties, with drooping eyes and a strongman's legs, he appeared to speak no English. But whenever Reef departed from the official programme, Oleg would lean close and mutter something. Then Reef stiffened, and resumed the official patter. Salim had tagged him as KGB, and the man evidently ran the show.

The party was a short walk from the hotel. Reef's hands described irregular polygons as he pointed out historic buildings. As Salim had predicted, the temperature had risen, although it was still below freezing. The atmosphere was lively, with Saturday-night shouts and honking cars. Drew's embassy paranoia had almost dissipated and he was starting

44

to enjoy himself. The only irritant was Oleg, who trailed several feet behind them, hands thrust into the pockets of his leather jacket.

Leonid Petrosian met them at the door, led them inside and offered Russian champagne. He was a tall, elegant Armenian, who rhapsodized about jazz and claimed to have played trumpet with the Ellington Orchestra when it visited Moscow ten years before. Dressed in a good wool suit with a red silk tie, his dark hair brilliantined, he smoked cigarettes from a ceramic holder and listened attentively. He had done his homework: he knew each band member, their instruments, their collective history.

'And Mr Fisher, what can I say of Mr Fisher?' he said, tapping his cigarette above a crystal ashtray. 'A true disciple of my favourite jazz pianist.'

'And who might that be?' Salim said. Salim did not rate Bill Evans.

Petrosian didn't flinch. 'Bill Evans, of course.'

There was a moment of dislocation. Marshall and Salim, like many black musicians, missed in Evans's playing the blues and the barrelhouse. They might also have resented his success. Drew didn't argue with them. 'I like to think there's as much Monk in my style as Evans,' he said cautiously.

'A great tragedy, his death. He was Russian, as you know. Soroka, his mother's name. In Russian this is the name of a bird, the English word for the creature I do not know, but in

Russian tradition it is a symbol of sadness and joy. Like his music. We invited Evans here last year.' Petrosian sighed. 'But unfortunately his health . . . and his political feelings, we cannot deny it . . .'

Marshall glanced at Drew. They both knew that there had been other reasons why Evans had cancelled his Russian tour, but Marshall was not a man to speak ill of the dead.

Salim had no such compunction. 'Just like in '69, right?'

'Just so,' Petrosian said, and Salim smiled. Petrosian took an almost effeminate puff of his cigarette. 'We have all heard the rumours to which your smile alludes, Mr Jackson. But I still have in my collection a news clipping, from the *New York Times* I believe, which records Mr Evans's last-minute political reservations at Kennedy Airport on that trip. And we are all aware of the reputation for the truth carried by that fine newspaper.'

He smiled the knowing smile of the seasoned bureaucrat, daring Salim to contradict him.

Marshall wasn't about to let that happen. 'Where do you get your love of jazz, Leonid?'

Petrosian approached this question carefully. He was a man with Kremlin patronage who could publicly risk irony about politics and express without reservation his love of an art form that was not generally acceptable in a dictatorship of the proletariat. But the atmosphere, these days, was cold.

46

There was a war on – there were boycotts and embargoes. He couldn't be too free.

'My father was a diplomat all his life. He spent the war years in Washington and travelled often to New York on consular and commercial missions. When we returned to Soviet Union in 1956 he brought back many records, so I grew up listening to Duke Ellington and Benny Carter. He loved the music. He met many of these virtuosi, got to know them, called them by their nicknames. Prez and Bean and King.' Again the smile.

Marshall smiled back, an acknowledgement of how strange it was to hear the names enunciated in an Armenian accent in a baroque hotel ball-room beside the Kremlin. It was as if Brezhnev had stood at a Party congress and run down the Yankees' batting order. And if the boys wanted black credentials, well, it was clear Leonid could deliver. Yet Salim's face showed no expression.

The room was socialist shabby-genteel, with a faded floral carpet, ornate chandeliers, and panelled walls with mahogany marquetry and brass sconces. Flowers just past their prime decorated the tables, and an East German hi-fi played Louis Armstrong. Waiters in shabby tuxedoes offered champagne, vodka and Georgian wine to wash down black bread spread with salted cucumber and red caviar. The service was efficient, supervised by Leonid's auto-cratic wife, Luba, who had the face of an empress and the voice of a fishwife. Like her husband, she dressed well, in a floor-length gown of blue satin that swished as she moved about the room, haranguing the staff.

The other guests had an arty air: the men, long haired in corduroy, the women in French-cut slacks with bright scarves. They were in their twenties and thirties, children of Khrushchev, and exuded a social innocence long gone from America. Most smoked pungent Russian cigarettes, and a blue pall hung beneath the dim lights. His services no longer required, Reef had joined them. He looked like he was waiting for his dance partner to arrive. In fact, the room's atmosphere was anticipatory, with the hum of a good party about to happen. Clearly out of place, Oleg skulked against a back wall, chain-smoking and glancing about.

Leonid shifted to business: he handed out a mimeographed itinerary and reviewed the band's schedule – two concerts over the first week in Moscow, a week of appearances in Leningrad, then back to Moscow for two more gigs at local institutes, and workshops at the music department of Moscow State University. They'd be kept busy, with Oleg along to keep them out of trouble. The pianos, Drew was assured, were first rate, and the venues had been chosen for intimacy and good acoustics. The experienced Dr Timoshenko, who was expected at any minute, had arranged it all.

Drew listened with one ear but had been distracted by a sudden stillness around the record-player. Reef and his friends were listening to a young woman with Tartar eyes and curly black hair as she sang Russian words over Armstrong's version of 'St James Infirmary'. Her doleful vowels, hovering above the song's funereal chord changes and Satchmo's silvery trumpet, were incantatory. The ghosts of the New Orleans masters marched through the room.

But other, more disturbing ghosts closed in on Drew. His mother. Jessie. And Bill Evans. In Baton Rouge the turned earth on his grave had been still fresh, his name on the headstone newly chiselled. With the scent of magnolia in his nostrils, Drew had made his promise of a song.

'Ah, at last,' Leonid said. 'Dr Timoshenko.' A woman several years younger than Drew was walking towards them. She had fine fair hair gathered at the back of her head and eyes of such depth that, even in the dim light, he could see in them welcome, excitement and discomfort at being late. As she approached, she shifted the satchel of papers in her arms the better to offer her hand. Her gait was awkward, almost flat-footed, but Drew could see that she had what his mother would have called breeding.

'Leonid, I am so sorry for delay,' she said. 'It was . . . unavoidable.' As she searched for the right English word, her eyes crinkled and she glanced at Drew. She had full lips, an efficient manner, and a pleasantly freighted figure. The schoolteacher you had a crush on. 'I am Katya Timoshenko, cultural administrator for your visit, and I am at your service.' She shook their hands, bobbing her head girlishly and smiling with such shy charm that Marshall bowed in reply.

'Dr Timoshenko is, as you say, my right hand,' Leonid said.

'Right han' plays the mel-o-dee,' Salim said, so that only Drew heard.

'Until some years ago she arranged all our musical visits. I am happy to say that for your visit I have coaxed her out of retirement.' He smiled as he spoke. Perhaps the irony of the phrase, applied to such a fresh young woman, had struck him as it had Drew. Her cheeks were ruddy, and cold air clung to her clothing, with traces of the street that gave way to stronger scents as she relaxed in the warmth. She was wearing a simple red silk dress, but wore plenty of makeup and jewellery – several rings on both hands, silver bracelets, a necklace and earrings. Maybe she wasn't the schoolteacher type after all, Drew thought.

'I see you have agenda,' she said, pointing at the mimeographed pages in their hands. 'Good. First recital is on Thursday, Mayakovsky Hall. I have arranged for rehearsal time on Tuesday, six to eight, and again Thursday morning. I think you play at US Embassy tomorrow?'

'Yes,' Marshall said. 'They insist.'

'By Tuesday you will be ready for a Russian audience. Mr Fisher, you will be pleased to know that hall has Steinway, one of only few in Moscow. I

50

will have it tuned before the curtain lifts, I assure you.' She waved away his attempt to thank her, bracelets sliding into her sleeve. 'By our standards minimum conditions for world-class pianist.'

At that Yoshi laughed, but Katya had meant it seriously: her voice had dropped an octave, her eyes had narrowed and she lifted her chin – the correct expression for earnest discussion, Drew mused. 'I appreciate it,' he said.

A laugh swirled from the group around the record-player, and Katya looked across at them. 'Is that Reef?' she asked Leonid, as if she had forgotten where she was.

'Yes. Our little prince.'

'Please. You must excuse me. I have not seen him for many months.' Absentmindedly, she handed her satchel to Leonid and crossed the room.

Salim bumped Drew's shoulder. 'Table grade.'

'C'mon, Salim.'

'You getting a conscience on me?'

Throughout the evening Drew kept an eye on her. He drank vodka and champagne indiscriminately. The chandeliers twinkled; the mahogany glistened. The music moved up the twentieth century: Duke Ellington, Benny Carter, Miles Davis (Marshall – Leonid must have known – had played with them all). Dancing started up around the hi-fi. Salim sat in the corner, drumming his fingers in time to the music. Oleg hovered. Katya flitted from group to group, sometimes gay, sometimes purposeful, always theatrical but without a trace of self-consciousness.

Drew sidled up to Reef and asked about her. 'I have known Katya for many years,' he said, vodka in hand, swaying slightly. 'We studied together at the Institute for International Relations where she earned her doctorate and I . . .' he lifted his glass in her direction' . . . and where I did not quite achieve my ambitions.'

'What were they?'

Reef blinked. 'A doctorate as well, of course – what every well-educated young Russian pursued in those days. A life, perhaps, in the diplomatic corps. You see, Drew, opportunities for Soviet citizens were limited. *Are* so. One must make of them what one can. I did not.'

The language remained impeccable but slurred at the edges, and louder than Drew thought prudent. After less than a day's acquaintance he felt protective towards Reef, who seemed balanced between puckishness and melancholy. He noted Oleg's position in the corner, well out of earshot. Though who was to say Oleg was the only snitch? What about the dancing innocents in their flat pumps and berets? Perfect cover. 'You seem to be doing all right,' he said.

Reef was on the brink of a response, but evidently thought better of it. He drank before he resumed. 'The Cultural Exchange is a good place to work. I have a pleasant apartment, thirty square metres, in Toplistan. Use, of course, of the Exchange's *dacha.* A Lada Zhiguli with only two hundred thousand kilometres on its clock.' He smiled wanly, and tilted his head – *You see how it is?*

When Katya appeared, flushed but demure, he brightened. 'Mr Fisher,' she said.

'Drew . . . if you please.'

'Drew. Would you mind if I asked your translator to dance?'

Drew extended an arm. Reef slipped his glass into the outstretched palm and took Katya's hand.

Drunk as he was, six inches shorter than his partner, Reef danced with *élan.* But Katya was on another level. The curious, flat-footed gait was gone; the ample body cut its tether to the earth. She spun, swayed and pivoted, laughing. She was freed as Drew was when he made music. It was some time before he became aware of the tune – 'Someday My Prince Will Come', the classic Miles recording from 1961, with John Coltrane blowing away Hank Mobley. That rare bird, a jazz waltz. It was a song Drew had urged Marshall to include in their repertoire, but he seemed tacitly inclined towards Salim's blunt verdict: 'That jive Disney shit.' It hadn't helped that Evans had recorded it before Miles.

Katya danced to the song as Drew liked to play it: subtly, without flourish, squarely on the beat, celebrating the simple melody and indulging in its romanticism. The grace and balance of her movement created a quiet intensity that sent the rest of the room into orbit around her. Like dancers in a painting by Renoir. Drew finished Reef's drink and stared at her. The more exclusively he focused on her, the less she seemed to move, although her necklace still jumped and the room swirled. Gradually she reached a point of perfect stillness and all sound disappeared, but for the glorious muted tone of Miles's trumpet and the richness of her laugh.

At the end of the evening they spilled out of the hotel and gathered on the front steps, gazing across Red Square at the Kremlin, pulling their coats tight against the cold. Released from the airless confines of the ballroom, their voices expanded. A policeman stood in the middle of the empty square, slapping his thigh with a baton. Cleared snow sat at the corners in dirty piles. A black Volga pulled up to the steps and parked, engine running. In the darkness behind its windshield a cigarette flared.

The Russians loitered, half-way down the steps, reluctant to let the party end. They all promised attendance at Thursday's performance. Katya was at the centre of the group, making arrangements and giving directions, looking chic in a full-length coat of soft brown fur. Drew looked heavenward, breathed the clear air, and felt himself approaching a place where nations were not in conflict, death lost its terror, and love did not fail.

Katya kissed them all in the French style and reminded them of tomorrow's rehearsal. Marshall thanked her with Southern excess, while Leonid and Luba looked on, arms linked. Salim and Yoshi left while Marshall was still talking, heading across the intersection towards the hotel. Reef told Drew and Marshall he would accompany them.

As they walked away, Drew glanced back and saw Leonid helping Katya into the Volga. She pulled the trailing fur in after her and he closed the door. The sharp air, the sound of doors slamming, the piled snow, the Volga's exhaust stained red by the tail-lights – these details sparked in Drew the memory of a moment that was clear in the feeling it evoked but vague in circumstance, except that it was from his high-school days in Montana: watching his parents head out for the night, perhaps, returning home after a track meet, or approaching the raucous school gym across a frozen parking lot on the night of a basketball game. A pulse of nostalgia, a whiff of loss. The car pulled away, and Katya waved from behind the glass, shadowy, desirable.

Out of the darkness, walking in Drew's direction with his hands in his pockets and a cigarette between his thin lips, came Oleg. With Reef, he saw the men back to the hotel, making sure they reached their rooms safe and sound.

CHAPTER 6

On Tuesday morning Katya went to Gorky Street to buy nylon stockings for her mother, who, although she had buying privileges in the city's finest diplomatic stores, insisted on a brand carried only in the special shop that catered for the upper ranks of the Red Army and their families. And she had to have them today. Any week now she would be returning to Ethiopia to join Katya's father, who had travelled back three days after the new-year holiday to resume his duties as third secretary in the Soviet Embassy in Addis Ababa. God forbid that she should not be wearing new French stockings when she returned to her husband. It would not do to look less than one's best, especially in one of the poorest countries in the world.

Leaving Volodya illegally parked, Katya rushed into the shop, showed her pass and made the purchase. She was running late again – this time for the band's first rehearsal at Mayakovsky Hall. The staff there had been less than competent, and she wanted to be on hand to smooth over any creases. Today the Americans would have their first working contact with Soviet life. She wanted them to come away with a good impression.

America was much in her thoughts today, and not just because of the musicians. Yesterday the hostages who had been imprisoned for over a year in the American Embassy in Iran had been freed and a new US president inaugurated. Not entirely logically, the Soviet papers saw the coincidence of the events as an opportunity to rail against Ronald Reagan and his warmongering ways. Even that morning's news bulletins, usually sedate, had had a paranoid tone, and Katya had asked Volodya to switch off the car radio.

She knew enough about America to be bothered by Reagan's election. The US swing to the right was dangerous, she was certain, but her own country's propaganda was unpalatable. The world was growing harder and colder. Everywhere extremists were taking over where reasonable leaders had once governed. Twenty-five years ago she had caught a Bluebird school bus each morning and shared her lunchbox with girls from the suburbs around Washington DC. When she had told her own children about those years, they had thought it was fantasy.

She hoped the musicians would restore her faith in simple human politics. Wasn't it the purpose of cultural exchange to rise above propaganda? These men were hardly Communists, but neither were they Reagan supporters. That much she could tell from the way they dressed and spoke.

It was difficult to determine much more about them, though: they were unlike any Americans she had ever met. They were sensitive, yet coarse. Wary: their language was careful and private, and they were governed in their relations, she sensed, by a subtle, alienating irony. The opposite of the puckered diplomat or the blinking, energetic tourist. Almost Russian, she thought, with irony of her own, but there was no mistaking them for natives. They stood out on the Moscow streets even more than the Cuban and African students who attended the political institutes and rode the Metro in their khakis and sandals.

The Japanese man wasn't American at all, in spite of his jazz slang and Bohemian clothes. He wore his strained smile like a *kabuki* mask, and was of a type Katya had learned to recognize on her travels: a man of some cultural confusion, stranded uneasily between the present and his past. No doubt he was a fine musician, at home in performance, but so far Katya had seen the men only in social settings where Yoshi was a minor character.

The black men were centre-stage, but she had no focus with them. They were truly alien. Marshall was a man of some elegance and awareness, whose very fingertips seemed to register waves of data from the ambient air. Salim, large, brooding and vulgar, was superficially his opposite but, like him, intensely conscious of the surroundings, his appearance, and the convergence of the two. Each man

58

faced the streets with a demeanour that was both proud and aggressive, as if he was forever challenged. Their faces had the fullness she associated with an American diet, but they held an expression she had not seen in the black men and women who worked at the US Embassy or visited the institute from Ivy League colleges. It was closer to the modern African look, of hauteur assumed against the impulse to deference.

Yet here, too, there was a difference. She had been to Africa many times, for the occasional conference and on visits to her parents in Addis Ababa. Her father had been there for five years, part of the Soviet diplomatic expansion that had followed the revolution, which had overthrown a black aristocracy, and the installation of the Derg. Although she didn't pretend to know the subtleties of the country's history, she sensed that in black Africa race was less of an issue than class. But something in the way that these American blacks squared up to the world told her that, for them, race was still the issue. Theirs was a different revolution.

Then there was the pianist. Shy, hesitant, sidelong, at ease with the black men yet removed in the essential, inevitable respect. He had a wide face, eyes far apart, and large teeth that reminded her of a horse's, though not unpleasantly. His fingers were long, with closely trimmed nails, and his boxy shoulders tensed against an unseen force. He looked strong across the arms and chest, but she had sensed in him a familiar vulnerability.

Something around his eyes spoke of pain both long-lasting and unAmerican. An intelligent, flickering fear of what raw circumstance could conspire to drop on a person of unusual tenderness. A fatalism, she mused, of Slavic dimension.

These men were her responsibility: she would be spending much time with them over the coming three weeks. But as Volodya negotiated the Chaika through the thickening traffic on Gorky Street and Katya marked the minutes that tolled her lateness, it was Drew Fisher who rose above the others in her mind. She had to admit that her excitement about the trip centred on his performance. She thought of his hands. She wanted to hear him play.

Volodya parked across the street from Mayakovsky Hall in front of the entrance to the Peking restaurant. As she gathered her things he set his arm on the seat and faced her. 'Shall I take the shopping to your mother?'

'No. I'll see her on Thursday. If you go to her today, who knows what errands she'll have you running for her?'

'When does she travel?'

Katya raised her eyebrows as she put on her fur hat. 'The bigger the decision, the less predictable she is. Though why she stays here in January when she could be somewhere warm, I have no idea.'

'Too warm for her, I think.'

'Yes, yes. Too warm, too cold. I don't know which she enjoys more – suffering or telling people about it.'

They made arrangements for him to collect Katya and she got out of the car. The cold air brought tears to her eyes, and the low sun glinted on the baroque façades of hotel and hall. The violet sky was dense with winter haze. Daughter, mother, grandmother, all looked to Katya when they had a grievance to air. But to whom could she turn?

An Oriental man in a white smock stuck his head out of the restaurant door, looked at the sky and retreated. When Katya was sixteen her mother had taken her to the Peking for lunch and told her she didn't love her husband, Arkady. As she spoke, she had been peering at the menu through her English reading glasses, her tone matter-of-fact, her mouth a pout of indecision.

At the time Katya had been reading *Anna Karenina* and was enraptured by its heroine. She had seen her mother's revelation in the light of fiction, not life. Did she have affairs? Did Arkady? Did the grand passions so clearly missing from the household lie elsewhere? Her heart had filled with a peculiar, theatrical self-pity. Her mother, she concluded, was like the cold society women of Anna's Petersburg, for whom love was secondary to appearance and acquisition. Her father was obsessed with rank, a prig. In her mind, she arranged these conceptions of her parents like dolls on a shelf. With the fierceness of youth, she resolved always to follow her heart, even if, like Anna, she was doomed by her surroundings. It was many years before she saw the sadness of the moment: the calculated timing of the revealed secret; her mother's despair at the incomprehension of her audience.

The hall was dark, except for the performance lights, and from the rear Katya saw the Steinway in the middle of the stage, angled as if for a solo recital. The four musicians were grouped beside it, like actors, and a short man in a quilted jacket faced them, gesticulating crudely. The other instruments were still in their cases, stacked to the left of the stage. Something was amiss. Why had she let herself be late? She hurried down the aisle. The KGB man, Oleg, sat in the second row, smoking. She avoided his eye. As she skirted the orchestra pit she heard argument. Reef, she saw now, was with the group, overshadowed by Marshall, who stood tall and straight, hands in his coat pockets. She hurried up the side steps and crossed the stage.

'There is nothing to be done,' Reef said, in English. 'It is the regulations.'

'Fuck the regulations,' Salim swore.

Katya stopped outside the ring of light that circled the piano. Reef fidgeted. Marshall pivoted, and bowed to her with stiff grace. Yoshi smoked a long-tipped cigarette and, to her dismay, allowed its ash to fall on the polished wood of the stage. Drew's baseball cap was pulled low so she could not see his eyes.

She waited a moment, then stepped into the

light. The man in the quilted jacket looked at her but said nothing. He seemed to be waiting for the translation of Salim's remark.

'The regulations apply only to classical repertoire, Vasily,' said Reef. 'These gentlemen play jazz music and require a different configuration of instruments to suit their distinctive tradition.'

Vasily had the quick eyes of the petty bureaucrat. Assistant deputy to the deputy stage manager, or some such position, his job was to enforce meaningless rules until his palm or ego was stroked. He rocked back on his heels and looked from Reef to Salim. 'A long translation for so few words in English,' he observed.

Katya cleared her throat and removed her gloves. 'Dr Timoshenko,' she said to him, in her richest institute voice. She did not offer her hand. Vasily failed to meet her eye as he nodded. 'I have direct and official responsibility,' she continued, 'for all arrangements concerning our visiting artists. Guests of the city of Moscow . . . guests of the Soviet Union.'

Vasily gestured at the piano. 'The regulations are clear, Doctor. The piano must occupy the central position beneath the spotlight, all other instruments at least one point eight metres distant . . .' He trailed off, pointing lamely at an arbitrary space where, presumably, the piano must not sit. The huge stage, which could have held an orchestra large enough to play a Mahler symphony, framed his limp hand.

Somehow she had set his quibbling in context

and elicited a tone of self-defeat. She turned to Marshall. 'Mr Powell, you have explained your requirements?'

Marshall glanced at Salim. 'We'd like to have the drums in the middle of the stage.'

'Rhythm be the rock,' Salim said, arms folded.

'It's a question of group dynamics, Dr Timoshenko,' Marshall added.

'Please. Katya.'

'Katya. We have to hear each other properly before the audience can hear us as a group.'

Behind him, Drew was looking at his feet. She had to listen to what Marshall was saying, but she was uncomfortably conscious of Drew's long-fingered hands and hidden eyes. 'Of course.' She turned to Reef and said in English: 'Our guests must be ready for refreshment. Please, Reef, take them to artists' dressing room.' Then, to the musicians: 'Reef will show you where you can enjoy coffee and cigarettes in proper surroundings while I prepare the stage to required specifications.'

She heard the ring of authority in her voice and felt larger than usual. Imposing. Vasily would have heard her tone and wondered what she had said to get these intransigent foreigners moving so quickly.

'What do you think?' she asked Vasily. 'The piano two metres stage left. Good acoustics preserved, the spirit of the regulations maintained.'

'Well, it seems to me—'

'You have staff available to make the necessary arrangements?'

'Staff, yes, but—'

She moved off. 'We will need to start rehearsal in twenty minutes, if you please.'

Salim was muttering to Marshall as Katya walked into the dressing room. 'It is all arranged as you wish,' she said. 'We will begin in twenty minutes.'

A slender girl, eyes downcast, set a tray of coffee-cups and pastries on the makeup table. It was flanked by a mirror lined with small, bright lights. In its reflection Katya saw Yoshi eyeing the girl's hips as she poured the coffee.

She hung up her coat and joined Drew to the right of the table, away from Salim. He took off his cap and blinked, as if emerging from the dark. The skin around his eyes looked bruised, and a slick line of matted hair showed where the hat-band had pressed against his head. His right hand was rubbing his thigh in a nervous motion. 'The piano will be ready in a few minutes,' she said. 'The tuner has been in, but you will wish to try it before the rehearsal, I am sure.' The girl handed her some coffee, which she drank. The quality was poor.

'Fine,' he said. He looked as if he wanted to tell her something. The wide-set eyes appeared sensitive, sun-battered. His skin was pale and stubbled, his hair unkempt. He held himself as if surrounded by unseen obstacles, as if his nerve endings were too close to an abrasive world. Not suffering, perhaps, but hypersensitive. She wanted to soothe him.

'I played in this hall,' she said.

'Piano?'

'How did you know?'

'You hold your arms like a piano player.'

She laughed, and saw by his quick smile that he liked the sound. 'And how does a pianist hold her arms?' she asked.

'Like you do.'

When she had met him on Saturday evening, at the Moscow Hotel, he had said little. Standing apart from the restrained gaiety that marked any Russian party attended by foreigners, he had piqued her curiosity and stirred something within her that she connected with her years in America. Today he maintained that observer's air, but the quiet phrases he uttered were intimate in a Russian way and oddly penetrating. She felt as if he was looking inside her. 'I played in youth competition. Rachmaninov. The second concerto.'

'Tough.'

'If you play well, tough piece perhaps. But I was not so good.'

Tough had been her mother in the front row, looking aghast at the mistakes she made. Tough was the reception afterwards, when her mother ignored her and fawned over the winner, a girl from Katya's school with golden arms and an air of assured disdain. Now Katya recalled the hot lights and the way her good brown dress had chafed her armpits as she played; the noise at the rear of the hall that had distracted her during the second movement and led to a string of missed notes; the fifteen roses the winner clutched to her breast in this same dressing room.

The other musicians had finished their coffee and left the room. Drew twirled his cap on his finger, a gesture she saw as distinctly American – an unconscious, male ease that often spilled over into something her culture found hard to comprehend. *Hey, Dick, pour me a cup of coffee there, will ya?* To a Russian this question was a command, but she had heard it uttered in a Kremlin antechamber by Melvin Laird, then Secretary of Defense, to the President of the United States. The response had been phrased in language you would not have heard in a Moscow tavern – by the President of the United States! Not that Brezhnev wasn't capable of vulgarity, but the social norms could not have been more different. Yet there was nothing vulgar about Drew. He was polite in the way of those from the American Midwest. His accent was soft and nasal, the muscles in his face relaxed, yet there was an edge to him that in her experience many Midwesterners lacked.

She gestured towards the door. 'Please,' she said, 'you must test the piano.'

It had been moved, and Salim was setting up his drum kit in its place. Yoshi was reading sheet music and Marshall sat beside Reef on a slatted wooden chair, explaining the mechanics of fitting a reed into a saxophone mouthpiece. Vasily had turned on the footlights, and she could see Oleg's silhouette across their bright divide, the movement of hand to mouth as he smoked. The piano stool was missing. She told Vasily to fetch it. When he had slid it into place she gestured to Drew to be seated, but he did not move. 'Please. You must test.' Her voice had not lost its commanding tone.

'No. You do.'

'I?'

He lifted a shoulder and bobbed his head, the gesture of an athlete or a Hollywood actor. 'Sure. A little Rach, maybe.'

The heat rose in her face. 'Is not possible.'

'Everything's possible. I can judge the sound better if I hear someone else play first.'

He kept smiling. In a Russian man she would have taken his insistence as rudeness, but instead she was flattered. Behind him she could see Salim, one knee on the ground, tightening the pedal of his bass drum and looking up at them, brow furrowed.

She sat because she had no choice – the spell of her authority had yielded to Drew's calm, encouraging smile – and considered what to play. But his expectation, expressed in his silence and stillness, confused her and, as more time passed, she felt silly – after all, she was only testing the piano. Without further thought she plunged into what she knew best: a rondo by Tchaikovsky, learned by every schoolgirl in the country.

She played by rote. The piano had been tuned properly, but her fingers were heavy on the keys and her tone was flat. She was about to stop when she reached what had always been her favourite passage, a couplet as simple as the refrain of a peasant song. A fragment she often hummed while she was cooking dinner. Suddenly she caught the spirit of the tune: her hands lightened and its delicate mood emerged. She was moved, by the piece itself and by the associations it had gathered for her over twenty years. Drew's hand was on the piano, his fingers tapping soundlessly, mimicking the progress of her right hand. She sensed that he, too, was moved, and a knot of shared feeling gathered around the notes that transformed the music. He was her audience, and she knew the other men were aware of the intimate connection between them, but she could no more suspend her performance than stop breathing. She played the final chords with trembling hands.

When she looked up from the keys, his face was reflective. His eyes were on her hands, and filled with something beyond admiration. The hall was quiet. Drew stood very still. She had been fascinated by *his* hands, looked forward to *him* playing, yet it was she who had performed, however unwillingly, and was now enduring observation on several incompatible levels. She had been manoeuvred, she thought, into an inappropriate revelation. Not by Drew's request so much as by circumstance. His eyes mirrored her confusion, as if he feared what intimacy might unleash, as if he, too, had been caught unawares. The mixture of public and private, easily accommodated in an American context, was dangerous for her in a way he could not appreciate. One did not, her grandmother would have been the first to tell her, betray to outsiders anything other than the most formal appearance. One did not take the risk. And when Marshall initiated a round of applause for her, she noticed, with a stab of fear, that Oleg was the only one not clapping.

MY FOOLISH HEART

CHAPTER 7

He couldn't get her off his mind. In Purgatory as long as he could remember, he had not expected to be visited by such feelings, especially here in Moscow, locked down by Arctic ice and Cold War politics.

First her dancing. She had been brisk and formal at one minute, then swirling, ethereal, elegant. The utter calm on her face and the songlike motion of her limbs. Amid the turmoil of that long first day, watching her had almost banished jet-lag and paranoia.

Then there had been her impromptu performance at the rehearsal, not so much the piece she had played but the way she had played it – the passion swelling beneath the conventional phrases, the look of remove on her face, as if she had been taken by the music to some intimate, distant place. Being close to her at that moment had been like composing music.

So why did he feel an irresistible urge to bury his feelings and run? Because he would screw up. As his father had with his mother. As he had with Jessie.

Drew stood with the other musicians in the hotel lobby, smoking a cigarette and watching the security staff, wondering whether Katya would show.

'Told me Lenin's tomb,' Salim said.

'Who did?'

'Reef,' he said, elongating the vowel with a show of teeth.

'More tourist trail, huh?'

'They like to keep us busy. Otherwise maybe we start snooping around.'

Salim mimed a pair of binoculars and surveyed the lobby. Yoshi emerged from the hotel's hard-currency shop wearing an unkempt fur hat. Salim, cackling, pointed at it. 'Tell me, Yosh – please – that you're being paid to wear that thing.'

'Ten below today.'

'I don't care it's a hundred below, you look like one comical motherfucker in that wig.'

Marshall cleared his throat. The security men were fidgety, playing with the collars of their leather jackets and pacing a circuit from doorway to cloakroom to reception desk. The lobby smelt of furniture polish and Russian cigarettes.

A few minutes later Reef arrived. On his own. 'Good morning, gentlemen. My apologies for being late.'

'Not a problem, Reef,' Salim said. Apparently he still got a kick out of saying the name.

'I hope you are well rested and properly break-fasted. We have a full programme today.'

'Gonna scope out the stiff?'

'I beg your pardon?'

'Lenin,' Salim said. 'We going to meet the man?'

Reef spread his hands. 'Yes, of course. To begin with. A visit to the mausoleum. But we must wait for my colleague.'

'Katya?' Drew asked.

Reef smiled. 'Much as she would like to join us, Dr Timoshenko is far too busy to be sightseeing. She is making the arrangements for your concert tomorrow night. Your first on *Russian* soil.' Mild-mannered though he was, Reef evidently couldn't stop himself making the point that their Sunday-night gig at the embassy – which had not gone particularly well – had not been sponsored by the Exchange. The tour, he implied, started now. He noticed Yoshi's hat. 'Ah, very handsome. Rabbit fur.'

'Rabbit?' Yoshi said. 'They told me mink.'

'Rabbit, I'm afraid. But very high quality, I assure you.'

As Reef spoke, Oleg came through the lobby door, coughing into a handkerchief. He ignored the Americans and spoke under his breath to Reef. Not once in four days had he looked any of them in the eye.

'So,' said Reef, reverently, 'to Red Square.'

Though cold, the morning was clear and brilliant, with a couple of inches of snow glittering in the sun. It was, as Reef put it, the perfect winter's day. 'Here in Moscow we prefer that the temperature remain below freezing,' he said, peering at the sky from beneath his scruffy fur hat. 'It keeps the streets dry and the air clean.'

The square was solid and dazzling. *Babushkas* in dirty head-scarves cleared snow from the flagstones with besoms. The buildings around the square were draped with massive Party banners and portraits of Lenin and Brezhnev, left hanging after the city's New Year celebrations. Rumpled policemen, looking bored and aggressive, lounged against portable barriers. The group approached the mausoleum as the bells of Spassky Gate tolled ten, just in time for the changing of the guard. They watched the splendidly uniformed soldiers manoeuvring in the sun with metronome precision, arms swinging, heads averted, bayonets glinting.

'Please look.' Reef pointed again. 'This is the viewing stand from which our leaders observe displays of national celebration.'

As if a film had cut to close-up, the wall of granite along the top of the mausoleum looked suddenly familiar, the scene of a thousand photographs and newsreels, the foundation of those imperial tableaux in which Stalin, Khrushchev or Brezhnev had waved to the world in grim confidence, shot from below against the mighty Soviet sky, leading ageing Politburos in a spectacle of power while tanks, missiles and smiling gymnasts paraded past. Drew looked at the austere line of red stone and tried to bring to life those images of empire, but felt instead a Baedeker hollowness, a sense of imposed history. Today pigeons wheeled against the wide azure sky, past the kaleidoscopic twists of the domes of St Basil's.

'Look at that line,' Salim said, under his breath. 'Gonna be the weekend, time we get inside.'

A queue stretched from a barrier at the mausoleum entrance to the middle of the square, where it angled right and kept extending, shaped silently by tougher, nattier police in collar tabs and blue epaulettes. The people in the line, Russians mostly by the cut of their clothes and the texture of their skin, were staring with undisguised directness at the Americans. Drew realized that he and his friends stuck out: six-foot-four Marshall in his camel-hair coat and kid gloves; Salim, black as obsidian, in Nehru jacket and sunglasses; Yoshi thin and stooped, face lost beneath the rabbit-fur hat. His own broad Dutch face was ineffectively hidden by the baseball cap, pulled low. 'We going to join the line?' he asked.

Reef looked at Oleg, who nodded almost imperceptibly at the sharp-jawed cops at the barrier. 'Please,' Reef said. 'This way.' He led them to the front of the queue.

Marshall was embarrassed. 'Hey, Reef. Tell our man here this isn't necessary.'

'You are distinguished guests of the Soviet-American Cultural Exchange. It is all arranged.'

The special cops paired off the visitors as they walked through the barrier, past the honour guard and down into the dark mausoleum. They all removed their hats, Salim his shades. A guard in

77

military greatcoat signalled hands out of pockets. They moved quietly into the black marble interior, redolent of floor wax and disinfectant. Beneath the hush of fear and respect they heard the efficient hum of machinery. Every few feet there were soldiers. At the entrance to the main crypt, a guard stood with legs apart, cradling a Kalashnikov. Salim whistled a death march, and another guard shushed him quiet.

Abruptly, in a flood of harsh light, they came to the waxy body of the great man – small, yellow-skinned, resting stiffly in the raised glass coffin in black suit and red tie. Soldiers with fixed bayonets stood sentry at the corners. Beneath the glass the high brow gleamed, the thin beard tapered stiffly to its tip. The hands lay on the jacket, fingers slightly curled. The military provided the security and the aura of respect, but it was the scientists, Drew knew, armed with their chemicals and computer programs, who kept the body intact, preserving it for the adoration of the masses. But the shuffling line had only a few seconds to inspect the icon. In moments Drew was outside again, squinting in the bright air, the after-image of the face fixed before his eyes.

'I have been to the mountain,' Salim intoned, putting on his sunglasses with both hands.

'You believe.'

'I have seen, Fish. I have been in the presence. But happy are those who have *not* seen and yet believe.'

78

They had emerged behind the mausoleum, on a tree-lined path that ran alongside the Kremlin wall past the burial sites of civil-war heroes and former leaders. As they waited for the others, Drew noticed Reef nearby, in the shadow of a blue spruce, cleared snow heaped on either side of him. He was hunched and tentative, still holding his hat. He stared down the path, biting his lower lip, his stance suggesting suppression. Drew hoped he had not heard the banter. But as Marshall and Yoshi approached, Reef shook off his abstraction, put on his hat and fell into step beside them, pointing out the fresh memorial to Alexei Kosygin, buried in the wall only four weeks previously.

Drew's own mood shifted in the shadow of these tombs. His eagerness to see Katya was grounded by an awareness of death. He thought of his parents: his mother, mouldering in her Boston grave; his father, still alive yet crumbling into fragments of loneliness and regret. Of course he could have done nothing to keep their marriage from disintegrating, but he felt only shame when he remembered how at their worst moments he had been thousands of miles away, mired in addiction. Digging a hole for himself while he betrayed those closest to him. With Jessie it had been even worse. He could have helped her. He was on hand for her final descent, yet he had done nothing.

They reached the end of the path and stepped back on to the square. With Reef as a prod, Oleg gathered and guided them down the gentle slope beside the windowless brick wall of the Historical Museum. Through iron railings to their left they could see the tomb of the unknown soldier, the eternal flame pale in the sunlight, the grey-slabbed memorial piled high with wilting flowers. The fortress walls of the Kremlin rose above the bare trees. The birds were silent here and mortality permeated the stone they walked on.

Salim had his eye on Oleg, whose step had added authority. For once his hands were out of his pockets, and he glanced from side to side. 'Cat's up to something,' he said softly.

'We will view the exhibit in the Historical Museum devoted to the life of Lenin,' Reef said, 'and then we will have lunch at the hotel.'

'Think we might get some chicken today?' Salim asked.

'I cannot promise, but it is possible.'

At the bottom of the slope they turned the corner and approached the museum entrance. A group of protestors, mostly women, stood beside the steps. They held hand-painted signs and framed photographs of young soldiers. A full-bearded man with wild eyes leaned over a wall beneath the portico, addressing the group with a megaphone. Oleg stopped, and the others had no choice but to pull up and observe. Reef shifted nervously from foot to foot.

'What we got here?' Salim said.

As he spoke a young woman in front of them

turned and smiled. 'They're complaining about your lot, actually,' she said in an English accent.

'Been complainin' 'bout my lot since I was born.'

She laughed. 'I mean they're protesting about American support for the Afghan rebels.' She spoke mischievously, eyes flitting from Salim to Marshall, one corner of her mouth lifted in a crooked smile. Her face wore its questions like a mask, and now it asked: Who are these black men and what are they doing here? But there was no suspicion this time, just curiosity. She was short and blonde, in a red wool coat and striped college scarf. Her head was bare. There was something lively about her.

Salim considered the Englishwoman from behind his shades. She withstood his scrutiny calmly. 'You speak the lingo, then?' he asked.

'A bit.'

'What's he saying?' He nodded at the speaker.

She listened for a moment. '"This week the imperialist government of the USA changes its leader but not its undeclared war on the Afghan revolution."'

Salim laughed. 'No shit.'

'"The capitalists condemn adventurism and hostage-taking in Iran, but support the forces of terror when aimed at the Soviet Union."'

'Fish, you hear that? Sounds like we got us a *discussion* here.'

Marshall glanced at Oleg. Yoshi had removed his hat and was scratching his head.

'Where are your minders?' the woman asked. 'I can't imagine they've allowed a pack of Yanks loose in Red Square without proper chaperones.'

'Where's yours?' Drew asked.

She considered before she answered, then said, 'I wouldn't know, would I? I'm at the stage of my stay here where they don't make themselves known.' She nodded at a group of men kerbside, who were smoking intently and observing the protest. 'One of them, you can be certain.'

Her accent was sing-song and guttural, more Scots than English to Drew's ear. She carried a Russian textbook. Oleg and Reef were conferring. Drew tilted a shoulder in their direction. '*Our* minders.'

'One who speaks and one who doesn't.'

'You know the drill.'

'Of course. I've been here a year.'

Marshall nudged Drew and Salim from behind. 'Why don't we keep to the programme and go inside?'

Salim nodded at Oleg. 'Don't you think this *is* the programme?'

'C'mon. Let's go.'

There was an uncharacteristic softness in Marshall's tone. Salim took it as a signal to resist: 'And miss this scene? Free speech in action?'

The woman laughed. 'You call this free speech?'

'Hey, no different from us, is it? Doing the dirt on Reagan just like we do back home and ain't nothing the man can do but take it on the chin.

Free country,' Salim said. Marshall leaned forward and grasped Drew and Salim by the arm. This time, there was no mistaking his firmness. 'Mothers,' he said.

'What's that?' Salim said.

Marshall indicated the women holding the photographs. 'Mothers, whose sons have died in the war.'

For the first time, Drew looked at the women's faces: withered, pleading, darkened by hardship and despair. Working women, by the look of them, they held the photographs below their chins.

'The Red Army has not returned the bodies,' the Englishwoman said. 'The men were reported dead, but they have no idea how they died. There has been talk of the rebels dismembering corpses.' The women's stillness was almost fiery.

Reef caught their attention and pointed at the museum door. Oleg had disappeared. On the steps Drew glanced over his shoulder and caught the Englishwoman looking at him. She lifted a mittened hand, a splash of red in the sunshine. A farewell smile. *Who knows?* it asked. *Maybe we'll meet again.* He thought of Katya. But behind the Englishwoman was the tableau of grieving mothers.

He followed Marshall inside.

Reef spoke softly: 'Concerned citizens. We all, as modern nations, have our problems. There are many complicated situations.'

'It isn't easy,' Marshall said.

Reef continued: 'Your hostages have returned from Tehran. A good development.'

There was still no sign of Oleg, but they all sensed that Reef's comment was risky. Drew took it as an apology, a moment of candour and sympathy seeping from beneath the official behaviour and political gamesmanship.

'Thank the Lord for that, Reef,' Marshall said. 'We don't need any more mourning mothers.'

As Drew filed past the exhibits in the museum, the women's eyes, their creased faces and chapped lips stayed with him. He circled back – inevitably – to his last conversation with his mother, a year ago, in a harshly lighted ward of the cancer unit at Massachusetts General . . .

'Does Dad know?'

She shook her head. 'No. And I don't want him to.'

He held her hand and stared into her haggard face.

'We haven't spoken in seven years,' she went on. 'I don't see any point in doing so now.'

A long silence. Her breath was laboured and she wheezed.

'I've written instructions.'

'Mom, please.'

'No fuss, Drew.' She patted his hand and looked out of the high window. He followed her gaze: the blurred edges of Boston brownstones, a cotton-wool sky. 'He never let me in, Drew, not even when he was rehabilitated.' She smiled coldly. 'He hated that word. The day he got the letter from the State Department – the letter he'd been waiting for for fifteen years – he drank himself into a stupor. That was when I decided to leave him.'

'Mom.'

She looked at him. 'You had your own problems back then, didn't you?'

He grasped her hand.

'Drugs,' she said.

He nodded.

'Drew.'

'I'm clean now. Been clean for four years.'

'I know.'

'How?'

'I could tell.'

All the words he had rehearsed, questions and explanations, remained buried. Her fingers were bluish and lumpy.

She nodded at a cassette-recorder on the night-stand beside her bed. 'I listen to the tapes you send me. Every evening I listen.'

He kissed her hand and held it to his cheek.

CHAPTER 8

'I have no eye-liner. I am trapped in this flat all day, no help to speak of, no one calling to see what I might need, your *babushka* on the phone every hour to complain of what you have not done for her – *you* who have turned your life over to her.'

Katya's mother delivered these sentences shrilly while her daughter hung her fur on a crowded coat-rack in the overheated hallway.

'I have no problem with Babushka.'

'And what of *my* problems? Does no one think of *me*?'

When she was with her mother she had no choice *but* to think of her – but Katya dared not say so. She had been working non-stop since seven that morning, dealing with printers, television crews, sound engineers, theatre personnel, and a host of petty bureaucrats with no function other than to place obstacles in her way. She had not eaten all day. With the concert ninety minutes away she had arrived tense and frazzled at her mother's flat on Kropotkinskaya Street and in no mood for the customary harangues.

'Do you want me to attend your precious concert looking like a harridan?' her mother said.

Katya sifted through her handbag for her own makeup. The air in the flat was stale: her mother refused to open a window in winter, even the *fortochka*.

'Nadia. Here.' Katya used her mother's given name when she was trying to be firm. She handed her an eye-pencil. Nadia examined it and flung it on to the sofa-bed. 'It is no use. You must send Volodya.'

'Volodya has gone for a bite to eat. He will pick us up in an hour. Now, please, get dressed. I have to telephone.'

The concert programmes, scheduled for delivery from the printers on Tuesday, had still not appeared. Everything else, touch wood, was ready. The piano was tuned, the sound check had gone well, the musicians were at the theatre. But the programme was her special project. She had designed it herself, using one of Elena's drawings on the cover. She should have known better than to act on Leonid's recommendation of the city council's printer. No doubt he would receive a kickback.

While Katya was on the phone, Nadia flitted from room to room, agitated and vocal. Every day she complained about her husband, but she was irritable and unfocused when he was not around. She had stayed on in Moscow to be with an old friend whose husband had died on New Year's Eve.

Katya ended her call and went into the kitchen

to prepare a snack. She had been promised that the programmes were on the way to the theatre, but she remained tense. Her mother appeared in a towelling bathrobe, holding out fresh-painted nails to dry and carefully smoking a cigarette.

'Give me that,' Katya said, 'and eat.' She took the cigarette from her mother and stubbed it out, then cut the bread and sausage into bite-sized pieces.

Nadia blew on her nails and motioned Katya to hand her a fork. 'Darya is inconsolable. Her daughter stayed for only three days after the funeral.'

'She is with the Taganka group. They are touring. If she misses even one performance her understudy takes over for the tour.'

'Katya, *three days*! It is not right.'

'It is life.'

Fingers splayed, Nadia chewed. The open neck of the robe showed the skin beneath her breast-bone, tanned and slack. She had been in Ethiopia for five years. The wrinkles around her eyes, deepened by sun and smoking, had tightened her acquired look of severity. She wiped her mouth with a napkin and pointed at Katya's dress. 'You're wearing this?'

'What's wrong with it?'

As she had worn her red silk dress to the party, Katya had had to settle for second best tonight with the chocolate-coloured poplin gown.

'It draws attention to your hips.'

'And that's such a bad thing?'

Nadia ate more sausage. Her silence invited a retort.

'And what are you wearing?' Katya said. She found it difficult to keep irony from her voice. The extent of Nadia's wardrobe was as legendary as her insistence on its paucity.

'I have a choice? Where can I buy clothes? Addis Ababa? There is nothing there. Nothing.'

'My dress is five years old.'

'So why wear it? Get your Hero of the State to spend some of his certificate-roubles on you.'

Katya chewed a piece of sausage. Nadia would wear her Chanel suit and the Bulgari necklace. She would don her party face and turn heads. At her age. 'My husband can buy nothing. He is in Kazakhstan.'

'Then you buy.'

A few months ago, all Nadia's considerable energy had been aimed at convincing her daughter to marry Ilya. She had implied that if Katya rejected him the family would suffer a blow from which it would never recover. Now, no conversation between them was without a sneer at Ilya. Her mother's cynicism lit a fuse of panic in Katya. What had she done? Why had she listened to her?

'On Monday,' Katya said stiffly, searching for a different topic, 'I go to Leningrad. With the Cultural Exchange.'

'How nice for you.'

'I will be away for a week. We have a full schedule.'

'Where do you stay?'

'The Oktyabrskaya.'

Nadia shook her head. 'Poor quality.'

'I was lucky to find anywhere at such short notice. Besides, it is a good location. Near Elena.' She put her plate on the counter and filled the kettle.

'Does Elena still doodle?'

'She has quite a reputation now. She has exhibited in West Germany.'

'Reputation among whom? Showing abstract pictures in West Berlin will not win her any friends in the Artists' Union.'

Anywhere else in the world Elena would have been celebrated. She believed in art as Katya believed in love. She painted with passion and talent. But the Philistines who ran the country agreed with Nadia's assessment.

Katya poured tea. Nadia's eyes glinted with mockery. But her thoughts had moved on from Elena. 'I believe you have a special guest on your excursion.'

'What do you mean?'

'Luba told me about Leonid and his latest conquest.'

Katya frowned. 'I am not interested in Leonid and his affairs.'

'You should be happy. Now he will leave you alone.'

'Mama! Please don't let's talk about it.'

Leonid was one of those men for whom seduction was second nature, what the French call *un homme à femmes*. He had been flirting with women for so long it had become an unconscious impulse, charming at first, then manipulative. He had asked Katya to include on the Leningrad itinerary a young, attractive assistant from the Exchange who had no reason to be there. And even as he had asked Katya to do this, his smile had suggested a continuing interest in her.

'You'd think he would at least be discreet,' Nadia said, 'but Luba has given up on him. The suffering that woman endures.'

Leonid acquired mistresses as capitalists acquire property. He was a master at blending the courtly and the political; he appealed skilfully to the vain and the ambitious, and the women who fell for him usually had a streak of both. He had tried to seduce Katya soon after she had left her first husband. She had been vulnerable, distraught – unwittingly, perhaps, she had encouraged him. When she had seen the nakedness of his intent, she had demurred: his wife and her mother were friends. Yet he persisted, turning his pursuit into a running joke, as if he didn't mean it. Because he had a generous nature and a quick wit, she forgave him the occasional attempt to bed her, but at times he became unpleasant.

'I'm concerned about Babushka,' Katya said.

'Why?'

'I haven't told her yet.'

'About?'

'The trip.'

91

'So tell her.'

'I am worried. She has not settled in.'

Her mother did not look up from her food. 'Where are the children staying?'

'With Ilya's mother. She is close to the school. But Babushka . . .'

'Tanya is there every day, no?'

'Tanya does not understand that Babushka needs a certain kind of attention. For years she had her routine, and now she is unsettled, sometimes confused.'

Her mother searched the pockets of her robe and came up with a packet of Benson & Hedges and a disposable lighter. She checked her nails and lit a cigarette. 'I think I know something about your grandmother's habits.' Arkady's mother had lived in their apartment and *dacha* for ten years.

'Of course,' Katya said. 'But she has changed. She needs attention every day.'

'Which is why she moved in with you.'

'Yes, but this week . . .'

Her mother stood up and waved away the implied request with her cigarette. 'Your father telephones each evening with all his petty crises. Darya is inconsolable. There are vermin in the flat and no one offers me the smallest bit of help.'

'What has this to do with Babushka?'

'Babushka, Babushka. My mother was a good Communist and died with nothing. Arkady's mother now complains because Ilya's mansion in the forest is not to her liking. I should have her problems.' Nadia's expression was harsh.

'We all have our troubles, Mama.'

'You don't know what trouble is. We have nothing out there, do you understand? It is a barbaric country run by sadists, and every day your father and I must entertain them with smiles, then return to the compound wondering if there will be ingredients for a decent meal or even someone who knows how to cook proper Russian food for us. Do you know what I am doing this month? Do you think this is a holiday for me? I have a list as long as a believer's beard – food, toiletries, clothes, pepper vodka for your father. He drinks more and more these days, you have no idea. Every day is a nightmare for me, what to get, how to get it, asking favours of everyone I know. And no one to help me. While you are out in your palace with its magic tablecloth.' She trembled with anger.

In her twisted face Katya caught a glimpse of what her mother would look like in twenty years – a face stripped to the bony essentials of bitterness and suffering, leathery skin taut over her small skull. She would be helpless, needy, expecting Katya to take care of her.

But what was so awful about Nadia's life now? Ethiopia was not an easy station, it was true. The weather was oppressive, the landscape harsh. Katya had visited two years ago, taking dried herbs, vegetable oil and oatmeal. Bribing the Derg cut heavily into precious hard currency – so how, Katya

93

wanted to ask, could Nadia afford designer suits and expensive jewellery if Arkady could not put food on the table? Her diatribe had been a diversion from the truth, which was that she preferred being away from family responsibility and did not want to think about her mother-in-law and her needs, even for a week. Perhaps she shunned contact with Babushka from fear of what she herself would become?

Katya felt suffocated – less by her mother's selfishness and bourgeois materialism than by the chilling sense she imparted that, in this time and place, love was not possible. Marry for money, marry for security, marry for any reason but love. It had been her message for as long as Katya could remember. In her mother, who was almost exactly the age of the state, passion had been channelled into Philistinism and self-pity. And as for her, so it was for the empire: six decades of socialism and what was there to show for it? A stagnant, corrupt élite who sealed themselves away from the people. A doddering General Secretary (addicted, it was said, to drugs), who presided impotently over an *apparat* gelded by greed. Whole ministries whose *raison d'être* was the destruction of privacy and the creation of an insidious intimacy. How could love flourish amid such barrenness?

Nadia finished her snack and went to her bedroom to get ready, leaving behind a trail of cigarette smoke and despair. For her, confrontation was blood. She could not live without it. But for Katya each outburst took its place in a chain that stretched back to her adolescence and added to the strain of being her mother's daughter. Nadia always made sure that the emotional balance tilted her way, always had the last word, never admitted that maybe she had a better life than the vast majority of her compatriots. No, she must suffer and be seen to suffer.

At six Volodya rang the bell, and Katya opened the door.

'The programmes?' he asked at once.

'They are on the way to the hall.'

It was a relief to see him. He tilted his head towards the car. Katya raised her eyebrows. He nodded and returned to his post. He knew Nadia.

It was half an hour before her mother had chosen her shoes, applied her makeup, done her hair, and put on her jewellery. She paused for a long time at the hall mirror, punishing her daughter for annoying her.

In the car they stared silently out of opposite windows. At such moments the city itself was tinged with the bitterness of their relationship. As Volodya drove down Kropotkinskaya Street and on to the ring road, Katya caught a glimpse of Borodinsky Bridge, where she and her mother had endured perhaps their most memorable confrontation. In the middle of a November snowstorm, snowflakes melting on Nadia's long lashes, she had warned Katya not to associate with certain students in her doctoral class. Out of the range of microphones, they shouted in the wind about loyalty, friendship and self-preservation. Nadia had heard from the wife of an internal-affairs lieutenant that two young men in her daughter's class had been observed speaking to unauthorized Americans in the lobby of the Ukraine Hotel. Katya had known them since her schooldays and had worked with them over a memorable summer, canning peaches in Bulgaria. With one – strong, quiet Mikhail – she'd had a brief love affair. Now her mother was asking her to disown them.

Katya refused to heed the warning. In those days she had had high ideals and went out of her way to associate with them and prove to herself that true friendship would not yield to coercion. A month later the men were expelled from the university without possibility of appeal. Their careers were ruined because of a casual conversation in a hotel lobby. Her mother, paralysed by anger and fear, did not speak to her for months. A more ominous silence was that of the university and the KGB, who left Katya to wonder if she had harmed her friends by flouting her mother's warning. She was never punished, and as her career progressed she found it impossible to discount that her faithfulness to her friends and to her ideals had helped condemn them.

She waved away her mother's cigarette smoke and watched the cold streets drift by. Her nerves were jangling. Let the Americans play well and please their audience. So much seemed to depend on tonight.

CHAPTER 9

Volodya left them at Mayakovsky Hall at seven o'clock, thirty minutes late for the reception hosted by Leonid and Luba, who met them at the door.

'Ah, Nadia,' Leonid said, kissing her hand, 'as beautiful as ever.' Nadia ignored him and greeted Luba.

Leonid turned to Katya, who was trying to take in the activity in the lobby and gauge what had still to be done. But she was really looking, she realized, for Drew. 'The programmes,' she asked Leonid, 'have they arrived?'

'Just this minute. Vasily has distributed them to the girls.'

The way Leonid looked at women was both predatory and flattering. He glanced up and down her body but never seemed to lose contact with her eyes. He clasped his hands loosely – expectant and deferential – but the leonine tilt of his head betrayed his desire for control. 'And you look quite splendid yourself, Katya,' he said. But even as he spoke he was staring at Nadia's calves as she and Luba drifted away, deep in conversation.

Katya felt the old, comparative link. Her mother was small-limbed, natural in her movements, socially confident. Tonight her hair was freshly cut and her jewellery glittered against her tanned skin. The anger had disappeared, and she played, with great skill, the role of her daughter's calm companion. Like her father, Katya had to work hard to appear comfortable in public, and though she knew that many men were attracted to her, when she was with her mother doubts nagged at her about her figure.

Leonid took her coat and handed it to an attendant. Across the room Salim, Marshall and Yoshi were talking to a group of journalists. Marshall was bending down to hear the questions of a small man in a corduroy jacket. Salim, in a bright yellow caftan, looked stern. Beside them, Reef translated. She could not see Drew.

'Everything is ready?' she asked Leonid.

'Everything.'

'Should they not be backstage?'

'Let them finish,' Leonid said, and added in English: 'Good publicity.'

The lobby had an air of high anticipation and privilege such as could only be found on a frosty January night in Moscow in a year when foreign wars and cold diplomacy had made such events rare. The old gas chandeliers sparkled. The conversation hummed expectantly, like an orchestra tuning up. Party bosses, foreign journalists and the city's artistic élite helped themselves to glasses of champagne and chocolates wrapped in coloured paper. Stalin's famous pronouncement in 1935, the year before her grandfather's execution in a Lubyanka basement, came to Katya's mind: 'Life has become better comrades; life has become more cheerful.'

'The journey to Leningrad,' Leonid said, 'all is arranged?' His tone was conspiratorial, faintly lascivious.

'Of course.'

'Train tickets, visas?'

'Exactly as you requested, Leonid,' she said tightly. She refused his offer of champagne. 'I must see to the performers,' she said, and left abruptly.

She crossed the lobby, inspected the programmes and looked into the auditorium. Television cameras were set up at the rear and along both side walls. Klieg lights warmed the stage. A still-life of piano, drum kit and prostrate double bass sat in front of the huge red safety curtain, gold-embroidered with elaborate Soviet insignia and a profile of Lenin. The first three rows, reserved for the highest rank of the privileged, had been marked off with loops of red ribbon. She turned back to the musicians. They had finished their interviews and were walking towards the door that led to their dressing room. She hurried to follow them and felt a hand on her elbow.

'Where you running to?' Drew asked.

She stopped short and flushed. It took her a moment to find the English words. 'Please. You must go to dressing room now.'

'Must I?'

He wore a freshly ironed blue shirt and white trousers. The look of vulnerability around his eyes had yielded to a narrow, focused vigour. He was drumming on his thighs with his fingers, lips parted to show a glimmer of teeth. She knew that he was preparing himself to perform but her mood allowed her to indulge the idea that she was the subject of his intensity. 'I will come with you,' she said, and led him in the direction of the dressing room. 'It is nearly time.'

She had lived too long to fool herself. She knew the difference between a light flutter and the rare pulse of deep attraction. She couldn't think of anything to say.

'Kept looking for you today,' he said, from behind her, as they passed through the narrow passage to the dressing room. Old programme posters lined the walls, lit by low-wattage lightbulbs.

She looked at the scuffed carpet beneath her feet. 'Today was most busy day,' she said, without turning. She could feel him gazing at her hips beneath the tight poplin; she worried that she would stumble. 'I had much to prepare for tonight.'

'Hey, there's a buzz out there. Feels like a hit. Hope they like the tunes, is all.'

She slowed as they approached the end of the passage and he bumped into her. She steadied herself against the dressing-room door and half turned her head. His right hand rested on her waist and lingered. She became aware of the rapid rise and fall of her ribs as her breathing quickened. He was close enough for her to smell a sourness on his breath. It matched the darkness around his eyes, and she did not find it unpleasant. 'Excuse me,' he said softly.

He took away his hand and she turned. 'Now,' she said – and the words came with great effort – 'you must join your colleagues. The announcements are coming.'

She expected him to speak, but he stayed silent. She opened the door, and he moved past her, his arm brushing her breast. Ahead, the other musicians were grouped in a mute triangle, avoiding each other's gaze, directing themselves to the performance.

Leonid arrived, script in hand. Stagehands and helpers scurried like shadows across the tension, whispering and purposeful. What are they all doing here? Katya wondered. Drew had become the only reality in the room. She stood calmly, her hand on the doorknob, watching the theatrical hubbub while, inside her, a storm raged.

She took her seat beside her mother in the front row. Nadia peered at her. 'Are you all right?' she asked.

'I'm fine.'

'Is Leonid bothering you?'

'Mama, I'm fine. Please, the music is about to start.'

The musicians emerged to desultory applause, led by Leonid across the stage. Drew sat at the piano, adjusted the stool, and ran his fingers soundlessly across the keys. She sensed her mother's sidelong inspection and tried to look elsewhere, but he remained at the centre of her gaze. While Leonid gave a dry, Russian-style introduction, Drew rolled up his sleeves and placed a clean white towel at his feet. He took a packet of cigarettes from his shirt pocket, set it on the floor beside an ashtray, cracked his knuckles, and gazed up at the suspended microphones. He seemed unaware of the audience. Then he bowed his head so that it almost touched the keys, and waited for Leonid to finish his opening remarks.

The music took Katya by surprise. She had listened to the band's records, been present at their rehearsals and sound check, but the reality of performance was different. Without cue, the four instruments crashed into activity, blaring and atonal. The men played frantically, without apparent reference to each other. 'We wailed', she had heard Salim say after one of the rehearsals, and the sound that now rolled out was an animalistic howl that caused the well-dressed audience to flinch. Katya could read the look on the faces of Leonid's privileged guests: what was this chaos bouncing off walls that had absorbed Tchaikovsky and Rimsky-Korsakov? How could it be called music?

But for Katya it was invigorating. It quickened her pulse and fell across her senses like a sprinkle of rain. It reminded her of Stravinsky – shifting, primal, highly rhythmic – yet had a power all its own. Soon the opening cacophony yielded to a steadier passage of craggy beauty. The drums hissed and exploded; the piano and double bass, plucked rather than bowed, repeated an insistent, trance-like figure. Over this tortuous beat the saxophone came to the fore, deep-toned and growling, sexual in its energy and sway. Marshall's long face was tense and contorted. He bobbed back and forth, improvising over the driving rhythm and, it seemed, inviting the audience to swing their limbs or shout, as if ancient ritual lay behind the flurry of notes.

Katya felt as she had when she first discovered literature: then she had been astounded by the riches the old masters could offer, the secrets they could reveal to a sixteen-year-old girl. And as she had surrendered to the great books, so now she gave herself to the music.

When Marshall finished his solo Drew took over, eyes closed. Whatever was flowing through him coursed through Katya as well. All her longing was suddenly given a context. *Take me*, her body said. *Make me free*. The tremulousness that had overtaken her at the dressing-room door, when Drew laid his hand on her waist, expanded. She was cut loose from herself, buoyed by feelings she allowed to happen, like breathing. And as his solo built, with breathtaking pace and variation, her own excitement mounted with a directness she had only experienced when making love, and she recognized that the music had shown her a vista of infinite possibilities, a landscape of startling chords and unexpected silences.

CHAPTER 10

Drew had been a miler in high school, and coming down after a show always reminded him of the first moments after a race, when his heart was still pounding. He was wide-eyed and edgy, no good for small-talk, eager for a drink. It was the time when he most missed heroin, the cool distance it created and the comforting bubble of isolation. The jagged energy of the music might flow within him for hours, and he usually preferred to be alone.

After the Mayakovsky gig, however, he went looking for Katya. Though the audience had been a dark blur in the large hall, he had sensed her presence. The fingers of his right hand, even as they had searched for the notes that shaped his solos, had tingled with the memory of her waist's soft curve. The accidental contact in the passageway had sparked a connection that had extended into the music. He had to see her.

The reception area was packed with guests in tuxedos and evening gowns drinking champagne and eating canapés. The room was oppressively warm, and a roar of Russian conversation enveloped him as he pushed through the crowd, acknowledging words of appreciation, braving stares and the press of flesh. Claustrophobia beat within him like a captured moth. Where was she?

He saw Leonid across the room, holding forth with sumptuous gestures and a charming smile before two dark-suited men. His cigarette, in its ceramic holder, described lavish arcs as he emphasized a point, and his hair shone in the light of the chandeliers. Drew walked up to him and interrupted: 'I'm looking for Katya. Do you know where she is?'

Leonid's audience turned to face him: Washington and Ahern, the political officers from the US Embassy.

'Hey,' Washington, the black officer, said, 'the piano man. Not bad tonight. Not bad at all.'

Drew stared at him, nonplussed. He could feel Ahern's slit-eyed stare riding the border of his vision.

'Missed your gig at the embassy, I'm afraid,' Washington continued. 'Mike and I had a meeting. But Mr Petrosian kindly asked us along tonight. So here we are. Had to check you guys out.' He widened his eyes to let Drew know that he was joking. Ahern rubbed his mouth with a pink hand. He didn't take his eyes off Drew.

'We are always delighted,' Leonid said, 'to welcome our esteemed guests from the embassy. To extend the hand of détente, as it were.'

Ahern flashed him a look – *Yeah, right* – pulled

106

at his tie and looked at the door. 'Rick, we gotta run,' he said. He slid away.

Washington tightened his lips. Drew sensed he had something to say, something friendly or helpful, but now had no time to say it. He tapped Drew's shoulder. 'Don't worry about Mike. Never went to charm school.'

'I'm not worried.'

'We genuinely wanted to hear you guys. Not a lot of American-style entertainment in this town. You gotta take it where you can get it. No offence, sir,' he said to Leonid.

'None taken.'

'Keep in touch.' He walked away, his jacket shifting between his shoulder-blades.

Drew discovered he had been holding his breath, and let it out in a long near-groan. He and Leonid took each other's measure. 'They are frequent guests at our events,' Leonid said.

'I'm sure they are. Do you know where Katya is?'

'Dr Timoshenko has gone to the television offices with the camera crew. To supervise delivery to the studio of your taped performance.'

Drew tried to light a cigarette, but his hand shook so fiercely he gave up. 'Leonid, I need a drink.'

'Of course. Please wait.'

While he was gone, Salim arrived. 'What's wrong?'

'He was here,' Drew said.

'Who?'

'The embassy spook. Ahern.'

Salim scanned the room. His large face bore a bloom of sweat and his eyes were bloodshot.

'He left,' Drew said.

'Black Brad with him?'

'Washington. Yeah. But he's OK. Ahern couldn't get out of here fast enough. Kept looking at me like I was a criminal. Like he was going to flash cuffs any minute.'

'Steady on, Fish. Don't go paranoid on me.'

'I gotta get out of here.'

'We can do that.'

'I need a drink.'

'Got you covered.'

Salim hijacked Maxim and the Volga and directed him back to the hotel. From a deep pocket in his *caftan* he pulled out a pint of Four Roses. They drank from the bottle, gasping at the whiskey and the frigid air.

The cold streets were empty as they glided past the huge, severe buildings. Lights were on in the government offices, and Drew imagined their occupants: strategists and *apparatchiks*, calculating coldly behind double-glazed windows the size of arsenals, budgets, missile bays, ailing factories, shortages. On the alert now that Reagan was coming on board, hand to his holster.

He was turning into his father. Seeing enemies at every post, conspiracies in every corner. At home and abroad. He had thought it would be different here, but loneliness echoed wider on these streets, beneath this sky, than it did at home.

The hotel doors were guarded on the inside by a cluster of dour young men in leather jackets, who smoked American cigarettes and eyed the guests with surly resentment. 'Wha's happenin', guys?' Salim chirped, waving his passport in their faces and matching the baleful stares. 'Know that look,' he said to Drew, as they dropped their jackets in the cloakroom and headed for the hard-currency bar. 'See it on corners in the hood, be looking to create a situation. Take it on, brother, only thing to do.'

'Easy, Salim.'

Salim, too, was jittery. No bourbon at the bar, so they settled for Johnnie Walker. Brisk and sullen, the barman took their money, his eyes as empty as the taiga. The room was high-ceilinged and dark but thin on character: plastic chairs and tables, each decorated with a wooden vase and a single artificial flower; a dirty floor of chipped tiles, with cigarette burns here and there.

Salim sipped his whisky. 'You all right now?'

Drew shrugged.

'What are you thinking?'

'I'm thinking how I flew five thousand miles from my problems, but here they still are, staring at me like a snake.'

'Ain't no problems here, just solutions.'

'You call Ahern a solution?'

'I call him an irritation. Like what you have to

deal with every day of your life when you walk the walk. Know what I'm sayin'?'

Drew knew. 'Walk the walk' was Salim shorthand for holding your head high while you handled adversity, keeping cool in a hostile world, staying clean when you'd like nothing so much as a hit of horse. Above all, avoiding self-pity, a cardinal sin in Salim's gospel.

'You thinkin' about Jessie?' he asked, not looking at Drew.

'What kind of question is that?'

'The straight kind.'

'A kind you don't ask.'

'I do, when I'm lookin' for a straight answer.'

'Being straight,' Drew said, 'is what fucked me up.'

Salim tapped the table with his fingers and worked his lips. 'That's a different straight.'

'Maybe. But it's true.'

'Don't bullsh me, Fish. You hear?'

'I'm not.'

'You forgettin' what the shit took from you, man?'

'I know exactly what it took from me.'

Salim's eyes went flinty. He was still except for his foot, which tapped furiously. 'You gonna make me say it? I'm hearin' strings. A hundred motherfuckin' violins.'

When it came to false feeling Salim had perfect pitch. Drew, who instinctively avoided even a trace of sentimentality at the piano, was less reliable in conversation. Anxiety threw him out of tune. Led to rash statements. And actions. 'I left her when I was straight. What kind of shit was that?'

'That was five years ago kind of shit, that was. Five years. And still you're peddling this jive. Kickin' was the right thing, Fish. Don't lose sight of that. The right thing, no matter what else went down. No matter what's goin' down tonight.'

He didn't need Salim's logic. Tonight history was working against him – looking for Katya and finding Ahern, looking for himself and finding his father. He lit a cigarette and drank his Scotch. Yes, he had kicked the habit, and a month later he had left the only woman who'd ever loved him. That was the kind of decision he made when he went straight.

Salim leaned close. 'Don't do the blame thing, Fish. You hear me?'

But Drew was running into himself, a tightening loop of self-pity that made him seek isolation. He knew this route well. At the end of it, always, was his father, throwing logs into the fireplace and soddenly addressing visitors: 'Behind the cold, clear gaze of a Montanan . . . lies absolutely nothing.' And then he would cackle, while Drew listened from the kitchen and wondered why he felt drawn to the vacant and spacious when his dad so hated it.

Blame had been in his father's voice and his mother's milk. In the air he breathed. America blamed Russia and John Fisher had been caught in the crossfire, so he blamed his wife and his son. He should have been living in the great cities of the world, advising presidents and princes. Instead he ranted at his family in the Rocky Mountains.

His father had made him a Montanan when he brought the family to Missoula in 1955. Drew had been twelve, and they had moved from Lima, where his dad had been third secretary at the American consulate, a tertiary position in a far-flung outpost. It had been as far away as the American government could station the once-great John Fisher from the halls of power and circles of influence that should have been bene-fiting from his knowledge and experience. But as bad as Peru was, Montana was worse. As Drew passed through adolescence he learned that his family was living in this distant outpost because his father was a pariah.

He became aware that over the previous seven years his dad had been investigated nine times by the State Department or Congress. That the last time, the year before their arrival in Montana, he had been the special object of Gunner Joe McCarthy's wrath. That he had been found guilty by the House Un-American Activities Committee of 'lack of judgement, discretion, and reliability'. His dad had been the object of a witch hunt. His dad, the most tough-minded, resourceful, cautious diplomat in the foreign service, had been subjected to poisonous hysteria, which had been upheld by the Secretary of State, John Foster Dulles, who let it be known that it might save everyone's embarrassment if Drew's dad resigned. But John Davis Fisher, who had marched through China in 1938 with Vinegar Joe Stilwell to look Chiang Kai-shek in the eye and tell him he was a fool, was not about to resign because Joe McCarthy said he should. He forced Dulles to fire him – then discovered that so-called friends shunned him and he was blackballed by the Ivy League.

In this way the State Department lost its top Asian expert, who came to rest at the University of Montana, where he taught political science and pretended that the dirty mill town of Missoula was where he wanted to be. He had moved from the bland consulate compounds to a ramshackle lodge on the banks of the Clark Fork river that was never warm enough and always smelt of woodsmoke. Money was tight. For Drew's sake they spent two hundred bucks on moving the piano out of storage, with the library and the China mementos, but Clare's antique furniture went under the gavel and the summer-house in Kennebunkport was sold to pay the lawyers.

The son of missionaries, John claimed that his boyhood years in China had prepared him for roughing it. He stomped around the yard in hiking boots and an Icelandic sweater, yelling at the dogs, chopping wood, building shaky fences. He loved Montana, he roared. But pain and cynicism surfaced. He let his hair grow, didn't bother shaving, and drank more with each passing year.

He hectored Clare mercilessly, and as she retreated into cooking, bird-watching and trips to her mother in Boston, he looked to his only child for love.

The timing was unfortunate. As his father discovered the unique loneliness of an influential man stripped of dignity and profession while still in his prime, Drew was stepping gingerly into a blank that was taking shape around him to swallow innocence like fog. But, like the long pauses he loved in Thelonious Monk tunes, the silence brought out the sound of life around him. There had been moments in his teenage years, which he could recall with absolute clarity over twenty years later, when the certainties of childhood yielded to a churning sense that desire and danger floated side by side. He heard it in the throaty laughs of the girls he watched from his seat at the back of the class. He smelt it on autumn evenings, walking to football games, the air fragrant with decay. He sensed it in his mother's subtle but distinct avoidance of physical contact with his father. Love will not come, such moments announced, without pain.

Well, he was a runner, and he ran: to college, to New York, to jazz, to Jessie. To heroin. The last step was so effortless, so logical. High, he could forget his father's need and his mother's pain. He could be with Jessie on her terms. And for a white kid from the sticks trying to make the scene, it was a badge of arrival.

114

Or so it had seemed at the time. But tonight Salim was reading his thoughts, daring him to express them so that he could spit on the sentiment.

There was a stir in Reception. An American laugh announced the arrival of another group. A man in a suit and a Stetson glided in, face like a boiled ham. He had the step of a someone who'd had too much to eat and drink. 'You got that right, Ivan,' he shouted.

A half-step behind him hovered a good-looking, bearded man in a Soviet fatigue jacket and new jeans. He wore Western aviator sunglasses but spoke with a Russian accent. 'Maybe you don't get other chance. Maybe she is last you see.'

'Well, I'll take the risk.'

The American leaned unsteadily on the bar and looked at Drew and Salim as he ordered. His pal led him to an adjacent table, and he set his hat on the third chair. 'Save this, case a *real* woman comes along.'

'I tell you—'

'I know what you told me.'

Salim stared at the plastic table with blank eyes and lower lip firmed just enough to drop the corners of his mouth. Drew knew the look well. It was a black man's wariness, the fear of being caught off guard, retreat in the face of white swagger. No evidence yet of anything other than oiled self-confidence, but no harm in taking its measure.

The man breathed deeply. Drew waited for the question.

'Something tells me you guys are from the States.'

Drew turned in his seat. 'That's right.'

'Where from?'

'New York City.'

'The Big Apple.'

'*Bolshoi yabloko*,' the Russian said, and the American barked a laugh.

'Hell, Ivan, you'd fit right in there, you know that? You and the rest of the Soviet empire.'

Salim was still staring at the table. Drew turned back to his drink, knowing he would soon have to choose between rudeness or boredom.

'From Latrobe myself. Latrobe, P-A. Home of Rolling Rock beer. And Arnold Palmer.'

'The old tractor,' Drew said, with some despair.

'You got it.'

The Russian leaned across the empty chair. 'Don is very particular American. Russian girls no good.'

'You guys watch yourselves,' Don said. 'Ivan's a man on a mission tonight.' The tone of his exchange with Ivan was light and repetitive, like a stone skimming a pond. Drew guessed they had just met. Don took a crumpled handkerchief from his pocket and wiped his forehead. He had the Southern sheriff's moist lips and fleshy chin, but his eyes revealed an alertness, a careful curiosity. Behind the banter he was sizing them up.

'What brings you to Russia?' Drew asked. Better to probe than be probed by a guy like Don.

'Steel.' The word rang in the high-ceilinged room. His tone snapped tight and his eyes narrowed. 'Blast furnaces and continuous casting. Slabs and blooms and yield. Another thing we know about in Latrobe.' He drank. Drew's ear marked the sharpened timbre, the stiffening of purpose that men of a certain cast assumed when the subject was business. And whether it was iron ore, platinum or wheat, doing business meant making money, and money was the American eucharist. 'Flying out to Magnitogorsk tomorrow,' he said, as if heading into battle. 'Biggest steel mill in the world.' He swirled the ice in his glass and smiled. 'If not the most efficient.'

'I think Magnitogorsk is closed city.'

'Not so, Ivan. Chelyabinsk, yes. Big defence industry there. But in Magnitogorsk they got nothing to hide but the sky. Nothing out there 'cept the plant and the smoke. Four hundred thousand people in this city of nowhere, and they all work at or support the mill.'

Salim had leaned forward, elbows on knees, head hanging like a vulture's. 'What's your gig?' he offered.

More a challenge than a question. Drew could tell that Salim smelt what he called the 'money stink'. 'Smell it on their breath, right? Comin' out their pores. But *they* don't sniff the whiff because they're inside it. Got the money stink risin' round them like skunkweed. It's their karma.'

Don took in Salim's yellow tunic and Uzbeki skullcap, the ridged brow and broad nose, and

117

cheeks nubbed with a couple of days' coiled growth. Easy, too, to guess what Don saw. He loosened his tie. 'My gig? Consultant. Lowest labour costs in the world and they can't compete on world markets. Yields been dropping year by year. Need a little American know-how to get them competitive again.' Again the thin smile and eyes stripped to expression of the essential.

'So they workin' with us?'

Don didn't like the *us* but kept moving. 'Well, they're working with me. And I'm not the only one. Let me tell you something: when it comes to politics you have to ignore the propaganda. It works both ways. And my experience? Not much difference between the two brands. We love to talk how they're full of shit, but same breath we're hopping on our high horse like the Lone Ranger. Afghan War, civil rights, the gulags. Carter putting on his preacher face and boycotting the Olympics. Hell, I was here at the time doing business. Got back from the Urals in time to see the finals of the men's hundred metres – biggest joke of the Games without our boys in there. Meanwhile we're selling them grain and processed food and helping them turn their industry around. Politics may be politics, but money talks.'

Ivan looked up from his wallet. He'd been counting green-backs, as if to illustrate Don's thesis. 'Don is very clever. He understand Russian people are like American people. We all want for same. For example, you gentlemen look for ladies.

118

I, Ivan Ivanovich, can make introductions. Best ladies in Moscow.'

Drew didn't bother to look at him. Just hearing the offer fatigued him. Where was Katya now? Had she expected to see him on her return from the TV studio? He should have ridden out his despair and waited for her. On this of all nights he did not want to be hustled. He wanted sleep. He wanted distance. But stumbling to his lonely bed held no appeal, and Salim was perking up with the prospect of a political discussion. 'What about the grain embargo?'

'What about it?' Don said. 'It's a joke. We shipped eight million tons here last year. Flag-waving farmers out in Kansas growing wheat for the Russkies. And you think Reagan the great middle-American is going to tell the farming lobby to swallow *those* profits? It's a no-brainer.'

'The man do love his capitalism.'

'Even more than he hates Commies.'

'Just like you, right?'

Salim's bait was subtler than it sounded, delivered with a comedian's timing, intended to shift the discussion to a higher level. He knew that Don knew what was going on. He had assessed the man as smarter than he looked.

Don responded with matching wryness, scanning the dark corners of the room with casual scrutiny. 'Oh, I love everybody,' he said. 'So long as they don't get in the way of me making a buck.'

'So you makin' a buck with the biggest mill on the planet?'

'Oh, yeah. They got a big Jap oxygen furnace and continuous casters. The latest and greatest gear. Paid for with natural gas pumped straight from Siberia. But they're still doing eighty per cent of their production open hearth because they don't have the technicians to keep the show on the road. Which is where I come in.'

'At top commercial.'

'I'd be a fool to do it for less.'

'No gain being a fool.'

'You said it, pal. No gain at all.'

They stared at each other like gunslingers. In Drew's tired head the exchange tolled with irritating resonance. The sly, jiving rhetoric he so loved from Salim had thinned to a liberal aggression that reminded him of his father's emasculated rage. He tried to tune out, but Don's voice droned on, and the plastic tables and moulded cement walls surrounded him like a sarcophagus. Too much tonight. Too many reminders of what was missing. In the old days heroin would have filled it.

Ivan seemed to pick up on the emptiness and leaned close, speaking quietly over Don and Salim's strident crosstalk. 'My friend has doctorate,' he said. 'Very clever, very intelligent.' Intelligent pronounced with a hard g. 'She will know what you need.'

'No, thank you, Ivan.'

'She warm and sexy. Tall. Soft hands.'

He was close enough for Drew to notice his own

reflection in the dark glasses. To smell the dill-scented breath. To see the damp strands of moustache clinging to the corners of the soft mouth. 'This how *you* make a living, Ivan?'

The Russian lifted his shoulders and spread his hands. '*Make a living*. In Soviet Union very strange phrase. No translation in Russian for "make a living".'

Temptation rustled. Against his will Drew was thinking of soothing words and soft hands. He had been with prostitutes. Sometimes it was good, sometimes not. Though what was good about it was not what he needed tonight.

'Make you very happy,' Ivan whispered.

Drew looked away. Several customers had wandered in, Germans or Finns, dressed in expensive suits, looking about the room as they shot their cuffs and tucked silk ties into jacket fronts. 'There you go, Ivan. There's your customers. Why don't you ask them?'

'They not appreciate, my friend. They are like Don. You . . . you have sense of a true woman. Russian sense. This I can tell.'

The voice at his shoulder hissed like an insect. The man's breath washed over him. Drew almost gagged. But Ivan knew how to play the waiting game. He had the pimp's patient persistence and radar for weakness. Or perhaps it was something else. He glanced at Salim, still engrossed in his discussion. 'Maybe other pleasures you like. I have the real good stuff. From Afghani mountains.'

Drew stiffened. 'What stuff?'

'You know. The thing you want. You miss.' His voice was a papery whisper.

Drew pushed him away and looked over to Salim, who was leaning back and laughing, revealing gold molars and a red palate. Don was smiling. In true American fashion, they had found common ground.

'You can see it here?' Salim said.

'Can't *see* it,' Don said. 'But you can hear it. On radio. Voice of America.'

'Got to *be* there for that. Got to hear them bohunks get their ragtag asses booted.'

'You will. Only one Super Bowl team in my state, and it ain't in the City of Brotherly Love!'

'Salim,' Drew said, 'let's go.' He could sense Ivan at the edge of his vision, waiting, beckoning. '*Salim!*'

But Salim had a point to make about a subject dear to his heart. 'Eagles too old-school,' he said. What he meant was they were too white. Blue-collar and rust-belt tough, but without the ghostly speed of the ghetto. 'Raiders gonna fly past them suckers. Cliff Branch. Kenny King.'

'Do that, they'll make Steelers fans very happy.'

Drew stood up, sweaty and claustrophobic. He wouldn't look at Ivan. 'I'm out of here, buddy.'

Evidently Salim noticed the pale panic in Drew's face. He glanced at Ivan, who was slowly tearing a beer mat in half. 'OK, Fish, OK. I'm comin'.'

Don lifted the hat from the chair and turned

the brim in his hands. He caught Drew's eye as Salim got up. 'Let me guess, you guys are some kind of artists.'

'We ain't sellin' wheat,' Salim said.

'Actors?

'Musicians,' Drew said.

'The music,' Salim said, imitating Marshall, 'we like to call jazz.'

Ivan snapped his fingers. 'Ah. Louis Armstrong. Ella Fitzgerald.' Again the hard *g*.

'So you dig jazz here?'

'Voice of America. Mr Willis Conover.'

'Hey, Fish, this Voice of America, man, Super Bowl *and* the tunes. We got to check this dial *out*.'

But Drew was walking away.

Ranged about the bleak space, the blond business-men waited, legs crossed, wide northern European faces in the overheated air, sipping their drinks and waiting for what chance, and Ivan, would throw their way.

CHAPTER 11

On Saturday morning Katya kissed her sleeping children and stepped through bitter frost to her car. Volodya and the Chaika had been commandeered by the space ministry for the weekend, so she had to drive her unreliable old Volga. The sky was infused with the shimmer of unreasonable weather. She was tired and distracted, doing her best to keep guilt at bay. Her day was fully scheduled, and though she would have a few hours with the children over the weekend, on Monday they would go to her mother-in-law's for the week of her Leningrad trip. Anna had stopped speaking to her, and even Sasha was sulking.

Leonid had summoned her to the offices of the Soviet-American Cultural Exchange for what she knew would be a morning of bureaucracy. She had much to do: paperwork and preparations, a gala dinner to oversee at the Praga restaurant on Sunday night, arrangements for the trip north on Monday. She would not see Drew until the dinner. And even then, how could she enjoy his company with Oleg peering at them?

The Exchange meeting was a nuisance. It had been arranged ostensibly to review the Leningrad itinerary, but Katya knew from experience that any such trip with foreigners had careful security protocols that must be drilled into accompanying Russians *ad nauseam*. As if the foreigners were the ones being watched.

The offices were in a pre-Revolutionary building on Kuibyshev Street, a few hundred metres from the Kremlin and within that triangle of old city that was the very navel of the Soviet empire: Nogina Square to the Lenin Library to the Lubyanka. She parked as close as possible to the entrance and walked carefully along the frozen footpath. In spite of the frost, the street's scrubbed cobblestones and granite façades stirred something deep within her. Here, she had watched the glitter of Red Square celebrations from her father's shoulders. Here, she had assembled to march in Komsomol parades. Here, she had peered from the curtained hush of a Zil limousine while her mother and father, stiff with fear and pride, prepared themselves, with whispered reassurances, for a Kremlin visit.

'My little blonde *pirozhki*,' Nikita Khrushchev had said to her that day, grinning and patting her head. Then he had turned to his fawning entourage: 'Our future, comrades. Our future.'

She had stood with her parents in the receiving line on the Parade Staircase of the Grand Kremlin Palace with other Party faithful to celebrate the launch of Sputnik. Khrushchev had been at the

125

height of his career: he had led the USSR to super-power status; a Russian spacecraft circled the earth; he had disposed of his enemies at a dramatic summer plenum to become the country's un-ambiguous leader. The electricity of influence crackled around him.

'Ah, Arkady Vasiliyich.' The most famous man in the world had noticed her father. He stepped around her and embraced him, kissing his lips. Nadia beamed. Tears in his eyes, the premier mentioned the name of Katya's grandfather. Nearly a quarter-century later, she could still see the black belt encircling his big stomach, the medals pinned to his breast pocket, the nicked hands gesticulating like a magician's, the bald dome and fleshy growths around his nose. Heard, too, his reverent tone when he whispered her grandfather's name.

Her family and her country had been at their zenith. Now, as the dull-witted building guard examined her documents and noted the details of her visit in his log, she was conscious of a long fall from grace.

She made her way through a warren of corridors lined with anonymous doors and peeling skirting-boards. Strips of cheap red carpet, dusted here and there with fallen plaster, were tacked shoddily to the wooden floors. As close to the centre of the empire as it was possible to be and the decay was evident, lit with clinical fastidiousness by fluorescent lighting. She felt pale and superficial within the dilapidated walls. Deep inside the building she arrived at Leonid's office and knocked firmly, resisting the malaise that was settling on her like dust from the mouldering ceiling.

The door was opened by his assistant, a peroxide blonde in heavy makeup whose ample figure was a year or two away from ballooning into peasant girth. She wore a wool sweater and too-tight skirt, and moved with the assurance of a woman who understood the simple power of surface sexuality. From the look in her eyes, pale and possessive, Katya saw at once that she was intimate with Leonid. She brushed past her without a word.

Leonid rose from his desk and Reef turned in his chair, smiling. Oleg was sitting at a small table off to the side, looking sickly and pale. He studied a volume of regulations and jotted notes on a yellow legal pad. A lit cigarette, Western by its mild smell, lay in the ashtray beside him.

'Katya. We have just been speaking of you. Please.' Leonid gestured towards an empty chair beside Reef. 'Coffee, tea?'

'Tea, please.'

He nodded to his assistant and, though Katya had her back to the woman, she saw a knowing smirk reflected in Leonid's eyes. This was the woman with whom she would share a compartment on the train to Leningrad. She removed her gloves and coat, handed them to Leonid, and sat beside Reef. Oleg coughed.

'Reef has been telling us about your husband,'

Leonid said. 'I had no idea he was participating in such an important mission.'

Katya frowned. For reasons she could not articulate, she did not like discussing Ilya's job, especially with other men. She did not trust their interest. Mention of him was usually prelude to tiresome political talk or an attempt to curry favour. He enhanced her status for the wrong reasons and with the wrong people.

'He is part of the back-up team with little chance of flight time.'

Oleg looked up from his notes and puffed his cigarette. He was definitely unwell. His eyes were bloodshot and rheumy, his forehead beaded with sweat.

'All the same,' Leonid said, 'it is a critical role. And any time one has such an opportunity to serve the motherland . . .' He tilted his head with the tiniest measure of irony to let Katya know he was teasing, but not so much that Oleg would prick up his ears – yet Leonid was far too protected to worry about someone like Oleg. He played the game but hinted with almost every gesture at the real story. The purpose of today's meeting was to air the familiar, to pay lip service, and to bring to the surface lines of control implicit in the exercise of playing host to guests from a rival superpower. Leonid's orbit of influence was far higher than that of the rest of them. Oleg could terrorize someone like Reef, but he was small beer to Leonid who, while he mouthed the platitudes, did so always with a play of superiority around his handsome eyes. It pained her to admit it, but Katya knew that today she had to stay on his good side. Or he might unleash Oleg.

'Believe me, Leonid, there is no one more eager to do his duty.' She smiled wanly as the assistant returned with tea. 'And the highest duty for a Soviet cosmonaut is to pilot a Soyuz spacecraft.' She spoke clearly and with obvious intent, letting it be known that she was the wife of an important man. She was capable of playing the card of influence when it suited her. By concentrating on the vulgarity of a KGB soldier who pretended not to listen, and the smugness of an office girl who had bought a trip to Leningrad with the dispensation of soon-to-fade physical gifts, Katya masked the self-disgust such a comment usually prompted. Though she could not hide from herself the echo of her mother in her voice.

Leonid smiled as the assistant placed the tea in front of her with an over-polite flourish, a little toss of her head and flip of her wrist. This *devushka* had her own card to play. 'Thank you, Larissa,' he said, hands folded at his chin as if in prayer.

Larissa sat at the corner of his desk, crossed her legs with a nylon swish, and took out a notepad, a parody of a secretary in an American film. Leonid drew an English cigarette from a silver case on his desk and inserted it into his ceramic holder. For a moment Katya thought the girl was going to light it for him.

'Larissa will be travelling with us to Leningrad,' Leonid said, through a puff of smoke. 'She will be providing . . . administrative support.'

No mistaking his smile this time. Reef pushed his glasses up the bridge of his nose and shifted uneasily in his chair. Katya stirred sugar into her tea. 'How nice,' she said.

A curious tone filled the silence that followed. It was as if they were waiting for others to arrive and had run out of small-talk. Oleg returned his attention to the pad. His clothes were carefully ironed and his bald pate was lustrous in the soft light. Unlike the corridors, Leonid's office was well maintained and elaborately furnished. So elaborate it had an air of unreality. Uzbeki carpets hung on the walls and Armenian *objets d'art* sat on the walnut desktop. Oak bookcases were lined with Russian and Western first editions and a vitrine was filled with Gzhel china. Velvet curtains framed windows frosted with condensation. Outside, blurred branches kept a still vigilance against the Russian sky.

Into the elaborate silence Reef tossed an absurdity. 'Larissa speaks fluent French,' he said.

Katya smiled derisively. 'That will certainly be a great help if we meet anyone from Paris.'

Leonid cleared his throat.

As Katya sipped the sweet, lukewarm tea she caught a glimpse of Oleg's pad: it was covered with doodles. Suddenly Leonid gathered together loose papers and bundled them into a neat pile.

'Well, we have much to do, much to prepare,' he said. 'Of course, we have started well. The concert on Thursday night was a great success. You are to be commended for your efforts, Katya.'

Uttered with perfect, or perfectly feigned, sincerity, the words disarmed her. Leonid was a master of the shifting posture. His face was attentive and graceful now, when moments before it had been all vulgar innuendo. 'Thank you,' she said.

'Of course, not everyone was impressed. Or, at least, not as impressed as you were.' His hands flowered from the desktop, palms offered to the ceiling like a priest's.

Katya was stung. He had set her up.

'The music,' Leonid continued, 'was – how shall I say? – strident. Yes, overly strident.'

'It was what they chose to play,' Katya managed. 'Their repertoire.'

'And the pianist, Drew Fisher.' She winced as he pronounced the name with casual disdain. 'I had such high hopes from his recordings. But so self-indulgent. Bourgeois in the extreme.'

His face was full of challenge. She had made fun of Larissa? Well, she would pay for it. She nodded weakly, but his eyes pressed for a spoken response. 'What he plays is different, yes.'

'Different?' he said. 'Is that what you call it? You like this difference, don't you?'

'I am open to what all musicians have to offer.'

'Ah, open. Open.' He spat the word, tapping his cigarette so forcefully that the ash bounced out of the ashtray. 'Be careful what you are open to, Katya. Be very careful.'

He glanced at Oleg, as if to confirm his meaning. Larissa was recording the exchange, lifting her chin between sentences and pushing out her chest.

Shame rose in Katya: it was not the shame of moral disgrace but the Russian shame of private feelings unmasked. She had dropped her guard at a critical time, insulting the mistress of the man she was obliged to humour. After a period when she had been less than discreet. Leonid might have delivered his warning later in the meeting, but he would have done it subtly; Katya had pushed it into the open with her jibe. She could not have been more foolish.

Reef's hand lay on the arm of his chair, inches from her own, trembling, it seemed to her, with sympathy. Slowly, she calmed down and forced herself to listen while Leonid moved to the business at hand. He reviewed the itinerary and protocols for Monday's trip. She contributed as best she could to the discussion, outlined the arrangements she had painstakingly made, nodded stiffly at the appropriate points. But beneath the surface her shame was as keen as her desire. Her fear greater still.

What had she been thinking? She had a life, duties, responsibilities, and she was dealing with men whose ability to humiliate was just one of many weapons. They could do so much more if they chose – to her, to her children. Twenty-five years ago the general secretary had patted her head and kissed her father. Her future had traced a perfect ellipse in the heavens. Today she was married to a Hero of the Soviet Union. Both men had more in common with Leonid than with her. Men in a man's world where love's currency had been devalued by ambition and the need for control.

Weren't they the fools, though? They had turned their backs on all that was important, quashing passion because it threatened. She knew. She had done the same herself, for the sake of the children. And in doing so she had grounded her future in an arid security. Then Drew had appeared, his bruised gaze suggesting intimacy of the most complicated sort, her response inviting censure and humiliation. Proof offered, as if proof were needed, of the bleakness of her marriage.

All week she had prayed that Ilya would make the flight team and disappear for many months into outer space. Kazakhstan was not far enough. Even before Drew's appearance her husband's fortnightly visit home had become unwelcome, even intrusive. Every other Saturday Volodya drove her before first light to Vnukovo airfield, where she would meet Ilya off the military flight and listen with strained patience to his obsessive analysis of imagined intrigues.

'Benyukh is against me.'

'I thought he was your sponsor.'

'He is, but he has been scheming with Evdokimov,

who drinks with the doctors. If Ganichev is ill, the doctors will pronounce, and who is to say they won't pass over me and send Rumyantsev?'

'How could they pass over you?'

Ilya fidgeted with frustration in the car seat. A silly question, of course, but what else was she to say? 'They do as they like. Or what it is in their interest to do.' He grimaced at his own indiscretion, gazing at the back of Volodya's head. 'Sokolnikov was at flight school with Evdokimov's son – they're as thick as thieves. I passed Orlov's office yesterday and Benyukh was on the phone, whispering.'

'So he was whispering.'

'*Rumyantsev!* I was in the programme when he was in short trousers.'

The names, familiar yet meaningless, threw up waves of weariness in her. Ilya could scarcely get through the social pleasantries before he launched into these monologues, often sustained for the full hour it took to drive from Vnukovo to Star City. At home he had an unvaried routine. Katya had learned early to send Babushka and the children to her parents' flat, awkward as that was. After he had unpacked his flight bag, Ilya walked the dogs, ate breakfast, then spent the rest of the morning with his mother. The children would appear for an hour after lunch, drink a glass of tea with their stepfather, and return to Kropotkinskaya with Volodya. Weather permitting, he and Katya went for a walk in the forest. If she could talk him into it, they drove into Moscow in the evening for the theatre or the ballet. He always fell asleep during the performance. They went to bed at midnight, had sex, and rose at five so he could catch the morning flight back to Baikonur. She no longer accompanied him to the airport.

So it went. And so the despair of her decision suffused her. Until recently she had worried about spending so little time with her husband. Now she didn't care. Neither did he. He knew his mission and did not mind becoming a visitor in his own flat. She became a host, and like all hosts looked forward to her guest's departure. And now there was Drew, his tender eyes and long fingers, the drama of his performance and the longing it had unlocked in her. The prospect of Ilya's next visit and his conjugal expectations filled her with disgust.

For the first time in the meeting, Oleg was speaking, his voice hoarse: '. . . separate environment and circumstances. Not as familiar as here in Moscow, so I want all differences from the routine noted and logged.'

He looked at her, as if expecting a reply. She nodded in mock agreement. He held his thin lips close to his teeth and twirled his pen in his fingers. 'There will be daily reports.'

Reef cleared his throat. 'Daily?'

'Of course.' Oleg tapped the leather-bound volume. 'It is in the regulations.'

'We have never had to submit daily.'

Oleg leaned across the small desk. His lips

worked, as if he was sucking bits of food from his teeth. His face was empty of expression, but the watery eyes were small and hard. Leonid sat back passively, stroking his chin, tilting the cigarette in its holder. Larissa scribbled.

'Perhaps you have never before followed the regulations,' Oleg said, with quiet menace. He was breathing through his mouth, and Katya could hear his chest wheeze. 'Perhaps they were not known to you. On this trip you will submit written reports to my room before you go to bed each evening.'

Katya sensed danger. Oleg's phrasing and tone were unambiguous. Events have been too loose for my liking, they said. I am in control and you will do as I say. Leonid's tactics were complex – they had as much to do with vanity and sexual politics as anything. He could be manoeuvred. But Oleg and his function were the raw face of the system. You confronted him at your peril, especially when he was ill and irritable.

'Why now?' Reef said. 'What is different now? I have been translating for the Exchange for eight years and have never been asked to deliver reports with such regularity. What will I have to say after one day? What is the point?'

He had appealed to Leonid. But the innocence of his question, his blindness to the dance of pressure and dominance that Leonid and Oleg had choreographed would enrage Oleg, Katya knew. The man's power rested on his ability to crush,

136

and the best defence was an awareness of that power. Reef lacked such awareness. He always had.

'The point?' Oleg said quietly. He looked away, as if distracted by a sound. Katya felt a cloud of apprehension in her breast. Suddenly Oleg banged the small table so violently with his fist that his teacup fell to the floor and smashed. Larissa dropped her pen. 'Do I need to spell it out?' he shouted.

Reef held his head stiffly, his beard quivering. He was scared. Katya's heart filled with tenderness, as it did when her daughter cried over a dead bird. He should have seen it coming. But had it ever been otherwise with him? He had been denied his doctorate because he had failed to include in his thesis formulaic Marxist-Leninist analysis at the appropriate points. He had courted Katya with flowers, poems by Pushkin, and love letters blooming with florid expressions of romantic doom, when it was apparent to everyone else that she wasn't interested. He absorbed the pragmatic realities of the world in slow motion, forever a step behind.

'So, Reef,' Leonid said deliberately, gazing down at the meek man who would not look at any of them, 'do you understand?'

'Of course I understand. I will supply Oleg with reports as he demands. Of course.'

With the heel of his boot Oleg pushed away the shards of teacup from the table leg. Katya's humiliation was mild by comparison. She had status, however compromised. She did not need the job. But the Exchange was Reef's livelihood. He had everything to lose, and everyone in the room knew it.

Oleg had a coughing fit. When he had recovered his composure he took out a cigarette and lit it, all the while staring at Reef. The cigarette triggered another fit and he left the room, gasping. Reef stared at the floor like a chastised child.

'Larissa,' Leonid said, 'get my leather case from the back office.'

When she'd left Leonid came to the front of his desk and leaned against it, arms crossed. He laughed, assuming his debonair look. 'The Exchange team, what? The three of us. Like old times.' Reef did not move. Leonid glanced at Katya, who was not about to pretend that the last few minutes had not occurred. 'It will be pleasant to get away from the dirty capital,' he said. 'Yes. Pleasant to take a trip.'

'Are we finished?' Reef said abruptly.

'Finished? Yes, yes. Tomorrow the banquet, Monday Leningrad. Life is good, comrades.'

Leonid's false bonhomie only deepened the gloom. Reef gathered his coat and scarf from the rack, his galoshes from the square of carpet beside the door.

'Our ministry friend is not in good form today,' Leonid said.

But Reef did not answer. He would take no comfort from oblique apologies. He bent forward to snap the buckles of his galoshes, and in the curve of his back Katya saw frailty. From his coat pocket fell a dirty, crumpled handkerchief. As he picked it up she stifled a cry. Illogically, she remembered Drew at the piano: his hair dancing before his eyes, his hands pausing before a crashing chord, the rolled cuffs of his blue shirt revealing wrists veined and white in the glare of the lights.

CHAPTER 12

'I didn't say I didn't like it. It's different, is all.' Drew sat directly across from Katya but spoke with his head angled towards Larissa who, three seats down, had leaned forward with busty confidence to ask why he didn't like the caviar. The restaurant light was yellow and blue. Waiters glided past the long table like sailboats. Drew held away from himself a small piece of rye bread, lightly spread with unsalted butter and finest Beluga.

'Impossible not to like with such tasty bread.' Larissa spoke with the syncopated precision of a woman who had drunk more than usual. A glass of champagne listed in her hand. She wore a strapless white dress, with a Greek cross dangling deep in her *décolletage*. Her colour was high. Leonid, sitting to her left, laid a hand on her arm, as if afraid the contents of the glass would spill on to his lap.

'Oh, the bread is good,' Drew said. 'Excellent bread.'

'Russian bread. So . . . so *krepkii*.' She blinked moistly, lost focus, resurfaced with a gentle jerk of her head. Around the table swirled voices liberated from the daily drudge of socialist gloom. The atmosphere in the pre-Revolutionary room (the same room in which Katya had celebrated her first wedding thirteen years ago) was taut with high spirits, buoyant on a breeze of good food and drink paid for by the Cultural Exchange. The room floated in its own dimension, leagues adrift from queues, shortages and shoddy vestibules. Oleg had not appeared.

Katya heard Reef addressing Salim and Yoshi brightly: '. . . a philosophical concern. A matter of the soul.'

'Ruskii hleb . . . ochin krepkii . . .' Larissa's voice swivelled away like a lighthouse beacon. She could have been reading from a menu, for all Katya heard. The words drummed, without meaning, like rain on a tin roof, dumb background to the rush of love within her. Nothing Larissa could say would dim what she was feeling.

Drew's eyes strayed to Katya. She avoided them, instead watched Leonid's fingers edging up the plump curve of Larissa's forearm.

'All the food's good,' Drew said. 'This is some feast.'

But it was Katya he was savouring, not the dinner. She sipped her champagne. If anything she would have been relieved if he had been distracted by Larissa's breasts. The grip of his attention was relentless. His gaze enveloped her. With Oleg absent and Leonid babysitting his tipsy escort, Katya felt free to yield to feeling, but it overwhelmed her. The laden table, the pastel walls, statuary and draped curtains of the Praga's finest dining room, all were incidental to her love.

She had arrived for dinner in a cautious mood, mindful of Leonid's warnings and steeped in her fears of the past few days. She kept her distance from Drew, avoiding the pre-dinner reception and timing her arrival carefully, a minute or two behind the guests. As they entered the dining room, she watched closely as Leonid conducted the musicians to the far end of the table beside Reef. She took a seat at the other end, next to a woman from the Ministry of Foreign Affairs, a vague acquaintance who had been a year ahead of her at the institute. She was catching up with her when Drew had seated himself across from her, surprising everyone with his breach of protocol. Her breath caught in her throat and a liquid warmth spread from her heart to her limbs. He busied himself with the cutlery, laid his cigarettes and lighter next to his plate, and snapped open his napkin with a deliberate flourish. Finally he looked at her. 'Unreserved seating,' he said.

'Pardon me?'

'Like a gig where you sit where you want. American-style.'

Conversation at the table found its gear again and roared away, leaving her breathless in its wake. Why had she avoided him? What did she have to fear? Under his scrutiny all rational concerns evaporated. The facts bent, like light through water.

'Where have you been?' he said.

It took her a moment to frame the question in her head. 'What do you mean?'

'You disappeared after the concert. And last night . . . well, I hoped you might show up.'

'I was with my children.'

'How many kids you got?'

'Two. Boy and girl.'

'How old?'

'Sasha is thirteen, Anna twelve.'

'Big responsibility, kids that age.'

'Of course responsibility. They are my children.'

To her ear her voice was dry and haughty, the words terse. Her hands stayed folded in her lap and her shoulders were motionless. But her face, she knew, would betray her agitation. She pictured it as it had been reflected in her bedroom mirror before she left the flat: her hair pinned back, the better to display her rouged cheekbones and opal earrings. Lips full, hinting at arrogance. Her eyes: brown with flecks of green, long lashes. Keenly expressive even when she tried to hide her feelings.

Drew's eyes looked less distant and vulnerable. His elbows were on the table's edge, sleeves rolled. His white hands dominated the space between them. He wore an open-necked shirt, revealing a pale red birthmark that ran along his collarbone.

Leonid stood and bowed. 'The ladies will not mind,' he asked in English, 'if I remove my jacket?'

Drew laughed with easy humour. He looked at her and said, so that only she could hear, 'You look good.' When she failed to reply, he picked up a soup spoon and looked at his upside-down reflection in its curve. She watched him rotate it. His bent wrist was long and thin, bound by a copper bracelet. Further up his arm, near the crook of his elbow and edging out from under the loosened cuff, was a stippled patch of tiny white scars, all tailed and pointing in the same direction, like a shower of falling stars.

Dinner unravelled, lost all sequence. She ate hungrily, drank all the toasts, but tasted only the flavour of his presence.

'I celebrated marriage in this room,' she said.

He looked around, as if noticing the surroundings for the first time. 'No kidding? Where's your husband tonight?'

'First marriage was here. With my children's father.'

He nodded. 'Sure.'

'Second marriage . . .' She lost her drift, shook her head.

When her silence continued he offered her a cigarette. She declined and he lit one for himself. 'So,' he said, shaking the match, 'Leningrad tomorrow.'

She quoted at once in English: ' "Of Northern lands the pride and beauty,/ A young, resplendent, gracious city". Pushkin. Our Pushkin.'

He smiled. 'Resplendent?'

'This English word I know like Russian. I was translator for US presidential visit and had many poetical phrases memorized.'

'What visit?'

'Two delegations of President Nixon: 1972 and again in 1974.'

'You met Nixon?'

'Yes.'

His interest in her yielded momentarily to something larger, and his dark eyes lost their narrow scrutiny. Larissa, rising from her chair with Leonid's help, slipped on her heels and nearly fell into Drew's lap. Hand to her elbow, he helped her on her way. 'What did Tricky Dick think of this place?' he asked.

'Who?'

'Nixon.'

She remembered the leader of the United States in St George's Hall in the Kremlin, scratching his stomach and looking at the salmon, caviar and suckling pig with greedy impatience while Brezhnev delivered an interminable opening toast. She shrugged. 'In my opinion, he was not one to find beauty in his surroundings.'

Drew laughed. 'No Pushkin, huh?'

'I don't think so.' She looked over her shoulder. 'But no Pushkins in Kremlin either.'

'So where are they?'

Now she smiled. The awkwardness was gone. 'Maybe in Leningrad?'

Around them the waiters moved with unhurried dignity, pouring Cognac and vodka, wedging platefuls of wrapped chocolates on to the crowded table. It was a classic Russian dinner, all the richer for the scarcity that gripped the frozen streets outside. The silver cutlery and bottles of mineral water sparkled in the harlequin light.

She excused herself and went to the lavatory, stepping carefully. Love and champagne had made her dizzy. Leonid and Larissa stood beside the dining-room door, arguing and smoking earnestly. Larissa's heel was broken; she looked lopsided and tired. Clearly drunk, Leonid stood close enough to her that the ruffled pleats of his dress shirt grazed her body. Where was Luba? She rarely missed a banquet. Perhaps their boy was ill. Perhaps she had had enough of Leonid's blatant adultery. When Katya returned from the lavatory they were gone. Neither were they at the table, where the plates had been cleared and Reef and the other Americans now sat around Drew. As she approached, Yoshi rose and offered her his place between Drew and Marshall. Salim had taken her chair, and Reef sat beside him, a tumbler of vodka in his fist.

'All about soul, huh?' Salim said, pouring a drink. His wide face – fleshy, large-pored, distended – glistened with sweat. He smoked a Russian cigarette. His gestures were curt and aggressive.

Katya felt disadvantaged at having arrived in the middle of a conversation. Marshall said to her,

'Reef has been giving us insights into the Russian soul.'

Drew tilted away from the table and casually draped his right arm over her chair back. She felt the touch of his fingers through the silk of her dress.

'The *suffering* Russian soul,' Salim said, scraping a bit of food from his teeth.

Reef nodded with exaggerated gravity, arms folded. His glasses had slid to the end of his nose and the thick lenses magnified his eyes comically. He could drink a lot for a small man, but after a half-bottle or so his gestures stiffened into caricature. 'Our history,' he said. 'Our tradition.'

Katya knew this mood: he was apt to spout poetry or break into song, gush sentimental Slavic tears. They were impulses she recognized in herself, and she worried that he would expose himself to ridicule, though in truth these men liked him and were as generous with his faults as few Russians would be.

'What tradition?' Salim said. 'Sufferin', or *talkin'* about sufferin'?'

'Both,' Katya said curtly. She didn't like Salim's manner and felt obliged to come to Reef's aid. Drew's hand burned on her shoulder. 'Suffering, of course. But also discussing, expressing, writing. We must know meaning.'

Salim's nostrils flared and his unshaven cheeks arched over his expansive mouth. 'Real sufferin', if you ask me, ain't got *time* for discussion.' The whites of his eyes flashed.

Marshall extended his long frame in the chair and lifted his face to the light. He leaned forward, hand on his tie so it did not touch the tablecloth. 'I wouldn't be telling these people what they can or cannot discuss, Salim.'

'Ain't tellin' nobody nothin', boss. Just talking about soul.' He nodded sideways at Reef. 'Man here tellin' us about Tolstoy and such. Shit, all those guys were aristocrats. Talkin' Russian blues while the serfs busted their stones. What the fuck Tolstoy know about tote that barge?'

Katya could not quite make out his meaning, but his tone was clear and the profanity stung like a slap in the face. Yet Drew laughed.

'Tolstoy did not have serfs,' Reef said.

'That a fact?'

'Salim would have been right at home at the Finland Station,' Marshall said, with a shade of irony more tolerant than Katya would have expected under the circumstances. 'He's a real revolutionary.'

Drew's hand had drifted from her shoulder. She wanted him to reclaim it, but something personal to the group was interfering.

'I will take you to the Finland Station next week, if you wish,' Reef said. 'We will have plenty of time for such visits.'

The suggestion was perfectly sensible, so why had it sounded absurd? Reef peered into his glass of vodka.

'The blues is an expression of suffering,' Drew said, his voice almost playful.

'No, sir,' Salim retorted. 'Miles called that jive a long time ago. Musical form is what the blues is. Don't need to suffer to play the blues.'

'It helps.'

'Listen to the white boy. *It helps*. Shit.'

Salim's tone was savage, but Drew did not appear to be offended. He leaned back in his chair, still smiling. For the moment Katya had left his thoughts, that was clear.

But Salim hadn't forgotten about her. He turned to her and pointed at Marshall. 'His granddaddy picked cotton all his life. Had his ass *owned* by another man.'

'Salim!' Marshall said.

'A slave,' she said.

'Shit, yes. *That* be sufferin'.'

Anger warmed her face. 'Here in Russia, Mr Jackson—'

'I ain't no Mr Jackson.'

She raised her voice, gave it an edge of authority. 'We know your history, Mr Jackson. Do you know ours?'

He stubbed out the cigarette and waved dismissively.

'Do you think only Mr Powell's grandparents were slaves?' she said. Reef was trying to interrupt, a finger raised. 'Do you think only black people know suffering? What kind of simplicity is this? Bad history, Mr Jackson.'

Salim was grinning. 'Showin' a little spunk,' he said to Drew. 'I can dig that.'

Maxim appeared at the door, his face pale and bored.

'Max,' Salim shouted, hand in the air. 'My man!'

'Is time,' Maxim said, pointing at his watch.

Beneath the table, Drew pressed her knee with his hand.

'Bad boys ready to kick ass,' Salim said, rising heavily.

The other men were also stirring, the heated words quickly forgotten. Drew's hand remained on her knee, less sexual than sympathetic. Her heart beat in confusion, resentment mixing with desire. How could they end the exchange so abruptly? Salim owed her a reply. 'Mr Jackson, I must tell you—'

'Sorry, girl. It's time.'

'Time for what?' she said.

'The game,' Drew said. 'The Super Bowl. Biggest football game of the year. We've been invited to the consulate to watch it. Via satellite.'

'Now? At eleven o'clock?'

'Three p.m. eastern standard, honey,' Salim said. 'Rise and shine, sports fans, it's Miller time.'

'How are you getting home?' Drew asked her quietly.

'He was wrong. To say what he said. Was wrong.'

'Salim?' Drew smiled. 'Just causing trouble. He's the drummer. Likes to keep things hopping.'

Drew's focus had returned to her, as if Salim's

harangue had never happened. She felt as if she had overreacted, but knew she hadn't. Had she missed the point of the discussion? It was as if Salim's words were not a debate but a performance. His language, his vulgarity and dense accent, his slang and bad grammar were all part of a show.

And Drew had been part of the performance. But now he was back with her. 'Do you have a ride home?' he repeated.

'My car. I have my car.'

Salim and Yoshi headed out of the door with Maxim. Reef followed without a word. With Leonid gone, all formal arrangement had broken down.

Marshall approached, hand extended. 'May I offer my thanks for a wonderful evening? And apologies for my younger colleagues. They get carried away sometimes, forget where they are.'

Her anger turned to embarrassment and she felt her cheeks redden. She stood up and shook his hand. Drew fidgeted, eyes flitting about the room. Beneath her confusion she could feel the force of his intent.

'Leonid must've had to leave early,' Marshall said.

'I don't know what happened to him,' Katya said. 'Perhaps Larissa was ill.'

'I'm sure everybody will be fine by tomorrow. I take it the previous arrangements stand? We meet at the train station?'

'Of course.'

'Good,' he said.

Drew, who had remained seated, said, 'There isn't enough room in the car.'

'What?'

'Maxim's car. He can only take four.'

Marshall was confused. Drew would not look at him.

'I'll take you there,' Katya said. She tried her best to sound spontaneous. 'You go with Maxim, Mr Powell. I'll take . . .' She gestured lamely in Drew's direction. Marshall looked at them, hesitating a beat. 'Sure. OK. See you there, Drew.'

When he was gone, Katya and Drew sat silently for a long while. A few government officials and hangers-on laughed at the other end of the table, oblivious to anything but their own good cheer. The waiters stood by the door with bored expressions, waiting for their evening drink and a cold trip to distant suburbs. He would have no idea of the risk she was taking, she thought. But the lack of scrutiny was a rare gift, and she shook with excitement. Fifteen years ago she had sat in this same room with the same trembling anticipation: free for once to explore the promise of a private, immediate future. Free to give herself as she wished.

Eventually she stood. 'Shall we go?'

At the cloakroom he helped her into her fur. It had been a long time since she was so aware of her femininity, the attention of a man who did not hide his feelings.

They emerged to the frigid night air like divers from the ocean. The sky was dense with stars and stained at the edges by the city's ubiquitous orange glow. Cars whooshed along the boulevard, disappearing into the underpass. Everything was still and crystalline except for a plume of dirty steam rising from a distant manhole. She led him up Kalinin Prospekt, where she had parked. She pointed to her car; it was too cold to speak.

She rubbed the windshield with a gloved hand as the Volga's ancient engine warmed. Hands in his pockets, Drew hunched into the dashboard. 'How cold is it?' he asked.

'Minus thirty.'

'*Man.*' He breathed deeply.

When next he spoke she had anticipated what he would say. 'I don't have to go to the consulate.'

'No?'

'No.'

She drove. The traffic-lights blinked amber in the clear air. At the end of Kalinin Prospekt she stopped and idled. Left would bring them to his hotel. Ahead were the bare trees of the Alexandrovsky Gardens and the sloping eastern entrance to the Kremlin.

She had an idea, and turned right.

'Where we going?'

'You are cold?'

'Well, yeah.'

She shifted gears and touched his arm. 'Let us be warm.'

She drove to the Kamenny Bridge, down the

153

ramp to the embankment, and along the river drive until they could see, directly beyond the viaduct, clouds of steam billowing into the clear sky, lit pure white by stanchioned arc lamps. She went through the traffic-lights, turned again, and followed heavy wire fencing until she reached Kropotkinskaya Square. She parked. Through the windscreen she could see her mother's apartment block. She counted up five storeys – the apartment lights were still on.

'So, what's happening?' he said. The car engine hadn't been stilled ten seconds and already the frost had invaded.

'*Bassein*,' she said.

'What?'

She pointed at the clouds of steam. Like ghosts, the silhouettes of several bare-chested swimmers passed behind the chain-link fence before plunging into water. 'Swimming-pool.'

He stared blankly.

'We swim,' she said.

'What – *there*?'

'There, yes, there. Of course.'

'You gotta be kidding me. We'll *die*.'

She opened the car door. 'Please. Hurry up. Closes at midnight.'

Against his protests she gave him instructions and went into the women's changing rooms. She put a two-rouble deposit on a suit, cap and towel, then changed quickly.

All her years in Moscow, and this was her first

winter swim here. At the pool entrance an old woman took her towel and warned her about the icy pathway. 'Don't touch the fixtures when you get outside. Your wet hand will freeze to the metal. I will watch for you and open the door.' Katya held her breath and dashed through the cold into the pool.

The water was wonderfully warm; the mist, two or three metres thick above the surface, kept the frost at bay. Through the cloud she saw the men's changing-room door open. Drew stood, smoking a cigarette, while his own old woman scolded him and pushed him out. The bathing suit was too large for him. He crossed his arms before his broad chest. His long legs were knock-kneed and pale. She waved him in, once, twice, three times. He approached slowly, feet arched, looking at the sky, shaking his head. At the pool's edge he took a last drag of his cigarette, flicked it into the gloom beyond the fencing, and dived in.

He surfaced like a seal, hair slicked to his head, the shape of his cranium delicate and childlike. He was a poor swimmer, and as he paddled through the mist, she felt like reaching out and helping him. But his face was alight and his eyes were wide. As he came near he gave a boyish whoop. 'I can't believe we're doing this. It's *thirty below*!'

'Yes. It's wonderful.'

'This steam! Look at it!' He steadied himself by grasping her arm. Beads of water clung to his thick eyebrows. 'So this is how you warm up, huh?'

'This I have not done before.'

'Never?'

'Never.'

He clutched her arm with his long fingers. She was aware of their damp skin and the vapour swirling about them. 'Come,' she said. 'Let's swim.'

She pushed off gently and he paddled alongside her, grazing her bare arm with his awkward strokes, breathing loudly through his mouth. There was a steady hissing sound, and behind it the rumble of Moscow traffic. She led and he followed, his awkwardness in the water so different from the way he usually held himself. They swam, alone in the huge pool, dwarfed by the limitless sky.

MY ROMANCE

MY ROMANCE

CHAPTER 13

The incident was as fresh in his memory as if it had happened that morning.

They exited the A Train at 34th Street. It was a hot August night, and stepping from the air-conditioned car into the acrid, girdered underworld of New York should have been intimidating. But it was not. Drew was riding with the king, high on some of the fine Thai heroin that had been flowing so freely through the city that torrid summer. This shit was some good. It turned the hiss of subway doors into a sublime fanfare. Jessie was a soft grey blur beside him. The underground lights whirled like pinwheels. Even the homeless, slack-jawed alkies propped against the stained tiles of the station wall looked cool. The train clacked southbound into the tunnel while Jessie rooted through her purse for cigarettes and Drew stood in the gloom, blissful and blinking.

They had scored and shot up at his dealer's apartment in Spanish Harlem. Going in, the scene was tense: Jessie was badly strung out; the dealer took his time answering the door. They paid much more than they should have, and Drew had trouble finding a vein. But by the time they left they were floating downtown in a bubble of well-being – until they hit the 34th Street platform and saw Benny Parsons talking to God.

Drew had played with Benny. Before his conversion to the needle, Benny the Lip had been a decent trumpeter in the Sweets Edison mould. In the sixties he was a regular at the Gate, where Drew sat in on an occasional Tuesday. Thin, hollow-cheeked, brooding, Benny had been fragile long before he sampled heroin. In him, smack produced ecstatic visions: eyes rolling heavenward, he raised scarecrow arms and loosed torrents of the Bible and the blues in the cracked voice of a radio preacher. He lived in a basement rat-trap in SoHo, emerging after dark to haunt street corners as far as Times Square.

Tonight Benny was in bad shape. In spite of the heat he wore a wool sweater and a tattered raincoat. His trousers were soaked with urine. There wasn't a glint of reason in his eyes. His right arm hung damaged at his side, and the left windmilled. When Jessie saw him she threw her cigarette on to the tracks and ran to his side. Drew wavered, trying to make sense of the scene beneath the high. He was always the slower to react.

Jessie was a slender woman, birdlike round the shoulders, with a long neck and straight dark hair she kept short. She wore black T-shirts and black jeans and smoked incessantly. Her hands were so thin from her addiction she had stopped wearing her rings – they lay in a silver cluster on her dresser top, beside the spoon, the lighter and other paraphernalia of her habit. When she was alarmed, her large eyes grew gentle and fawnlike. Now Benny's spinning arm knocked her to the concrete floor. A couple of the homeless stood up, stiff and wary.

'Be righteous, my brothers!' Benny shouted. 'The hour cometh, his vengeance is nigh.'

'Benny.' Drew helped Jessie to her feet. 'Benny, it's me. Drew Fisher.'

The arm stilled. Benny looked at them, his back to the tracks.

'You come on now,' Drew said. 'Let's get you a cup of coffee.'

Benny pointed at Jessie. 'There ain't nothin' in Chicago for a monkey woman to do.'

'Benny. Let's go upstairs.'

But he was drifting away from them, towards the edge of the platform. Commuters filed in, keeping their distance. The coming of the next train was announced by a stirring of stale air, heavy and charged. Benny looked over his shoulder. The roar of the train grew louder, and its pitch told them it was not slowing down. An express. For a moment Benny seemed to calm down. His back still to the tracks, he cocked his head as if someone in the distance was calling his name. Drew and Jessie stood perfectly still. Then he looked up at them, his eyes peaceful now, and they both knew what he was going to do.

He mistimed his jump. He was close to the

tunnel entrance, and the train arrived so quickly that instead of falling into its path he bounced off the corner of the first car and sprawled back on the platform. The train's noise drowned all other sound. The faces of the onlookers were pale and curious in the flashing of the passing cars, and Jessie's silent scream turned her face into a mask of fear. Benny lay unconscious, twisted and still like a dead animal. Blood trickled from his mouth. Drew straightened him out. Jessie put her bag beneath his head. The crowd gazed mutely as Drew yelled at them to call an ambulance, then pulled his coat over Benny's frail chest. 'I think he's breathing OK,' he said.

Jessie didn't answer.

'He's going to be all right, babe.'

He hugged her, as much for his own sake, and felt her bones beneath the cotton T-shirt.

After a few minutes a cop arrived, then an ambulance. Benny roused as the medics lifted him on to the stretcher. Drew and Jessie rode with him to Manhattan General, Jessie clutching Benny's arm, her tears falling on his raincoat.

Now, on another train, in another year, Drew sat on a leather seat, smoking a Kent and drinking a glass of tea. Shouts echoed up and down the platform. Departing lovers said last goodbyes. Stooping with difficulty, an old woman with swaddled legs cleaned a wooden bench with a dirty towel. Opposite him, Salim sat heavily, knees apart, the charts to 'Milestones' spread across a closed briefcase lying on his lap. Marshall had added the tune to the playlist for the next gig, and Salim bent his big head close to the sheets, annotating the margins carefully with a blue pencil.

The minute hand of the platform clock lurched, the stationmaster's whistle shrieked, and the train glided soundlessly out of the vaulted station and into a desolate jumble of overhead wires, broken bricks and disused carriages. It was snowing. Salim glanced up, then returned to the music. South-facing, Drew watched the gaping station exit fall away through the swirling snow and let the backwards motion fool him into thinking that time could indeed be reversed, mistakes undone, lost love rescued.

Benny had recovered. Apart from concussion and a few broken teeth, he was fine. The blow had seemed to knock some sense into him, and for a while afterwards they had run into him outside the soup kitchens on Third Avenue, sheepish and grateful. A couple of months later the demons returned and he landed in Bellevue. Drew was glad that he was off the streets. The guy had cheated death, and death did not take kindly to unpaid bills.

The night after Benny's accident, Drew and Jessie had held each other in her bed and promised they would quit. And so they did, for two weeks. Then Drew walked into her apartment after four days in Boston and she was sitting on the kitchen floor, her back against the refrigerator, her face puffy and content. So he went back on too. The year spun itself out in a spiral of false hopes and hard luck. Jessie's mother died at Christmas. In January she fell ill with hepatitis. Drew brought junk to her hospital bed and shot her up while she blamed herself for their habits. Then he really did kick, she stayed hooked, and everything changed.

'What you chewin' on?' Salim asked, without lifting his head.

'Just checking out the scenery. You're missing it.'

'Ain't missin' nothin'.' He concentrated on working out the rhythms in his head and making careful, personal symbols with the pencil.

'Yeah,' Drew said. 'I guess.' Leaving a city by train – was there anything quite so depressing? Cross-cutting the derelict, the neglected, the disposed. The falling snow was not cleansing but smothering.

The day hadn't started this way. He had woken clear-headed and refreshed. The radio in his hotel room, which he could turn down but never off, played Mozart, and he could hear the floor attendant pacing the landing, tapping on doors. He was up and gazing sleepily out of the window before he recalled the events of the night before. The image of Katya swimming in the mist rose in his mind as he surveyed, through falling snow, the grandeur of Red Square. Her oval face beneath the swimming cap. The freckled expanse of skin below her neck. Her smooth, sideways stroke through the water as she looked back at him and smiled.

And love swam through his veins. He was hooked. Five years since Jessie, here he was again. Against his will and against his better judgement, but in love. Salim, who knew him so well, could see the obvious and was trying, in his oblique, belligerent way, to warn him.

Drew had turned down the radio and packed his bag for Leningrad. His breathing was quick, his senses alert, as if at the start of a race. After the swim she had run from pool edge to changing-room door, huddled and dripping. On the way back to the car, his wet hair stiffened in the frost and his face stung. Bright-eyed, Katya pointed out her parents' flat. As they turned on to the embankment road, the arc-lamps were extinguished: the pool and its steam clouds were suddenly invisible. Outside the hotel she touched his arm. He leaned across and kissed her cheek. She would meet him at the station the next day.

Through breakfast and check-out the wonder of that interlude stayed with him. But at the station, where she directed porters with brisk authority and handed the musicians their tickets and instructions, she was nervous and distant, avoiding his eye. He felt a dangerous spinning in his heart, and the old vulnerabilities swarmed in. He grew pessimistic. How could they continue where they'd left off the night before?

Leningradsky station was old-world, dramatic and immense. Wizened women with gold teeth and tattered clothes sat mutely amid dirty children and piles of clothbound luggage. Drunks slept in filthy corners or brawled. A big-city railway station, marbled and ornate, but with a rural coarseness. Following Reef, Drew meandered through the crowds, bag in hand, spiralling into a paranoid funk. How could he approach her? It was perhaps best that nothing happen. But he continued to yearn, and he boarded the reserved carriage with mixed emotions.

Although the train was scheduled to arrive in Leningrad before midnight, they were put into their own sleeping carriage, two to a compartment. Porters piled their baggage and instruments in an adjoining car. 'VIP treatment,' Reef said, clearly pleased at his associated hike in status. He inspected the brass fixtures and wide berths with grave appreciation, then moved on to his own seat.

The compartment was comfortable but over-heated. Drew fidgeted, brushing ash from the seat and adjusting the window curtain. Salim sat down and went to work on his charts. Since breakfast, he had been cool and aloof. A girl in a brown uniform brought tea with lemon. Drew smoked and watched the sad tableaux of departure. Katya had not reappeared. His gloom hardened as the time to leave approached.

When the train was at last on its way, he opened the window a crack and threw out his cigarette butt. He sighed, and Salim looked at him. 'Dig this,' he said. He hummed the opening to 'Milestones', tapping the briefcase with one finger and going silent before the fourth bar.

Drew smiled. The missing bar played in his head, horn and piano suspending a long A flat as the bass chimed a quartet of half-notes that hung in musical space like a row of bells. 'Can the man write for the bass or what?' he said.

'Miles, man.'

'Miles.'

Salim described a series of gentle curves with his hand. 'I hear cymbals, right? Like waves.'

'Like waves.'

They laughed as they heard the same sounds in their heads, and Drew felt in himself the release from brooding that only music gave him. Salim made a note. The compartment door slid open.

'So quiet. You two so quiet.'

It was Yoshi, with Marshall. They carried glasses of tea in fancy pewter holders. The rising steam reminded Drew of Katya's floating form.

'Can you believe these carriages?' Marshall said.

'Big.'

'Wide gauge. Biggest in the world. You can stretch out in them.'

'Raider brothers stretched out last night,' Salim said.

'They did.'

'Kicked ass!'

Marshall smiled, for once sharing with Salim the pleasure of celebration. Salim's beloved Raiders had won the Super Bowl. 'Warm in here,' he said.

'You hear us complainin'?' Salim said.

Marshall handed his tea to Yoshi, took off his camel-hair coat, and sat beside Salim. He looked at the charts. '"Milestones"?'

'Yeah.'

He read the opening bars, the skin between his high eyebrows puckered in concentration, and pointed to Drew. 'Let's try this. You take the melody. Block chord it, and I'll run underneath.'

'Could do.'

They sat silently, blowing on their tea and running the tune in their heads. The train swayed. Outside was a blurred rush of white birch and dirty snow.

'Yeah,' Marshall mused. 'Block chords.'

Salim looked up, blue pencil at the corner of his mouth. 'How about that clyde in the suit cheering for Philly last night? Cliff Branch shut *him* up.'

'And Plunkett.'

'I agree. White boy can *throw*.'

'You missed a good game, Drew.' Marshall tilted his concave face towards the ceiling, like a radar dish poised to catch the most subtle atmospheric stirrings.

'Where did you go?' Yoshi asked.

'Hotel.'

'Fish wimped out.'

'I wasn't feeling so good.'

'Yeah. Musta ate some bad caviar.'

'Something like that.'

Salim looked out of the window. Marshall rubbed his chin. Drew's absence from the game was like a fluffed note, stalling the easy banter the group depended on to get them through long hours of travel and off-day idleness. Today he was the outsider, a role usually filled by Marshall. It threw them all off balance, and an uneasy silence followed.

'I miss New York,' Yoshi said at last.

Salim laughed. 'Spoken like a native, Yosh.'

'What do you miss?' Marshall asked.

'Yellow cabs, delis, Chinese food. Noise. So quiet here for big city.'

'I wouldn't mind a good cup of coffee myself.'

Salim opened the briefcase, took out a few sheets and peered at them. 'Women,' he said. 'I miss the women.' He would have phrased it differently had Marshall not been there.

Drew lit a cigarette and opened the window an inch.

'Some fine-looking women here, Salim,' Marshall said.

'C'mon. Bunch of Aunt Jemimas.'

Marshall frowned. A strict man, he did not hesitate to lay down the law about anything that might compromise the band's performance. But he had been a working musician for over forty years and knew well the realities of life on the road. Drew saw the conflict in his face. Marshall didn't like

Salim's vocabulary, but he was careful not to respond. It was an unwritten rule that if the boys kept their liaisons discreet, Marshall would not ask any questions. Curiosity past a certain level was not cool.

But as Drew watched, the long face betrayed a more complex struggle. The eyes were more active than usual, the moustache closer to the lower lip. He waved at the smoke, and Drew lifted his cigarette so it was nearer the window opening. 'You guys see Oleg?' he asked.

'Not if I can help it,' Salim said.

'He doesn't look so good,' Marshall said. 'The reason he didn't show at the dinner is he's sick. Got some bad virus.'

'My heart bleeds,' Salim said. 'I have to say, Marshall, I'm gettin' pissed off, him lookin' over our shoulders every day. Like a breath of fresh air when he didn't show up last night.'

'Careful what you say.' Elbows on his knees, Marshall eyed the corners of the compartment. 'The rules are different here.'

'You soundin' like the suits at the embassy.'

'And you, Salim, are sounding wilfully ignorant.' Marshall had slipped into preacher-tone. Salim raised his eyebrows but did not reply. 'I don't like being watched either,' Marshall continued, 'but this is not our house. We are guests. And if this gentleman thinks it important to accompany us on our trip in spite of being sick enough to stay in bed, well, then, it *is* important. Last night he wasn't there. Today he is. But whether he's there or not should not make a difference. How we conduct ourselves on this visit will determine whether others get invited in future. We are standard-bearers of a sort. Ambassadors. I want to make clear that I expect all of us to co-operate in whatever way our hosts deem appropriate. Whether you think they are being reasonable or not. Do you understand?'

'Hey, I'm cool.' Salim looked tense but unsurprised.

Drew was uncomfortable. There was a layer in Marshall's tone that Salim, contentious, literal, with a drummer's focus on time, would not have heard. It was spatial, harmonic, subtle. It played a familiar melody in an odd way, and Drew knew that he was the primary audience. Marshall was doing what he did best: improvising with the sounds given him, listening to everything that filled the air, leading.

There was a polite knock on the glass, and Leonid and Reef entered. Marshall stood and shook hands with them. He smiled broadly, but his crimped posture told Drew he was unhappy with the interruption. He hadn't finished his lecture.

'You are being looked after, I hope?' Leonid said. 'You have tea. Good Russian tea, a first-class carriage, snow at the window. The Red Arrow Express to Leningrad. As if in a novel by one of our nineteenth-century masters. Eh, Reef?'

'Yes, yes. Tolstoy would have approved.'

'I believe the dining-car even has sturgeon today.'

'Thank you, Leonid,' Marshall said. 'We're very comfortable here.'

Leonid's colour was high, his voice a little rough. Unlike Reef's drab quilted jacket and trousers of indeterminate fabric, Leonid's white turtleneck and dark wool trousers were supple and closely woven. Their easy folds caught the compartment's weak light as he gestured, and gave him the air of a prince from a small European country.

Leonid and Reef sat, filling the remaining seats. Legs crossed, Leonid drew a Dunhill from its red and gold packet and inserted it in his cigarette holder. 'Moscow to Leningrad. An historic run. The link between our two great cities.' He lit up, shut his lighter with a loud click. Reef sat forward, small hands clasped in his lap, fully attentive, as if compensating for his boss's relaxed form. Leonid's graceful pose declared privilege, satiety, escape from daily constraints. Though his mood made Reef alert, in Drew it sparked a vague discomfort. Today everyone he encountered seemed to be hinting at censure.

'I love travel by train. My father, he always spoke to me about your Pullmans in America. Such luxury. Such comfort.'

'Black folk know all about Pullmans,' Salim said, head still bowed over the charts.

'But Soviet trains are luxurious in their own way, yes?'

172

'I like the space,' Marshall said, throwing out a long arm.

'Russian gauge,' Reef said. 'Everything in Russia must be different. Bigger, usually.'

'Like Texas.'

Under the laughter Drew noted a peculiar tension, and couldn't read it. Agitation stirred him and masked any social subtlety he tried to apply. He pictured Katya, sitting with them, planning their visit. If she were to appear now, he would lose his composure. He felt like a young man, screwing up courage to ask a girl for a date.

'What do Russian trains do when they get to the border?' Marshall asked.

'They stop,' Reef said.

This time the laughter was less restrained. The sliding door was open a crack, and Leonid pushed the handle until it notched shut. 'Reef jokes, but there is truth here. The many differences between us and the West are . . .' he looked at Reef '. . . *izchislat*?'

'Calculated.'

'Yes. Carefully calculated. To prevent too much . . . cultural confusion, shall we say?'

The pause, the casual look in Drew's direction, the slow puff at the Dunhill – these details gathered and raised the pitch of Drew's apprehension.

'I think our music is confusing them,' Salim said.

Leonid looked for an ashtray and took a saucer from the ledge beside the door. 'To a Russian, of course, your music is strange. But there is an openness, yes?'

'Absolutely,' Marshall answered. 'And we're getting bigger crowds than we often do in New York.'

Without warning, music filled the compartment. Yoshi laughed. Salim frowned and looked at the ceiling. 'Shit, man.'

It was a vague instrumental, dull, ethnic, crackling with static. Leonid spread his hands, palms up, as if the sounds proved some point he was making. 'Of course, too much openness is not a good thing.' Leonid said this as if its context were obvious. Drew searched for the connection, but found only paranoia. The music maddened him. He excused himself and headed for the lavatory. Before he slid the door shut, Leonid said, 'You will find that the train's toilets are the exception to its general quality. Not as clean as we would hope, I'm afraid.'

Relieved to be moving, he made his way to the end of the carriage, passing Marshall and Yoshi's compartment. Yoshi's rabbit-fur hat guarded his seat, and the same music blared from hidden speakers. Where was Katya? He opened what he thought was the lavatory door and surprised the tea girl. She sat beside a steaming samovar, a paperback on her lap, and looked up at him with dark, frightened eyes. He apologized and moved on.

In the lavatory he raised the grimy seat and averted his face. The door handle rattled, but the lock held. He braced himself against the train's sway and pissed, imagining Leonid was talking about him in the compartment. *Too much openness is not a good thing*. Had there been a message for him?

His shoes squelched in the filth. When he flushed, the chute opened with a roar and he saw the pebbled tracks flickering beneath.

CHAPTER 14

Katya waited outside the lavatory, one hand gripping the wooden rail that bisected the dirty corridor windows, the other resting on her handbag, packed with tissue paper, toiletries, and a neatly folded hand-towel bearing her mother's monogram. One lavatory for the two carriages – typical Soviet planning. And such a lovely train! The famous Red Arrow. Why not get it all correct for once? That, she knew, would be too easy. Always there must be some little reminder of control. And inside – well, she knew what squalor lay beyond the door. It was why, in spite of her well-stocked handbag, she had waited until discomfort left her no choice.

She gazed down the corridor, wondering which compartment Drew was in, and thought of the week ahead. She had so much looked forward to this trip, had slept little in anticipation of the romance of a journey north in the company of a man whose silhouette made her tremble. His tentative paddling in the great *bassein*, his wet head, the surprising delicacy of his broad shoulders – these details had stayed with her through the rushed morning, had sustained her through a telephone conversation with her husband and painful goodbyes with her children. Then, outside the station, Oleg had approached her, eyelids drooping, breath stale. Forced from his sick-bed by a KGB conscience, he had even less patience than usual. He spoke with his hands in his pockets, eyes flitting from face to face as the crowd flowed past. 'I did not receive your report.'

She blinked at him, confused. 'Report. For when?'

'Yesterday.'

'When would I have had time to write one?' She peered over his shoulder as she spoke, looking for Drew.

He noticed her distraction and his tone sharpened. 'You seem to have forgotten. I will have reports each evening. It is in the regulations.'

'Yes, yes. Of course.'

She spoke too quickly. Worried about Drew's arrival – what her face might reveal, how Oleg's presence would colour her greeting – she had failed to attend to his words with the respect the situation demanded. She knew the rules. He peered at her, hunched and pale. Sickness and irritability had expunged any impulse to moderation – she could see that in his watery, bloodshot eyes. 'Concerns have been expressed,' he said. 'There has been looseness of association, lack of vigilance. Unauthorized excursions have taken place.'

She met his gaze, startled. Had he heard about last night?

'You know well the penalties for illicit association.'

He knew. He must! And in his tone were shades of meaning only a Russian of a certain class, of a certain time, could appreciate. A reminder, too, of past events. Of course. He would also have *her* file, with its notes on innocuous and suspect incidents, her schooling, her family tree, a footnote of importance for 1968 detailing the arrest of her former classmates at the Ukraine Hotel and, afterwards, her tacit betrayal of them, including Mikhail, whose muscled chest she had kissed among Bulgarian peach trees. With ominous insouciance he avoided her eye, yet stood firm, watchful, coiled, reduced this cold morning to the ruthless expression of his bureaucratic role. This man had a wife? Children?

'I do know,' she said, 'so I know the importance of ensuring the careful guidance of our guests. The attention they require.'

She had instinctively found the right words, the appropriate tone, but in context they sounded like mockery. For a long moment he stared at her, then nodded slowly. As he moved off, he added, 'The report. I must have the report.' The very air about his shuffling form seemed rank.

When Drew arrived at the station, minutes later, she was dangling in an airless space between him and authority. He greeted her with warmth and expectation. She responded woodenly. He paused, allowing Marshall and the others to collect their tickets from her and enter the station. She ignored him: she was frightened of allowing the smallest note of emotion to emerge, lest it expand into something obvious and dangerous. Drew was confused, of course, but what choice did she have? He followed his colleagues through the doors while Reef – gentle, observant Reef – gave her a puzzled look.

Now, peering down the corridor, knowing that Oleg, too, had his carefully selected place in the carriage, she said to herself that it was good he had risen from his bed to watch her and Drew – to watch them all. Last night she had let down her guard. She had neglected her grandmother's first rule of diplomatic behaviour. But there was no conviction in her self-admonition. She could not ignore her heart's urgings. Not even fear could disguise the truth of her feelings.

The door opened and Drew emerged from the lavatory. In the brief space before recognition she fixed on his eyes.

'Hey,' he said.

He was as he had appeared last night, as he had appeared all week. Tentative, oddly alert, as if he were about to mount a stage. But those eyes! Now she knew what made them so distinctive. Within their openness and depth there was something Katya had often seen in her grandmother's during her darker moods: a familiarity with inappropriate visions; an unwelcome intimacy with death.

'It's you,' she said.

He laughed. 'Yeah, it's me. Where'd they banish you to?'

'Banish?'

'They put you in a different car?'

'Yes. Next over. But no toilet there unfortunately.'

He looked over his shoulder at the filthy floor. She blushed and turned to leave. 'Perhaps I come back later.'

'No,' he said. 'Don't go.'

He laid a hand on her forearm. The train's sideways roll enhanced the contact. He was looking at her closely, as if he, too, recognized a depth he hadn't noticed before.

'You are comfortable, I hope,' she said. The sway of the train seemed part of a larger movement, something wheeling and astral. Yet he was before her, vulnerable, earthbound.

'Everybody asks that. Yeah, we are.'

There was a low cough. '*Izvinite.*' Oleg had appeared as if from nowhere. He waited for Drew to remove his hand from Katya's arm, then squeezed between them and passed into the next carriage.

Drew watched him shut the connecting door. 'Guy gives me the creeps,' he said.

Katya's pulse pounded in her ears. She moved into the lavatory. 'Excuse me,' she said.

'Wait. When can we talk?'

Oleg's appearance still gripped her by the throat. 'We must be careful.'

He touched her again. 'But when?'

'Later. Please.'

He nodded, his hand lingering in the space between them. She closed and locked the door.

When she returned to her compartment Larissa was brushing her hair. '*He* was here.'

'What did he want?'

'What do they ever want?' As she bent her head, Larissa displayed a handsome length of white neck, youthful and smooth. Katya could see her own image in the darkened window. She went to it and lowered the blind. On the middle seat, directly across from Larissa, an oval of puckered leather marked where Oleg had sat. Katya took a window seat.

'Reports, reports,' Larissa said. 'What can I tell them? What do I know?' Plump legs folded beneath her, shoulders draped by a Ukrainian shawl, she sat with ingenuous, feline complacency. Her voice whined, but her body basked in the privilege of the excursion. In the hour since leaving Moscow, they had moved past the restrained animus of their first meeting. She was, Katya discovered, a warm girl, not clever but quick to sense injustice and offer common ground. They were Russian women, and connected by a clear, undeniable condition. Oleg's attention, Leonid's expectations, their ostracism to a second-class carriage, the feminine intimacy of their compartment, all helped to establish a slender but frank alliance.

But Larissa did not fear Oleg. For a woman like

her he was a bureaucratic nuisance who got in the way of simple pleasures that were rightfully hers because she had paid for them with her innocence. It wasn't only that she had Leonid's protection: her origins and upbringing did not equip her for subversion, so the machinery of the state would never fear her.

Oleg, Katya knew, came from a pinched, Philistine tradition. His father would have been a provincial civil servant or deputy director of a state enterprise. He would have come up to Moscow in the mid-sixties, brooding and ambitious, during the freeze that followed Khrushchev's fall. She made the calculations effortlessly, well trained by experience and her institute education in the subtle measure of recent history. One of Brezhnev's children, in spirit and education, he had had years of special training in the manifold techniques of surveillance and interrogation. Ideology had crystallized in his professional life to the hidden exercise of a power both petty and terrifying. Katya's education, her position within the intelligentsia and her foreign experience would intimidate him. So he would intimidate her. That was how it worked.

'I know what they want to hear,' Larissa said. 'I know the game.'

'So tell him.'

She frowned. 'Writing comes easy to you. You are educated.'

'Not so easy.'

Larissa reached into her handbag and withdrew her cigarettes, an American brand. 'May I?'

Katya waved her approval. She liked the smell – it reminded her of Drew.

'We have our own rooms at the hotel,' Katya said. As soon as she spoke, she heard the *non sequitur*. Larissa responded with a sharp look, eyebrows raised and cheeks hollowed as she dragged on the cigarette. But Katya was not hinting at Leonid or probing for scandal: she wanted to keep the conversation going. She liked the sound of Larissa's voice, its homely vocabulary and unthinking lilt. Her undemanding tone was a refreshing change from the imperiousness of Russian men. Leonid. Oleg. Ilya. On the phone that morning her husband had been gruff and impatient when she had reminded him about the trip. 'Today? You travel today?' His voice, carried by frayed cable from Kazakhstan, crackled with dry disapproval.

'Yes. I told you last week.'

He would have been sitting in the cosmonaut's lounge, which she imagined as a sealed and featureless oval, a space capsule of bland exemption. It was there that he made his phone calls and wrote his letters. He described it to her always in negatives: no noise, no mess, no queues, no waiting for operators to call back with an available long-distance line. Thus had privilege evolved in the Soviet Union.

'Mama agrees to these arrangements too easily,' he said. 'She is getting too old for all this babysitting.'

'They're not babies. And, besides, they are at school all day.'

'And you?'

What was he asking? He was not a man of words, and the absence of his face put her at a disadvantage – the short nose, thinning hair, eyes narrowed in reflexive defensiveness. He had a practised bureaucratic smile and flared ears that were absurdly comic or irritating, depending on her mood. He was punctual, self-regulating. Every moment in his life was filled and apportioned. 'Without haste and without rest', he liked to say of his routine, not knowing – he would never know – that Alexei Karenin used the same cliché to describe himself.

'I am . . . I will be at work,' she said.

His silence allowed the tunnel of static and ghost-voices to offer its own commentary. She twisted the telephone cord round her finger. From the hallway she heard the dogs scrabbling at the inner door. Maybe he heard them too because he said, 'Did you talk to Makarov?'

'He'll take the dogs. As usual.'

'And charge as usual, of course. I must also pay for this Leningrad junket, I suppose.'

'You know that all my expenses are covered.'

Another whooping silence.

'What about Saturday?' he asked.

'Volodya will pick you up and bring you here.'

'As usual.'

She didn't need his face to see the sarcasm. Ilya

was a man of routine. He would miss her part in the weekend ritual more than he would miss her. She heard Sasha padding along the hallway in his slippers. He passed the sitting-room door and let the dogs in before she could tell him not to. The back of his head made her heart jump. Him she would miss.

'I will be at the Oktyabrskaya. Your mother has the number. Mornings I will be in my room, and I will check with the hotel operator at noon for messages.'

'I must go,' he said. His tone told her he had not been listening. 'Benyukh's briefing starts in . . .'

The dogs tumbled into the sitting room, their claws slipping on the parquet. 'Sasha, please.'

The boy laughed and the dogs yelped in response. *'Sasha!'*

'. . . that's all I ask.'

'What did you say, Ilya?'

'Too much you say?'

'No – what? The dogs are making a racket.'

'I must go. Goodbye.' He hung up.

For a moment she sat with the receiver to her ear, listening to the white noise of the Kazakh line. She saw him in his capsule, gathering his papers, straightening his uniform, whistling a vague tune. His mind on the day ahead, he would instantly have forgotten her.

It was even colder in Baikonur than it was in Moscow – she had listened in bed to the anonymous litany of Soviet temperatures announced

185

after the seven o'clock radio news. Minus twenty, minus twenty-five, minus thirty. Winter's count-down. Frigid in every corner of the vast contin-ent. Gradually her husband's image faded, and in its place arose that of her grandmother, hauling timber, with her ballerina frame, in Karaganda in those killing frosts. In the coldest times the dead of the labour camps could not be buried and were heaped away from the barracks in twisted clumps – but not so far away that they couldn't be seen. Prisoners stripped socks and underwear from the frozen corpses and traded them for crusts. Karaganda was not the worst, perhaps, but past a certain level of suffering what did degree matter? Karaganda. The name was like a curse. It was not far from Baikonur, it now occurred to her.

'He is always looking at other women,' Larissa whispered. The train rocked as she spoke, eyes wide as a child's. 'Compares me now to them.'

While Katya's mind had wandered, Larissa had descended from self-satisfaction to self-doubt, the emotional curve of tyrants, actors and mistresses.

Katya was moved by the young woman's frank-ness. 'Ssh.' She touched her arm. 'Don't speak about it.'

'If he should leave me . . .'

'He won't.'

But he was Leonid. He would leave her.

'You have your education, your marriage. What do I have?'

Katya felt the same maternal concern for the girl as she did when Sasha had skinned his knee or she was waking Anna in the dark for school. *Too much, you say?* Disquiet returned as she remembered Ilya's remark. It had not been his words but his tone that had disturbed her, flat and menacing, clipped and official – like the hunch of Oleg's back as he had moved along the corridor. Perhaps Ilya had not forgotten her after he had hung up. Any more than Oleg had.

'True love,' Larissa said, 'only happens in novels.'

Katya wondered if she really believed Leonid could love her, or that love was perfect in fiction. Leonid would always chase other women: it was his nature. Ilya would chase the stars. And as for fiction . . . Katya remembered how Karenin, thin-faced and hard-hearted, cracked his knuckles as he planned Anna's punishment for loving another man – and for failing to pretend that she did not.

CHAPTER 15

Katya's best friend, Elena, lived with her husband on the third floor of an eighteenth-century building on the Ekaterininsky canal, near Bankovsky Bridge. Pushkin was said to have spent his last night next door, in number twenty-seven. The next day he met his second on Nevsky Prospekt and proceeded to his duel with Baron d'Anthes. Elena claimed that each year, on the night of 7 February, she could hear his ghost pacing the floors beyond her studio wall. It was her sole brush with the occult; in all other respects she was a rational woman.

Katya visited her at least once a year, but rarely in winter. On Tuesday morning she rang the bell and waited. A sharp wind blew along the frozen canal, whistling through the ornate ironwork of the bridge. The sky was clear, the light pale and diffuse. It was the kind of day when the sound of church bells travelled beyond the city limits. The low sun glinted on the golden wings of the griffins guarding the bridge entrance, and the terraced façades of the elegant street stretched along the embankment in a stylized rhythm of column, cornice and pediment. Leningrad: St Petersburg. Katya felt the city's stirring contradiction – remote, marginal, reclaimed, yet the very heart of her Russia.

Elena buzzed her in and met her in the hallway. 'Katya.'

'Elena.'

They kissed three times, then held each other loosely, taking in the small changes good friends notice after even a brief absence.

'The coat.' Elena fingered the fur.

'The coat.'

'Come in. Peter is making coffee.'

The apartment was a treasure – sixty square metres, south-facing, in one of the city's finest locations. Childless, Elena and Peter had secured the family-sized space through her father, a friend of Andropov and a diplomat of good standing. Two generous rooms overlooked the canal. They slept and lived in one, worked in the other. Both artists, they shared this space within a refined code of professional domestic conduct that was strict and detailed. Several finished works – Elena's, judging from the broad strokes and bright colours – were packed in a scaffolding of rough pine, ready for shipment.

'I've interrupted,' Katya said.

'No. And even if you had, you would be most welcome.'

Katya could not get over the light. At this time of year the sun barely edged above the horizon, yet the room was radiant, touched with the metaphysical glow that some Neolithic tombs were designed to catch during the winter solstice. She looked out of the window. 'I forget this view. No, I forget how beautiful.'

Elena linked her arm. 'You see it on each visit as an artist should – with a fresh eye.'

Below them spread the city's gently angled roofs, iced at the edges and covered with a dazzling swell of fresh snow, squat yellow chimneys, now capped and unused, poking through. A few hardy birds – unidentifiable at this distance – perched on the television aerials. Beyond them were the Great Bazaar, Pushkin Theatre, the Palace of the Pioneers, the great bend of the Fontanka canal, and the magnificent onion domes of the Church of the Resurrection, always more beautiful to Katya than St Basil's because of the perfect setting. 'Those trees,' she said.

'Above the statue of Catherine the Great?'

'Yes.'

Peter emerged from the kitchen with a jingle of china. He smiled and set a tray of cups and saucers on the coffee table. He and Katya kissed. 'A working visit,' he said.

'But a visit.'

'Of course.'

'Peter,' Elena said, 'show her the letter.'

They drank strong Italian-style coffee and talked about the invitation Elena had received from a gallery in Riga. Peter spoke in long sentences, with slow, sweeping gestures when he struggled for the right word. He had a large-featured face, and a sturdy body beneath paint-stained overalls. His eyes were always half closed, and set unevenly, the right slightly higher on his face. As if to compensate, he tilted his head as he spoke. A soft, careful man, the perfect foil to Elena's swift intelligence. Painting back to back in their light-filled studio, they depended on each other's judgement of their work but had agreed, long ago, never to offer an opinion unless asked. They had lived, worked and loved together for over a decade.

'We drive to Latvia tomorrow – in our heap of a Lada, can you believe it? With my precious work in the boot.' She pointed at the paintings.

'But a good gallery.'

'Yes. Independent. Dealers visit there from West Germany and Finland. The authorities close it down for a month or two every year – always a good sign.' She shrugged with practised irony. Behind her, their large collection of books reached to the high ceiling. At college Elena had written poetry in the style of early Akhmatova: passionate, elegant, dense. She played the oboe with professional skill and belonged to a renowned choral group. Leningrad had drawn her not just for its history and splendour but because there the individual arts did not exist in isolation. She and Peter mixed with writers, musicians, sculptors, fellow painters; they discussed aesthetics with volcanic passion, distributed *samizdat*, and risked the

191

censure of the city council. It was not always prudent to visit them, but in their apartment Katya felt lifted above the inferno of the Soviet quotidian. The place was a haven.

'You've heard about the new *Seagull*?' Peter asked her.

'Where? At the Pushkin?'

'Yes,' Elena said, 'but not inside.'

'What do you mean?'

'You must see it,' Peter said. 'The company performs in the square out front.'

'The Alexandrinsky Players,' Elena added.

'At this time of year? You cannot be serious.'

Peter laughed and placed his empty cup on the tray. 'Oh, very serious indeed. They have big heaters set up, and terraced seating. And you can buy hot chocolate and Cognac. The actors wear overcoats and gloves.'

'But it is a summer play!'

'Not another word, Peter,' Elena said. 'Katya must see it for herself. You know the Alexandrinsky tradition. They make it work.'

Peter stood. 'And I must work, Katya, Please excuse me.' He bowed. Visitors – or perhaps it was just Katya – brought out in him an old-world politeness.

Elena watched him move into the studio at his considered pace. When he was out of the room she leaned forward, elbows on her knees, and gave Katya her full attention. 'So. How's life?'

Katya took a breath and spoke in French. 'I'm in love.'

Elena's upper lip drew away from her teeth – an almost imperceptible movement of surprise.

'I'm in love,' Katya repeated.

'With *Ilya*?'

'An American.'

'One of the musicians?'

'Yes.'

'Ah, Katya . . . So quickly. Not like last time.'

Her tone was a complex mix of irony, interest and support.

When Katya had retreated to Leningrad after Ilya's proposal, Elena had sat up late with her every night for a week, listening to her arguments and doubts, assessing her needs and fears. Unexpressed but ever-present was the question of love. As admirers of the Russian classics, their belief in love's primacy was absolute. And yet they were Soviet citizens, well schooled in the arts of survival and compromise. Elena would not point out potentially mercenary motives in Katya any more than Katya would accuse her of hypocrisy when she preached dissidence from the luxury of an apartment secured by her father's friendship with the head of the KGB. And because Elena had the devotion of a dependable husband, she could not push the argument against love without appearing artless. So it had always been between them. *Don't draw attention to what cannot be altered. Don't make it any harder than it already is.* Elena knew the obstacles – and how lucky she was.

She knew, too, the bargain Katya had struck, the risks in her decision. Risks that were now appearing like rooks in spring.

'So far we are holding back.'

'Holding back?'

'Saying little, I mean. But his eyes! What they are telling me, and not just about his present feelings. His history, his passions, his suffering.'

'It appeals to you that he has suffered.'

'There is something Russian about him, yes. Something fatalistic.'

'Do the others know?'

'How can they not? Such feelings are like radio waves. The official antennae pick up every blip.'

'So you suffer too.'

Elena's face was open and warm, lit by sunbeams that skimmed a vast Arctic emptiness before illuminating the tops of the city's elaborate avenues. Up here, where the highest forms of civilization bordered earth's bleakest vistas, faces did not shirk contrast. Elena's experience was there to be read, though her small, square teeth gave this mature look a girlish cast, and her eyes changed colour – hazel to green to brown – as the sun made its short descent.

Katya had been right to come here. She could speak to Elena about matters she could raise with no one else. But she paid for this intimacy with a measure of self-questioning. She could not avoid comparisons. She had never, in her own mind, fared well beside her friend, who was slim, purposeful, alert. Her natural beauty was at its best when unadorned; she did not wear jewellery or makeup, and her clothes were simple, utilitarian. The purity of her ideals, political and aesthetic, informed her movements. She always knew what to say, what to believe, as easily as she found the right gesture or tone. With her, Katya felt clumsy and inarticulate.

They had been friends for more than twenty years. On her first day at the Kutuzovsky Gymnasium, Katya had walked into her biology class and seen their namecards side by side on their double desk: *Rostova/Volkonskaya*. Something about the careful calligraphy and the run of vowels told her that they would be friends. From the beginning they were the cleverest in the class, and tacit competition underlay their quick friendship. They shared music and dance teachers, and belonged to the same Komsomol troop. They read the same books. Their *dachas* were within a kilometre of each other, and in summer they collected mushrooms and swam naked in the cold river while admiring the heroines of Turgenev's later stories. They were talented, precocious and very close. When they fought, their rows were brief and fierce, followed by periods of wary haughtiness. But they always made up.

As they grew older and went to university, their emerging differences somehow brought them closer. Katya excelled in academics, social life, love. Her style tended towards flamboyance. The men she chose were Byronic and brilliant. Elena discovered her twin passions of art and politics, and was uncompromising in her definitions and pursuits, which were never those of the establishment. She was a quiet, determined girl, who admitted you into her private circle by showing you her poems. She was dissident; she wore old clothes, cultivated a Bohemian look, smoked French cigarettes and was always pale. The men she slept with were distinguished more by their beliefs than their looks or intelligence, and Katya rarely liked them.

But she never stopped liking Elena. In summer, when the pace of study slackened and the distractions of the academic year ebbed, they sought adventure away from home, in the Urals, Bulgaria and the Crimea, where they worked, found love, read aloud their favourite poems and stories. Their final student trip was to Odessa, where they swam in the warm sea and sipped local drinks flavoured with juniper and lemon grass. They had picnics in public gardens. During the evenings they walked along the esplanade, where dark boys in bright shirts shouted compliments and proposals. Katya reread 'Lady with Lapdog', 'Gooseberries' and Ivan Bunin's diary *Cursed Days*, written, Elena told her, in post-revolutionary gloom at tables in the cafés where they drank Turkish coffee and Moldovan wine, and laughed at their own jokes. Throughout that fortnight, Bunin stared at her from the book-jacket photograph, brooding, moustachioed, romantic. Katya imagined meeting him on the esplanade or on the deck of a cruise ship, following him to his room for a night of passion, then parting from him the next morning, sunstruck and anonymous.

'So they know,' Elena whispered. 'What now?'

'They watch. They wait. They remind me. One in particular . . . well, you know the routine.' Katya pointed at the ceiling and Elena nodded. The place was bugged – how could it not be, given her history? Though safe from decipherment, the whispered French would attract suspicion. This visit would only heighten the scrutiny of Elena and Peter, but Katya had to speak.

'His music?'

'Beautiful. Contemporary. Like Stravinsky I think, primitive but sophisticated.'

Elena laughed. 'You're becoming a critic – but not an objective one, I would say.'

'You're wrong. Subjectivity has nothing to do with it. Music, love – one did not precede the other. They happened at the same time. Like one of his improvisations.'

Elena waved away the analysis. 'As I said. What now?'

'Elena, I don't know. I'm scared.'

They fell quiet. In recent years silences had become common between them, hollows of time and reflection. In a police state, Katya had learned, where speech is compromised and stripped of intimacy, silence is enriched.

'But you said nothing has happened?' Elena asked. 'Nothing?'

'You have not made love?'

'I am frightened we will and frightened we won't. What do I do if we . . . ?'

'If you must be together?'

'Yes.'

Their voices were barely audible. Their foreheads touched and they clasped each other's hands. From the studio came the sound of Peter hammering.

'Then he must stay.'

'They would never let him.'

'And they would allow you to go?'

'Eventually. Yes. I believe they would.'

The exchange was softly expressed but highly charged. In those cautious times one did not discuss such possibilities, even with the most trusted. To do so was to tempt Fate. Elena seemed to realize the danger and lifted her head. 'But not the children.'

'What do you mean?'

Elena's face darkened. As a dissident, she was used to expressing unwelcome truths. 'Do you think they would let the children go?'

'Of course. Why not?'

'Katya, they would never be issued with passports.' Elena, childless, spoke with casual authority, unaware of the impact of her words.

Katya felt betrayed – not by Elena but by circumstance. She had not imagined a future with Drew beyond physical intimacy: even his caresses seemed

198

too much to hope for. In the Soviet Union you learned to limit your imagination. It did not pay to dream. Elena pushed limits, but this dream was Katya's. Elena had what she wanted, including, Katya reasoned uncharitably, protection from consequences. She had spoken of something that had to be aired – but too soon. The conversation reached a cul-de-sac, as conversations did in this country – as life did. Another type of silence.

Elena sensed her blunder and made up for it by hugging her friend.

'I just want to be happy,' Katya said.

'I know.'

After a while, Elena stood and went to the window. The sun had set. Her back to Katya, she surveyed the darkening streets and quoted from Akhmatova: ' "Tomorrow will be better than yesterday/Over the Neva's dark waters/Under the cold smile of Emperor Peter." ' She turned and smiled sadly. 'Last week Peter and I went to Chavesky's funeral.' She spoke in Russian, more than loud enough for the microphones to hear. 'Our last great poet, you know? The bastards were there ahead of us. Uniformed militia and plenty of the boys in leather jackets. They took all the seats so we had to stand in the back. Dmitri Ivanovich's friends were not allowed to speak, but the puppets made sure they said their piece – Petrov, from the Writers' Union, Bulgarin, from the Ministry of Education, other swine. You know the type. All platitudes for a man who never wrote a trite word.'

The move from private to public, so typical of Elena, nevertheless felt like a defection from the hard question of Katya's plight.

Peter appeared at the door and was gazing at his wife. 'Do you know why they control these events so carefully?' Elena continued. 'They see for themselves that feelings are running high. They see the power of death. We are too disheartened by the system to act. Gathered together, under the spell of death and the uncompromising example of a great poet, we could be moved to action, so they surround us with police. Death lays bare the truth, and when an honest man dies the little men are full of fear. They are scared of the truth. They are scared of death and they are scared of love. That is real fear, Katya. Not what you're scared of. You have no need to be frightened.'

She had balled her fists. Peter walked slowly from the doorway and took her in his arms. Katya, though moved, was not reassured. At one time Elena's outburst would have driven away any other preoccupation – but how could it help her now? Elena had enemies – but she also had Peter, her art, her ideals. Katya had Drew and her children. In spite of what Elena said, she also had every reason to be frightened.

They calmed down with brandy. Peter toasted the coming exhibition. They talked about old friends and the literary life. The street-lamps flickered on and Elena shut the curtains.

When it was time for Katya to return to the

hotel, Peter helped her into her coat. She kissed him and followed Elena into the hall. At the door Elena handed her a set of keys.

'What's this?'

'For the apartment. If you need it while we're away.'

'Elena—'

'Ssh. Take them. Use the place or not, we won't be here. Until next time.' Elena's eyes shone in the gloom of the hallway.

Outside, the wind blew from the north and the Arctic sky glittered. The scrolled railings of the bridge trembled with an iron whinny and the golden griffin-wings glistened. Katya walked carefully along icy footpaths towards the Metro station, thinking of Drew and the night ahead. Deep in her pocket she fingered Elena's keys.

CHAPTER 16

Half-way through the week in Leningrad, Drew woke abruptly in the middle of the night. His throat was dry and his limbs sweaty. He reached for the bottle of water beside his bed. Not once on this trip had he slept through the night, and the routine of gulping water and shedding bedclothes was tiresome. Behind the drone of the hotel heating system he could hear a frantic buzz, like the sound of a wasp caught in a jar. An unremembered nightmare clutched at his chest.

He rose, used the bathroom, then peered out of the window. The night was empty and snowbound. The moon drifted through thin cloud, and the wind sang against the window. Across the street the pillars of Moskovsky railway station stood behind electricity and telephone wires.

He drank some more water but couldn't wash away the taste of loss. In Montana, on those rare days of real blizzard when school was cancelled and the ploughs took hours to reach their lodge at the far end of town, he would sit at the window sipping hot chocolate and watching the slow buildup of snow on the branches of the Douglas firs while his mother wrote letters at the big mahogany desk beside the woodstove. He had felt cared for, at peace, safe. Tonight's vantage yielded no such reassurance. His spirit was chilled by the streets below. In their gleaming snow-packed emptiness, they looked as they would when he, Katya and everyone else in the world were long gone. For all their vacancy they made him feel he was being watched. He pulled the curtains and returned to the twisted sheets, hoping he could get back to sleep. The buzz, he realized, was coming from the radio, which he could not turn off, and which he was now convinced could transmit in both directions.

As his head hit the pillow he remembered his nightmare. He had been a bird, soaring above a stylized urban skyline, a dream version of New York, with the music of Charlie Parker soundtracking his ride. Then the location changed. He was himself again, climbing subway stairs towards a rectangle of bright air, knowing that when he reached the street he would see something horrible. Sure enough, the bird he had been lay dead on the top step, its cold eye gazing up at him, its tiny shoulders crushed.

As he lay in the buzzing darkness he looked for a way to dispel the aura of despair. Katya. Her soft gaze and round shoulders. Her trembling breath. How they might soar should circumstance loosen its lock. But every moment of contact had been caged by suspicion and scrutiny.

Since their surprise meeting in the carriage

corridor, when the train's rolling rhythm had created a fluent, improvised intimacy, she had been absent or at arm's length. Days, she spent a step ahead of him, on reconnaissance, preparing for the evening's gigs and workshops. Nights, she was always in the background, peering from the rear of hall or class-room, her face blurred by cigarette smoke and, it seemed to him, a willed distance. Oleg, it was true, had been steadily vigilant, coughing and wheezing ever more noticeably as his sickness worsened. But even when Drew managed to catch a private word with her she was nervous and remote.

She did not appear at breakfast. At ten a minibus rolled up to take them to the Hermitage. The Hall of St George was featuring an exhibition of nineteenth-century Russian paintings, and Leonid, claiming special expertise, was to lead the musicians on a guided tour. The day was bright and cold. The bus smelt of dust and diesel. The six men waited, with the engine running, for several minutes. Drew assumed that Oleg was holding them up, but it was a breathless Katya who finally boarded and sat at the rear, beside Yoshi.

As they pulled away from the hotel, Salim took off his sunglasses and said to Drew, 'Don't tell me Dr No's off the job today?'

As if he'd heard, Leonid said, almost imme-diately, 'Oleg will not, unfortunately, be joining us. The hotel doctor has confined him to his bed.'

Salim grinned. Behind them, Drew heard Katya laughing at a remark Yoshi had made.

She remained out of reach when they arrived at the museum and as they made their way round it. The echoey hall was all wood, marble and open space. The murmurings of the visitors floated above them. Just a few feet away from him, heels tapping on the burnished parquet, Katya was inaccessible. Leonid was in florid form, his voice roughened by late nights and too many cigarettes, but Drew wasn't listening to him. The paintings, arranged on panelled stands that ran in diagonal rows across the wide room, were a haze of long beards and turbulent landscapes, whose skies were filled with ominous birds – grackles, rooks, jackdaws. He recalled his nightmare, and anxiety flooded him.

He dropped back and fell into step beside Katya. Yoshi moved ahead. When she said nothing he stopped her in front of a picture. 'Katya,' he said. 'Look.' The painting was familiar to him from some book cover or poster: a pile of human skulls, bleached and gaping beneath a high sun, ravens descending from a cloudless sky.

'Vereshchagin,' she said. '*Apotheosis of War.*' She looked at him, brow creased. 'Are you all right?'

'Yeah. Why?'

'You look upset.'

'Maybe it's the painting.'

'Is disturbing, yes.'

Ahead of them Leonid was unreeling a long-winded commentary.

'Or maybe it's you,' he said.

'Me? How me?'

'I've missed you.'

She looked ahead. 'Let's follow,' she said. She moved slowly, looking at the floor.

He kept pace with her, his eyes on her profile. 'Is this how it has to be?' he asked. 'All of us together, all the time? Like a flock of sheep?'

'It is the Soviet way.'

'Where did you go last night after the show?'

'What does it matter where I went? The concert went well, no?'

'It was fine.'

'So.' Her measured walk and studied expression matched the curtness of her reply.

He grasped her by the arm and spun her towards him. She wore slacks, flat shoes and a kind of artist's smock, simple but elegant, with deep pockets and a drawstring near the neck that she had left untied. Beneath a grey beret her hair was tied back. She had no choice but to return his gaze. A shiver ran from his shoulders to his knees, and his throat dried.

'What is it?' she said.

Drew wondered what had happened to the promise of the first few days in Moscow – when she had danced with Reef and played the piano at the rehearsal. But when he looked into her eyes, as he had on the train and as he did now, he saw the fear she was trying to suppress. Her mouth tightened fractionally, and her head tilted.

He took her arm and led her to a narrow aisle lined with portraits. She didn't resist when he pulled her towards him. Under Kramskoi's *Unknown Woman*, they kissed.

'I don't want to make it hard for you,' he whispered. 'But I've never—'

'Ssh,' she said, and held a finger to his lips. 'What?'

She leaned forward and kissed him again. Her beret fell to the floor and he felt her breasts against his ribs, smelt the fragrance of her hair. Then, behind him, he heard a gasp. Katya pulled away and he turned.

Reef was standing at the entrance to the aisle, frozen by what he had seen. He spoke in English: 'Please . . . I'm sorry, please.'

They let their hands fall to their sides.

'I'm very sorry,' he stammered, then darted away.

'Katya,' Drew said, but she had already run after Reef.

An hour later Yoshi and Salim had moved on to the museum's Oriental collection and the others were drinking black tea in the museum cafeteria. Drew and Katya sat apart. Reef peered at the tabletop and rolled crumbs with his fingertips. The waitresses bustled around in tight caps and spotless uniforms, their faces round and ruddy.

Leonid seemed jittery. His hair was ruffled and he drew quick drags from the cigarette in his ceramic holder and tapped ash into a paper napkin. His eyes flicked from Reef to Katya and back to Reef.

'A cultural day, yes?' Drew heard him say.

'An excellent day,' Marshall said.

'They say that if you spend one minute at each exhibit in the Hermitage it will take twenty years to see everything.'

'Wish I had twenty years.'

Drew struggled to concentrate.

'And on Saturday night Katya is taking you to the theatre. More culture.'

'You're not coming?' Marshall asked.

Leonid blinked. 'A previous engagement, I'm afraid. But you will be in capable hands.'

'Of course. We look forward it.'

'I must tell you,' Katya said, 'that it is not an ordinary production.' She swallowed, then continued: 'Chekhov's *Seagull* is to be performed in the open air, in the square outside Pushkin Theatre.'

Her voice came to Drew from somewhere else, like a ventriloquist's. His chest felt tight with desire.

'Outside? In this weather?' Marshall said.

'It won't be as bad as it sounds, I assure you.'

'We are a hardy race,' Leonid said. 'Frost is no barrier to art.' He smiled stiffly. That he and Larissa were sharing a room in the Oktyabrskaya was no secret, but to Drew he seemed a man with something to hide.

'You are our ambassador of jazz, Marshall,' Leonid said.

'I like to think so.'

'Well, Dr Timoshenko seems to be on a similar mission. Bring Soviet culture to the Americans.'

'Russian culture,' she said.

Had it been pride or challenge in her voice? Drew chanced a look at her. Her face was flushed.

Leonid paused. 'Ah yes. The critical distinction. Too bad Oleg is not here to hear you make it. Sick in bed, reading his reports.' He sipped his tea. 'What do you think, Reef?'

'Think of what?' Reef looked lost. His voice had been weak and defensive.

'Our friend Oleg,' Leonid said. 'Not the most cultural of men, would you agree?'

'I wouldn't know.'

'No?'

'I'm sure he has his own taste.'

Another silence intervened.

Leonid lifted his glass. 'To cultural relations,' he said. 'To all that brings us closer together.' He drank, looking carefully at Reef over his glass.

CHAPTER 17

As if inspired by Leningrad's artistic glow, the band's playing cranked up a gear. Shaking off Moscow lethargy, they blew the roof off concert hall and classroom for young, hip audiences who were thirsting for jazz.

Marshall set the tone. He began each gig with a consecration: a solo version of 'Goin' to Kansas City' – his American clarion, his sprinkling of the holy blues. Pale Russians with straggly goatees, horn-rimmed glasses and bright cravats crowded the stage, drinking in his vigorous, muscular tone, his superb range and technique, his deep knowledge of the tradition. Here was a man who had both power and finesse. You didn't need to be from New York City to know that. He was a man who could swing with the best of them.

On Saturday they played an afternoon gig at the Kirov Theatre, followed by coffee and champagne in the foyer, then a question-and-answer session in a low-ceilinged meeting room backstage. The room was jammed and overheated. The musicians filed on to the dais, taking their seats with Reef and Leonid around an old-fashioned microphone.

Another stood midway down the centre aisle. The atmosphere was charged.

Leonid addressed the crowd in Russian and the room quietened. The light was blue with cigarette smoke. Towards the back, men stood with their hands in their pockets, scanning the room and scowling. Drew saw Katya enter and make her way up the side. She stopped near the front and leaned against the wall.

Throughout the day, they had engaged in a conversation of discreet glances. The spaces between them crackled with their attraction, and distance had turned from obstacle to aphrodisiac. His playing that day had been aimed at her alone.

'And if I may repeat in English for the sake of our guests,' Leonid said, looking over his shoulder with a smile, 'one question, please, at a time from the floor.'

A queue of people stood behind the audience mike. The first leaned close and said sheepishly: 'Excuse. For Mr Marshall: please tell influences.'

Marshall sat on the edge of his chair, relaxed and smiling, long legs angled wide. He held a white handkerchief in one hand and a glass of water in the other. His posture reminded Drew of jazz photos of forty years ago: black men sitting on beer barrels in an improvised dressing room, hats tipped back, talking and laughing. He reached across and disconnected the mike from its stand. A loud crack of static made the whole room jump. The audience laughed, and Marshall smiled broadly. He wiped his forehead with the handkerchief. 'Influences? Well, let me tell you. I'm from San Antonio, Texas, and I play what they call Texas tenor. Big sound. Deep tone. Lots of blues.'

'Amen,' said Salim.

'When I was a young fellow there was only one band in the Southwest that anybody serious about jazz wanted to play for. That was the Oklahoma Blue Devils.' He paused, allowing Reef to translate. 'By the grace of God I secured a place in the reed section, beside Lester Young. Not for nothing they called him the President. Now, Pres had a tone alien to a Texan, but his taste and his swing and his improvising ability were unparalleled – to this day. The man taught me a lot. I ended up in Kansas City where I joined Bill Basie's band—'

'Marshall, please?' Reef intervened, hands lifted in mock exasperation. The audience laughed.

For the first time on this trip Marshall's face revealed a freedom usually unexpressed in public, a release from the self-censure and careful rigour that, in America, talented black men of a certain generation and temperament had had no choice but to assume. It was hard to shake the habits of a lifetime, especially when they had helped you rise above Jim Crow. Despite his life on the road, Marshall was more the preacher type than a musician: he had that clerical hauteur. You heard it in his precise diction and careful vocabulary; you saw it in his meticulous manners. It was black consciousness of pre-war vintage. In comparison Salim had come of age in

212

the sixties, when religion gave way to black power and anger was no longer a deadly sin. But he wore his own masks and, maybe because of his age or character, was even less inclined than Marshall to shed them. He sat like a Buddha on the low stage, sunglasses on, hands on his belly. Marshall and Salim. Not a bad partnership.

But today they were on the fringe. Throughout Marshall's speech, Katya had been gazing at Drew. As the room's energy gathered she became his sole focus. Everything else dissolved as they stared openly at each other. The emotion that was usually confined to her eyes filled her face. Her head was tilted back and her lips were parted. The scant light of the room seemed focused on her – she was an icon, dynamic yet motionless, clear yet unfathomable.

With his eyes he told her what he wanted.

There was laughter. 'Come again?' Marshall said.

An old man, grizzled and unshaven, stooped at the microphone. His nose was bent, his mouth toothless.

Smiling, Reef repeated the man's introductory remarks: 'My name is Yefim Anfimovich Torfyanov. I was born in Chelyabinsk in the year of the revolution. I played alto saxophone.'

'Yefim Anfimovich,' Salim said, savouring the name. 'My *man*!'

The man continued, and Reef translated: 'I played as a child in a marching band. As a young man I came under the influence of . . .' Reef looked at the speaker. '*Krolik*?'

'*Nyet*,' the old man said irritably. '*P' Angliskii.* Rebbit.'

'Under the influence of . . . Rabbit?'

'All right!' Salim said.

Marshall smiled. 'Reef, please tell the gentleman that I played beside the great Johnny Hodges for five years.'

He didn't have to translate: the man nodded. He took off his cap and smoothed his thin hair. His voice was fierce, yet full of respect as he spoke.

Reef translated: 'During the Great Patriotic War I served on the front lines. I was a tank commander. I would sit on the turret and play my saxophone and soldiers came to listen. Some had their own instruments and played with me. I was proud to do my part to defeat the Fascists, and with my comrades I pushed to the Elbe river in April 1945. There we met American soldiers. It was the finest moment of my life. When we saw the American soldiers, we knew we had achieved victory. We embraced them with joy. I played for them "Sophisticated Lady" and "Jeep's Blues", and they gave me Lucky Strike cigarettes and Kentucky whiskey.'

Marshall's eyes were moist. Salim took off his shades.

'You still play?' Marshall asked.

'No. I stopped in 1949.'

'Why?'

He answered, but Reef hesitated to translate. He looked at Leonid, who spoke quietly in Russian. For the first time since she'd entered the room, Katya looked away from Drew. Her face closed as she listened to the quiet exchange on the dais.

'Why?' Salim said. 'Why'd he quit?'

Reef sat up straight and pushed his glasses up the bridge of his nose. His feet were tucked beneath the chair. Beside Marshall, he looked like a schoolboy. 'As Leonid points out,' he said slowly, 'the fact is disputed. But Yefim Anfimovich claims that saxophones were banned in Soviet Union in that year.'

Yoshi laughed. 'Must've been listening to Boots Randolph.'

The comment raised a chuckle, but Salim, whiffing controversy, shifted in his seat. 'Ask my man Yefim here what kind of government bans a musical instrument.'

Reef said nothing. The room was as quiet as an empty church.

'Reef. You ain't gonna ask?'

The old man resumed speaking. Still Reef said nothing, and Marshall asked, 'Well?'

Leonid answered: 'He says that minor scales were frowned upon. That our leadership wished for music to be upbeat, to look to the future. That even the word *jazz* was banned by the authorities.'

'Is that true?'

Leonid shrugged. 'It would not surprise me. In Stalinist times many innocent activities were outlawed. Music, literature – all the arts became part of a war of ideology. And such restrictions . . . well, back then they were the least of our troubles.'

Marshall nodded. Everyone was looking at him. He cleared his throat. 'Well, tonight is evidence that if, in the past, there was such discouragement, it does not exist now. I think we all heard a few minor scales tonight.'

Reef translated, to applause. Salim chewed one of the arms of his sunglasses and frowned.

The next questioner was dressed like the others but his forehead was ridged into two tiers, giving him an aggressive, beetling aspect. He strode to the mike purposefully and spoke in English: 'Perhaps respected guests would comment on high percentage of black musicians in jazz music.'

'There you go, Fish,' Salim said. 'One for you.'

But Drew knew better and stayed silent.

'Good question,' Marshall said. 'I see it as cultural. Jazz and its associated traditions, such as gospel and blues, are part of the black experience in the United States. We grow up with it. It surrounds us from birth and has meaning for us in the deepest sense. And in the early days, of course, a classical music training was not always easy for our people to obtain. But black music was everywhere – in our churches, our parties, at our places of work and leisure.'

'So jazz is black art form.'

'I didn't say that. It is an art form with roots in the black American experience. But obviously you

216

don't have to be a black American to play jazz.' He extended a hand towards Yoshi. 'Mr Takata is native Japanese. You know after listening to him today that he is one of the finest jazz bassists in the world. Anyone can play jazz if they feel the spirit and learn the craft. And if they have the talent.'

'But blacks are best,' the guy persisted. The room's atmosphere had shifted now: something astringent pervaded the air. Drew saw that Katya, like the men at the rear of the hall, was still and alert.

Marshall thought for a moment. 'Musicians are not athletes. There are no world champions. To compare is legitimate but to rank is absurd. Was Duke Ellington better than Charlie Parker? Of course not. Nor the other way around. And as for race, it strikes me as irrelevant when you're talking about art. Alexander Pushkin was black, correct? Maybe not as black as me or Salim here but closer, if I'm not mistaken, to his African roots. What had that to do with his poetry?'

The audience stirred. The man at the mike made as if to leave, then spoke again: 'Comment, please, on racial situation in United States.' The bluntness of his tone verged on disrespect.

'Now we talkin',' Salim said softly.

Marshall looked the guy over. 'As it relates to music?'

'As it relates to oppression of black man in America.'

'How long we got, Leonid?' Salim said. 'This room booked for the night?'

217

Leonid sat back. He was letting this stream run its course. Katya's composure had been disrupted, and she shifted from foot to foot, avoiding Drew's gaze. Salim smiled, but Marshall's face was serious and his shoulders were up.

'The racial situation is not good,' Marshall said, 'but it's not as bad as it was.'

'Some would say is worse,' the guy fired back.

'And who might that be?'

'Many Americans, in your own publications.'

'Good. Nice to see free speech in action.'

Marshall's eyebrows rode high with irritation. His long torso was fully extended and his hands rested on his knees. Drew knew the signs well: his boss did not like being contradicted, especially in public.

'Free speech does not change fact of injustice,' the man said. 'South Bronx is war zone. Americans are making war on own people for racial reasons.'

'You been to the South Bronx, my friend?'

'I have read analysis.'

'And I've read about the gulags, but I'm not going to start preaching to you about them.'

Marshall looked squarely at Leonid, making it clear that if he was not going to intervene then he himself would not hold back. But before Leonid had a chance to speak, the man at the mike was pointing at Marshall and continuing, in an angry voice, 'America boycotts Moscow Olympics and creates economic sanctions against Soviet people.

Yet America kills a million Vietnamese and leaves in disgrace. Poverty in US as bad as third world, and black neighbourhoods like war zones—'

'You can leave it right there, pal. Unlike you, I know what it's like to be a black man in the United States. I don't need a lecture, especially from a guy who doesn't know New York any better than I know Siberia. But these people came here today to talk about music, not politics.'

'Everything is politics.'

'I beg to differ.'

'Everything *must*,' the man shouted, pointing at the ceiling, 'be political.' He swivelled smartly and left the room. His last phrase hung in the smoky air like the close of an up-tempo tune.

There were no more questions.

On the way back to the hotel, Marshall spoke quietly from the passenger seat of the minibus. The four musicians were with the driver, who spoke no English – Marshall had made it clear to Leonid that they wanted to be alone. 'The kid had it rehearsed,' he said. 'The whole spiel.'

'You get these types everywhere,' Drew said. '*Everything's political.*'

'It was more than that. Did you see Leonid? Sitting back with his arms crossed. He wasn't surprised. It was a setup.'

'He may not have been surprised, but what was he going to do?'

'Shit,' Salim said, 'shoulda pulled him into the action. See the hard men at the back? I bet they'd make it hot for old Leonid if we held the fire to *his* feet.'

'Bad enough it went as far as it did,' Marshall said. He shook his big head and stared at the streets. The bus tyres sizzled through wet snow.

Drew was in his hotel room, getting ready for the evening, when there was a knock at the door. It was Reef. 'A nice room, very nice,' he said.

Since Reef had seen Drew and Katya kiss, he had kept a tactful distance. When they had had to speak, his words had been shadowed by a darker layer of awareness. Ordinary phrases resonated with ominous shading. This new dimension wasn't menacing – if anything, Drew felt even safer with him – but there was an acknowledgement of a crucial difference, a change that bound them closer in a way they could have done without. For his part, Drew responded with an ambiguous forthrightness, which challenged Reef with its tone but avoided real confrontation.

'C'mon, Reef,' he said, 'same as yours, right? Didn't you tell me they're all the same?'

'So I did. And my room is nice, too.' He smiled, holding his fur hat with both hands. He looked tired around the eyes, as he asked, 'Would you step downstairs with me for a minute?'

'Why?'

'I would like to show you something.'

They walked down to the lobby. Reef pointed to two easy chairs, and went to fetch coffee.

'So, what's to show?'

'Not to show but to tell,' Reef said. 'Safer here.' He sipped his coffee and assessed the lobby traffic: tourists, cleaning ladies, prostitutes, the ubiquitous men wearing sharp clothes and suspicious glances.

'I'm afraid to say that Oleg has returned to Moscow. The doctor here diagnosed pneumonia.'

'What a shame.'

Reef inspected Drew's face to confirm the irony. 'As our great writer Pasternak said, "It is only in bad novels that people are divided into two camps."'

'This the same Pasternak who wasn't allowed to collect his Nobel Prize?'

'Yes. So he knew something about our system.'

They were moving out of the shadows now, and they both knew it.

'I guess,' Drew said.

'Even someone like Oleg—'

'Yeah, yeah. Got a wife and kids. Loves his family. Me, Reef, I don't have a family. Just an old man who's drinking himself to death in the mountains. So when love comes my way I don't look over my shoulder.'

'Love.'

'I love Katya. I love her, Reef.' Drew spoke with despair. 'But what chance have we got with guys like Oleg hanging around scaring the shit out of her? So he's back in Moscow. Another one will pop up to take his place, right?'

Reef struggled up from the deep cushions and

set his cup on the table. He did his best to disguise his emotion, but his wispy beard trembled as he looked for the right words. 'Please, Drew, I must warn you. Be careful.'

'All I've been is careful.'

'Not careful enough. This is a very dangerous situation for a Soviet. Katya is married to a man of distinction, a Hero of the Soviet Union.'

'I really don't want to know.'

'It protects her from the small things, yes, but also makes her more vulnerable. You go back to the United States. She must stay here. Oleg is nothing, I tell you. You are right – the country is full of Olegs. They are instruments only.' He blinked and swallowed. His speech had run away with him, he implied, but he stood by it.

'Look, Reef, I appreciate your concern. And I don't know what's going to happen tomorrow or the next day. But the last thing I want is for her to be hurt.'

'What is hurt? Hurt feelings? Lost love? I know about this hurt, and I tell you it is nothing – *nothing* – to the bigger pain. Better to lose love than lose your identity.' He stood and said neutrally: 'We meet in lobby at seven. For the play.'

'I will not see her hurt, Reef.'

'Seven o'clock.' He walked away.

CHAPTER 18

No stars tonight, but the right sort of evening for outdoor theatre: temperature hovering around freezing, the threat of snow, a glowing mist. Drew walked down Nevsky Prospekt as if he were in a film. The bare trees glistened in the gloom, their shadows long and purple. Young people clustered in front of dark statues and Metro entrances, smoking and watching passers-by with the detachment of minor characters. In Moscow they would have appeared menacing. Here they were local colour.

He had held Yoshi back on some flimsy pretext while Marshall, Salim and Reef walked ahead – Katya had gone early to arrange seats. Drew did not want to be with anyone who would bother him with unnecessary talk: Yoshi's reticence arose from a nexus of culture and temperament that made his silence natural and reassuring. With his fur hat, gabardine and tight smile, he floated down the wide street like the exile he was, sizing up the women in belted raincoats and wool berets.

'You checking out the talent, Yosh?'

'Ai.'

'Good as New York, you think?'

'Not bad for Communist country.'

But every woman reminded Drew of Katya. In a few minutes he would be with her, and he would be transformed, as this street was transformed by mist, darkness and a city's nocturnal expectations. The scattered voices of his past would come alive, as if to show that his whole being was resurrected by her presence. With her, his memories became bearable. Fortune and misfortune were levelled.

They walked from square to square along the wide avenue. The closer they got to the theatre, the more his stomach churned. In the fog the street-lamps threw down cones of amber light, and the headlights of the traffic thrust into the night. Trolley-buses glided by, the cross-wires above showering blue sparks.

'Listen,' Yoshi said.

'What?'

'Music.'

Yoshi had the keenest ears in the band, to go with his perfect pitch. They stopped walking and, sure enough, heard martial strains, the oompah of tubas and the thin tone of marching-band trumpets.

'Brass band,' Drew said.

Yoshi doffed his cap and lifted his head. 'High up.'

'High up?'

'Big bandstand, maybe. Sound coming over trees.'

They turned the corner and saw, past the bare trees and stage furnishings of the square, Pushkin

224

Theatre, magnificent, imposing, proclaiming in all its classical glory the primacy of order, taste and art. It was crowned with a statue of Apollo and his horses, galloping, it seemed, out of the mist. They realized that the music was coming from its mezzanine, where military musicians were spaced between the columns, the splashes of red in their caps and perfectly ironed uniforms standing out against the subtle white and yellow of the theatre façade.

'Ah,' Yoshi gasped.

'Something, all right.'

'Drew!' Katya was approaching through the swirling fog. He could not remember her saying his name before – it sounded like a birdcall. 'Please. Quickly. Snow is forecast and players wish to begin at once.'

She stood before him in a short lavender jacket and a long skirt, swaying slightly, as if resisting the impulse to embrace him. Something about her suggested pain, and he ached to comfort her and to be comforted.

When he did not reply she glanced over her shoulder at the square. Her hair was fixed at the back with a leather clasp and wooden pins like chopsticks. Yoshi looked on with polite reserve.

'What about the others?' Drew asked.

'They are seated. Reef will translate for them and I for you. Quickly, come!'

They took their seats to the left of the set. Bare trees in giant pots lined a gravelled, S-shaped path across the square, and a rough stage, too small to allow for any real action, stood at the rear. Big electric heaters with glowing orange bars had been set at the corners. The low mist was like a curtain. Katya sat between the two men, and Drew was conscious of their shoulders touching. The army band played a subdued waltz and he saw that they were there to play the incidental music for the show.

A few workmen appeared, laughing, coughing, ignoring the audience. They drew tools from their belts, stuck nails into their mouths, and started straightening and hammering the floorboards of the stage-within-a-stage. A couple in old-fashioned coats and hats soon followed them, walking out of the shadows and down the path, and Drew realized that the workmen were actors and the play had begun.

It took a while for Katya to get right the rhythm of recited lines and translation. She was conscious of others in the audience and spoke in a whisper. Sitting between the two men, she had to speak straight ahead, so they were forced to lean close to hear her. Her nearness didn't help Drew's concentration. Though he kept his eyes on the action, the smell of her perfume dizzied him, and stray strands of her hair tickled his cheek. He sensed the fullness of her body and saw her hands twisting a scrolled playbill. Her translating voice was burred and iambic, and several scenes passed before he paid attention to the sense of what was being said.

'"I am drawn to this place, to this lake, as if I were a seagull."'

'Did the girl say that?'

'Ssh. Yes.'

By the end of the first act Drew had grasped what was going on – unhappy characters, most in love with others who did not love them, talked pretentiously and watched a bad play by a temperamental artist, who stalked off the set when his mother offended him with a joke about his work. The language, as Katya translated it, was natural and comic. The women were beautiful but bored. Yoshi, too, was bored and took advantage of the interval to wander off. As the second act began they could see him in front of the theatre, hands in his pockets, peering up at the musicians. He might have been a character in the play.

Katya's soft, whirring accent, her careful articulation and the way she modulated her voice to represent the speech of different characters were like music. As the second act progressed and the narrowness of small-town life descended like evening fog on these sad, isolated lives, the magic of her whisper made its way into the story, and he could hear the writer's craft of sound and silence that lifted the slightness of the action to a level he knew well from musical performance.

In the middle of the act a shot rang out offstage, and Katya clutched his arm. But she didn't miss a line. The young actress sat alone on a garden seat beside the footpath. The playwright entered, carrying a gun and a dead seagull.

'"Are you alone here?"'

' "Yes, alone." '

He laid the seagull at the actress's feet.

' "What does this mean?" '

' "I was despicable enough to kill this seagull today. I'm laying it at your feet." '

' "What is the matter with you?" '

The man waited a long time before he replied. The scene before them was fiction, but Drew felt the horrible presentiment he had experienced just before Benny Parsons tried to throw himself in front of the A Train.

' "Soon I shall kill myself in the same way." '

The act ended, but Drew and Katya did not speak. The smell of gunpowder lingered. Her hand still rested on his arm. The air had grown colder, and they huddled together, like lovers on a park bench, watching intently as if the whole world was a performance for their benefit.

'Can you smell the snow?' she asked.

The spell of the play was such that he thought she was translating. When he didn't answer she said, 'It will be here before the end.'

The players appeared, and the third act began. Masha, dark and lovely but bored to the point of hopelessness, looked forward to her marriage: ' "What is the point of love without hope, of waiting whole years for something – one doesn't know what. But when I'm married there'll be no time for love, new cares will drive out all the old . . ." '

Katya knew the play well. She recited lines as if from memory, and as the action meandered with invisible art from comedy to despair, the range of her expression extended. When a significant passage approached, she increased the pressure on his arm, and her voice deepened with emotion.

' "If you ever need my life, come and take it . . ." '

' "My heart's been aching for you. I see it all, you know. I understand it all . . ." '

' "She ran away from home and had an affair with Trigorin. You knew that, didn't you?" '

' "What really matters is not fame, or glamour, not the things I used to dream about – but knowing how to endure . . ." '

As she translated, she spoke to Drew beneath the meaning of the words. Towards the end of the play, the second offstage shot exploded, but Katya did not flinch. As she'd predicted, snow was falling. She sat, seemingly impassive, snowflakes melting on her long lashes, and let the final lines tumble quietly in a tragic whisper: ' "Take Irina Nikolayevna away from here somehow. The fact is, Konstantin Gavrilovich has shot himself." '

Applause cascaded as the players returned and bowed in the thickening snow. But Katya did not clap. She stared at the dead seagull, now stuffed and standing on a card table, while tears and melted snow ran down her cheeks, streaking her makeup.

Drew took her hand, but it remained limp. Without thinking, he led her away from the square. Snow swirled around the street-lamps, melting blackly on the pavements but leaving a thick border on the kerbs. The chord changes of the closing music followed them and reminded Drew of another piece – an Evans tune, played solo, its title just beyond the edge of memory. Unprompted, the notes sounded in his mind, improvised, elegiac, like a flock of pigeons gliding to roost at twilight.

Invoked by the music, the three light sounds of Evans's ancestral name also fluttered to mind. *Soroka*. Russian for 'magpie', he now knew – Reef had told him. Then Jessie. Helpless, birdlike, crushed by the weight of the open sky. Finally the greatest soarer of them all, Charlie Parker, dying in the penthouse apartment of Baroness de Koenigswarter, confused, ulcerated, played-out. All in pursuit of something out of reach. All, like Drew and Katya walking hand in hand towards Nevsky Prospekt, in flight from narrowness and despair.

The city contained their movement like a great stage, a classical set built by slaves on a frozen swamp. Hunched against the driving snow, ghostly figures trailed beneath the street-lamps. When they reached the statue of Catherine the Great Katya stopped and peered into his face. 'Come with me,' she said. She put her hands on the lapels of his coat and kissed him.

He struggled to respond. 'Where?'

'Just come.'

She led him west, away from the hotel. They turned left at the canal and walked arm in arm past Kazan Cathedral and heavy residences guarded by granite entryways and oak doors. Opposite, the blurred white strip of the canal swelled into the distance, its railing posts capped with snow. At number twenty-five she took keys from her jacket pocket and opened the door. The vestibule was dank and unlit. They shook the snow from their shoulders and she whispered, 'Quietly, please.' She took his hand and led him up two flights of stairs, through double doors into a warm flat. She turned on a lamp and hung their coats in the hallway. 'Whisper only,' she said.

In the sitting room she lit candles and set them on the bookcase and window-sill. The flickering light showed rows and rows of books, an old-fashioned radio, abstract paintings, an exotic rug covering the wall behind the couch, bluish jars of preserved fruits and vegetables on the ledge above the window.

Katya had become brisk and domestic. She enlisted Drew's help in extending the sofa-bed and making it up with sheets taken from a drawer beneath the radio, then fetched a bottle of white wine and glasses from the kitchen. She went into the bathroom. Left alone, Drew uncorked the wine, took off his shoes and sat on the bed.

She returned in a thin cotton bathrobe, the makeup rinsed from her face, the leather clasp removed from her hair so it fell to her shoulders. 'You are still dressed. Why do you wait?' She helped him out of his shirt and trousers. The windowpanes rattled and the candle guttered. He touched her hair and they embraced. Through the bathrobe her body felt free and full. She tasted of toothpaste. She removed her rings, and when she leaned across to set them on the nightstand he saw a gold cross and chain dangling between her breasts.

He poured the wine, took off his underwear, then slipped the bathrobe over her shoulders to reveal her breasts. She lifted herself so that the robe fell away, then pushed him back on to the bed.

They made love as he never had before. There had been brief, unsatisfactory encounters in his twenties, then Jessie, women on the road – the perfunctory frenzy of casual sex. With Katya love was like the best jazz: patterned but unpredictable, intense, arcing, varied, and earthy. It was like being inside a Ben Webster solo. They improvised within the dancing shadows, and he felt as if pierced by blades of light.

Outside, the snow swept across the dark city. The candle on the window-sill burned, and snowflakes seemed to flock to its flame. Poised above him, she whispered her love.

MILESTONES

CHAPTER 19

Making love with Drew changed everything for Katya. Every detail of her day
glowed with him. His presence in her
mind gave even her quietest moments a certain
breathlessness. She felt him on her skin; she saw
him in the snow-packed streets and frozen air; she
heard him in radio music and in the two-toned call
of the hotel elevator. Yet love also brought fear. She
worked it out with Russian logic: their affair was
fated; fate was at odds with earthly power; earthly
punishment was inevitable. So it had been for Anna
Karenina and Katerina Izmailova. So it must be
for her.

Their love had nothing to do with pursuit, protection or will. It was selfless and empirical, like the
snow on the canal or the sound of church bells. It
had arrived of its own accord, and the power of
their attraction lay in the mystery of its origin.
When she pictured his wide jaw, his tentative smile,
his eyes, her hands shook, her vision blurred, and
she found it hard to swallow. It was his fragility
that moved her most – and warned, *What we have
will not last. And what lasts will bring us only suffering.*

In Leningrad, her distance from her everyday life, and the city's own physical drama – the clash of art and nature, stone and sky – allowed romance to take her over, but on the way back to Moscow, as the Red Arrow raced through the sordid suburbs, reality returned: children and parents; husband and home; politics. The wide horizon she'd glimpsed from Elena's window was gradually obscured by the high-rise clutter of the capital. She was not, after all, a character from nineteenth-century fiction but a modern Moscow woman, whose children's security depended on her ability to maintain the goodwill of powerful men. The danger was real. She had not been discreet.

The train approached the station. Larissa brushed her hair and gathered her bags, sighing with boredom. She had yielded nothing to Katya's sly probing. Questions easily suppressed in Leningrad endlessly repeated themselves: What did Leonid suspect? How had Reef reacted? Where could she see Drew alone? What would happen when he had to leave? She might not have chosen him, but she had no choice now but to fold him into a life that, in its closely observed privacies and personal compromises, would not accept him without rupture.

Blackened walls rose to screen the train's final approach, and she examined her reflection in the now dark glass of the window. In it she saw her daughter, a girl heading into adulthood, at the centre of her mother's life, yet outside it. And what about me? she asked herself. The urge to protect competed with the desire to shed all responsibility.

Volodya picked her up at the station and drove her directly to her mother-in-law's house in Star City. On the fringe of the cosmonaut complex, Ariadne's home was less than two years old but locked in that state of near-completion that made the newest Soviet structures look dowdy: missing tiles, screw-less hinges, exposed wires. Snow-capped cinder blocks were hunched in a pile beneath the bay window. A shoddy, gap-toothed structure, yet typical – even of Star City, one of the most coveted neighbourhoods in the empire. Home of the privi-leged and their less privileged relations.

'Mama! Mama!' Her children's voices welled in the hallway.

She went inside, and hugged them hard, moved by their delight. Their fate was bound in hers, and she trembled to think of what might happen to them all.

'Mama,' Sasha said, 'can we get the dogs now?'

'I want to go home,' Anna said.

'Children, please. Let me in.'

Ariadne loomed over their tousled heads, arms folded across her large bosom, iron-grey hair cut close to her head in a style that reminded Katya of photographs from the war. She sent the children off to gather their things.

'They are spoiled,' Ariadne said, with a little lift of her chin. She and her son shared a clipped manner, a peasant brusqueness that Katya must have noticed before but which today caused her to recoil. Ariadne frowned perpetually, brows arched above her eyes. She dressed plainly and wore waxy makeup. She had never been outside the Soviet Union and distrusted the diplomatic pedigree of Katya's family.

'They haven't seen me for a week. They're excited.'

'You enjoyed Leningrad,' she said accusingly.

'I don't know. Work was steady. Exhausting.' Katya looked at her rings. The children were squabbling now. 'Sasha! Anna! Put your bags in the car.' She looked into Ariadne's observant eyes. 'You must be eager to be on your own. We won't be long.'

'Take as long as you like. I'm an old woman with no one to talk to.'

'We will go.'

'No. You must stay.' She touched Katya's arm as if testing fruit. 'I'll make tea.'

'Don't bother. Volodya is waiting.'

'Volodya?'

'Our driver – Ilya's driver.'

'I'll start the samovar.'

They sat in near silence. Outside, Sasha talked to Volodya. Anna passed back and forth from the car to the kitchen door, making faces at her mother and tutting. The refrigerator hummed. The windows dripped with condensation. Ariadne kept the temperature unbearably high. Katya drank the hot tea quickly, and became flushed and uncomfortable.

'They will be making their decisions soon in Baikonur,' Ariadne said, tapping the table with all ten fingers. 'Finalizing the flight crew.' When she spoke of matters relating to her son her speech acquired a sheen that reminded Katya of voices heard in newsreels.

'Let him stay on the ground,' Katya said, looking at her hands. 'Do we need the worry?'

'It would be a great honour.'

'Of course.'

Ariadne peered at her, hands on the table like spiders. 'His flight log is his future – *your* future.'

Panic leaped within her like brushfire and, as if to quench it, she said the opposite of what she wished: 'Just let him be safe.'

'Duty first. Best for him. And for the family.'

The family. Katya could take no more. She stood up. 'Ariadne, my grandmother will be home soon—'

'Sit. Finish your tea.'

'I have already.' She felt suffocated. She wanted her children near her.

'I spoke to Ilya this morning,' Ariadne said. 'He told me you can phone him tomorrow. Early.'

'Fine. Good. Thank you.'

Ariadne was scrutinizing her.

'You are very good,' Katya said. She leaned across and kissed her mother-in-law with dismissive formality.

Outside, the children smiled up at her with pink noses and guileless eyes. She clutched Anna's shoulders and steered her into the back seat of the Chaika. She had expected her claustrophobia to fly away in the open air, but it remained. As Volodya drove off she glimpsed Ariadne looking out of the window, above the mound of useless cinder blocks.

'The jack of diamonds,' Anna said, 'is not to be trusted. He is too wealthy. The jack of clubs is the head of the municipal soviet. The jack of hearts is the lover, of course.' She laid the cards with exaggerated precision on the living-room floor. Sasha sat across from her, cross-legged, chin in his palms, watching with heavy-lidded concentration.

Katya unpacked her suitcase. She handled her clothing reverently, aware of new associations for each article: where she had worn it last, what she had been doing and thinking at the time, what Drew had worn at the same moments. The stages of their miraculous week were marked by a blouse, a scarf, a torn stocking. Her pendants and rings. How she had worn her hair. She remembered again the sound of her hat hitting the floor as they kissed in the museum; their discarded clothing surrounding them as they made love in candlelight. She trembled as she put away her things in the built-in drawers. Ilya was in Kazakhstan, four thousand kilometres away, but she could smell his aftershave and sense his lumbering presence. He might as well have been in the next room.

'I don't like the king of spades,' Sasha said. He

240

pointed at the cards, his mouth crooked and his eyes screened by his long fringe.

'Why?'

'He scares me.'

'Spades is the royal suit. The grandest.'

'I don't like him.'

The house had received them grudgingly, shaped to the haste of last week's departure – dirty coffee cups, piano music upside-down on its stand, the ironing-board standing before the television. The static sadness of the rooms was like a missed opportunity. Ilya's official photograph stared at her with frigid admonition. The letters and citations hung around it like dead stars. She wanted to get back into the car with the children and leave this place for ever. To go to Drew, escape this withered house, the noose of fear round her throat.

Sasha rose, went into the hallway and put on his coat. 'Where are you going?' she called.

'Out with the dogs.' He reappeared in the doorway. 'I'm taking them for a walk.'

'Don't go far. Babushka will be home soon. She'll need your help.'

He smiled, and she saw a look his father used to give her before they were married – puzzled, affectionate, charming. 'Where do you think I'm going to take them?' he said. Had he grown up in the last week? A mature shadow seemed to have fallen across the full lips and smooth chin.

She walked across the room and took his head in her hands. 'Sasha. I love you.'

Anna stopped shuffling the cards and looked at them. Katya let him go and took the leashes from the hook on the wall. The dogs barked as the door banged shut behind him.

The phone rang and her heart pounded. But it was Leonid.

'You are home safely?'

'Yes, of course.'

'Good to be home.'

Something in his voice alarmed her – an oily bonhomie that slid beyond the standard artificiality, the accustomed awareness of those listening in. She was even more attuned to it than usual. 'Leonid,' she said curtly, 'what are the arrangements?'

He took an audible breath. 'Our friend is still ill.' He meant Oleg. 'He has gone to hospital.'

She chose not to respond.

'We will have a new colleague,' he continued, 'and until his official appointment . . .' His voice trailed away. That was how the most obvious conclusions were communicated over Soviet telephones, the better to create deniability.

'So tonight's programme? Am I to—'

'Tonight, tomorrow . . . enjoy your children, Katya.'

'And Wednesday? The concert – I have made all the necessary arrangements.'

'Yes, you have done an excellent job. So don't worry. Enjoy that big *dacha* of yours.'

She could sense his smile, his face stretched with irony. The panic that had ebbed and flowed all afternoon engulfed her afresh. Her throat tightened.

'I'll phone,' he said. 'I'll let you know the latest situation, everything that develops.'

'Leonid!'

But he had hung up. Like that it was done.

Knowing it was foolish, she telephoned the hotel. Anna gathered her playing cards, watching closely from her spot on the carpet. After several attempts, Katya connected with the hotel operator, assumed her most authoritative voice and asked for the room of Mr Fisher. A long wait, and the operator informed her that there was no reply.

She set the receiver gently in its cradle and looked outside. She could hear the dogs barking faintly through the double-glazing. Beside the firs that marked the edge of the property, Sasha trudged after them, knee-deep in snow. She waved, but he couldn't see her. Anna stood up, slender-limbed and alert. She set the cards on the table and came to her mother. 'Mama? Are you all right, Mama?'

'Babushka will be here soon,' she said, lips in her daughter's soft hair. 'Tanya will bring her and we must have lunch prepared.'

Anna pulled away. 'What's wrong?'

'Nothing, darling.'

'Are you going out tonight?'

'No, I'm staying here with you and Sasha. Go across to the Kopolevs and ask for their soup cauldron. And see if they have any mail for us.'

After Anna had left she called the hotel again.

Still no answer from Drew's room. Wretched, alone, she went into the kitchen and chopped onions until her eyes stung.

The phone rang. This time she was certain it was Ilya. Again she was wrong.

'It's me.'

'Where are you?' Her stammering breath echoed in the receiver. 'I have been telephoning you.'

'I'm at a payphone. Reef showed me how to use it.'

Now that she had him on the line, she worried about security. She didn't know what to say.

'Are you off the job?' he asked.

'What do you mean?'

'Leonid said you weren't going to be at the show on Wednesday. At the university.' Traffic sounds hung behind his voice.

'I must see you,' she said.

'So you *are* off the job?'

'Later, please. Not now.' Her body trilled with anxiety. 'Tonight,' she said. 'What are you doing tonight?'

'Rehearsal. Then they have us tied up with some big shots from the ministry.'

'I heard nothing of this.'

'Can you come to the hotel? Afterwards.'

'It is impossible.'

'How about tomorrow?' he said. 'I'll come to you. Reef claims he can get me past the leather jackets.'

'Ssh. Be careful what you say. Yes, tomorrow.'

'Where?' he asked.

She discovered she had already thought this through. She struggled for a neutral tone, a directionless reference. 'Where we swam? Do you remember?'

'How could I forget?'

'Ten o'clock tomorrow morning. At the entrance.'

She could hear him breathing now.

'I love you,' he said.

'Yes. Please. Tomorrow.'

She hung up and stared at the phone, scrutinized by Ilya's photograph.

CHAPTER 20

Drew arrived at the pool entrance at ten sharp. Behind the fence, bathers floated beneath steam that curled towards a pale sky. The smell of chlorine cut through the cold air, and the concrete apron leading from changing rooms to pool edge was cracked and stained. The romance of his night swim was missing: the real world was too much in evidence.

He hunched his shoulders against the weather, looking for Katya with tentative side-glances. Elderly men and women left the pool, their step light and faces ruddy. A man with a schnauzer crossed the square, pausing to stare while the dog urinated. Since Leningrad, Drew had acquired a Russian suspicion of strangers: he stared at the ground. A tall American in a bomber jacket, loose corduroys and a baseball cap, standing by himself in cold so intense it could crack metal, how could he fail to attract attention?

As a kid, whenever he got into a funk his mother would ask, 'What's wrong?' and he always answered, 'Nothing.' His mother would shake her head and say, 'It's not nothing – I know when something's wrong.' Well, he had learned over time that the worst of all wrongs *was* nothing. Only music had filled the emptiness – until Katya. Her voice on the phone had lifted him above despair as if it were a chord. His need to be with her was more acute than the most bitter cold.

'Drew!'

She was calling from across the street. The dog-walker was gone. She moved ahead of him quickly until she reached the high wall of the embankment and turned the corner. He followed and reached for her, but she pulled away. The frozen river bend curved before them.

'Katya!'

'No,' she said. 'Just walk alongside. Look straight ahead.'

'What's wrong?' His voice squeaked. Her face was slack and pale. She shook her head. *Nothing.*

They passed beneath Kamenny Bridge. In its shadow she stopped and embraced him. He could feel her tremble. 'Where are we going?' he asked.

'Where is there to go?'

He realized he had expected her to have a place arranged where they could make love. Disappointment crashed within him.

'What will happen to me?' she cried.

Trucks rumbled overhead. The space between them was like the air before a thunderstorm. Her face was pale blue in the girdered light. He clutched her shoulders with his gloveless hands. 'Tell me. What's wrong?'

'They called. They know.'

'Who? What did they say?'

'They say nothing – that is the point. Drew, they *know*.'

Her body seemed pulled towards the earth: eyes and mouth downturned, shoulders sagging, hips splayed. Instead of her buoyant fur, she wore a grey cloth coat with a frayed hem. She was shivering. Her face pleaded for comfort.

He moved close to her and they kissed. 'I'll talk to Leonid,' he said. 'Get you back on the job.'

'It is not possible.'

'I have to see you.' He bent his head and peered into her desperate eyes. If they could make love, he knew, all would be well. 'Can you come to the hotel now?'

'How can you suggest? You have no idea.'

'I just want to be with you.'

'And I with you. But this is Soviet Union, Drew.'

As she said his name her gaze flicked restlessly beyond his shoulder and across the river. They disengaged. She walked away and he followed. He was aware of his difference: the cut of his clothes, the way he moved, the thrust of his expectations. A new distance had sprung up between them, a new void that fluttered like panic against his ribs.

He wanted to comfort her, but his mood had shifted. He had absorbed her tension. 'When?' he asked.

'You don't think I want to make love with you?'

'Then when?'

'We must be careful.'

'We were careful in Leningrad, weren't we?'

Abruptly she stopped walking and faced him. 'You go back to America in a week.'

'I'm not thinking that far ahead.'

'How can you not?'

He took a deep breath and looked at the colourless sky. 'What is so wrong with being in love? What interest does your government have in our feelings? Don't you realize how absurd this all is?'

His frozen words floated skyward. He could hear that he was being unreasonable, but frustration gripped him.

'Why do you ask these questions?' she said. 'Do you think I can answer?'

'Are you telling me they're watching us out here? Do they have microphones in the stone walls?'

'Anything is possible.'

'What you mean is, everything is *im*possible. If anything was possible then we wouldn't be having this conversation.'

He stared into the Moscow distance. The sky smelt of snow. Birds swooped past and came to rest on the bridge trusses.

She spoke so quietly he had to strain to hear her: 'Is it possible that you will not have to leave me?'

'I don't know. Maybe you could come with me.' The words were out before he knew it.

She blinked. 'And my children?' Tears were streaming down her cheeks.

'Listen to me,' he whispered. 'I love you. I will love you for ever.'

'Drew! Be careful what you say.'

He took her face in his hands. 'I mean it.'

'*Do* you?'

'It sounds like an old song, but it's true.'

'What are we going to do?'

Above them, along the bridge, people walked, looking down on them. People out walking in this cold!

'Can you get us a place?' he said. 'A safe place? Like in Leningrad?'

'That was not so safe.'

'Safe enough for love, right?'

She covered her mouth with her hand and swallowed. He took a handkerchief from his pocket and dabbed her eyes. 'Safe enough for love,' he repeated softly.

If they could be together, skin to skin, the future would become clearer, he was certain. Out here beside the frozen river nothing seemed possible.

'I'll try,' she said. 'Perhaps Reef can help. But please – say nothing to anyone. If you try to do anything, situation will only get worse.'

He nodded and brushed her damp cheek with the tip of his thumb. 'When?'

'Tomorrow. Perhaps Thursday. As soon as it can be arranged. I'll talk to Reef, and he will tell you.'

For a long while he looked at her. Tomorrow. Thursday. She might as well have said next year.

Finally, he took his cigarettes from his jacket

pocket and lit up. 'Reef. OK. I don't know how I'm going to play tonight. I need you there, Katya. It won't be the same.'

She touched his lips and leaned against him. 'And I need you,' she whispered. 'I will talk to Reef.'

'Yeah. OK.'

He put his arm round her and blew smoke into the vast sky.

CHAPTER 21

Reef agreed to see her that afternoon. They met outside Novodevichy Convent, where artists set up their easels and sold landscapes at market prices. If they were seen, she told herself, she could say they were buying paintings for the Exchange offices.

He was waiting for her at the convent gates. After a midday flurry, the sky had cleared and the bare trees were filigreed with snow. Their backs to the sun, artists in quilted jackets and fur hats sketched the frozen pond and clean lines of the convent walls. Within the grounds, she and Reef walked with false aimlessness along the paths, far from microphones, while sparrows hopped beside them and strains of plainsong floated with anachronistic grace from the high thin windows of the ancient buildings.

'Moscow was once filled with such music,' Reef said, 'before Stalin levelled the churches.' His precise, lisping Russian took Katya back to her student days, when she had sat before her life as the artists did now before the Russian winter.

'In there,' he said, pointing at a hexagonal building

in the middle of the complex, 'is the room where Sophia was imprisoned by Peter. When the Streltsy revolted, Peter hanged the ringleaders outside her bedroom window and left them dangling there all winter.'

'*Plus ça change . . .*'

'Come, now, Katya.'

'Come now, what?'

Her glance caught him at a vulnerable moment: his thin beard was raised defensively. He was nervous, of course. This meeting was as dangerous for him as for her. More so, in fact: he was not married to a Hero of the Soviet Union. She knew he wanted to help her. She knew he valued the human above the bureaucratic. But he was scared – for her and for himself – so he retreated into history and nostalgia while she waited for the right moment to ask her favour.

'Do you remember the time during our second year in the institute,' he said, 'when the lecturer in Marxist theory—'

'Popov.'

'Yes, Popov. He turned up drunk and told us we needed Stalin back. To re-establish discipline.'

' "Bring back Koba," he said.'

'Yes. In the class where we sat beside each other.'

She decided to ignore the personal reference. 'We never saw him again, did we? After he made that comment.'

They were silent. They could hear the dry snow crunch beneath their boots. Above them spanned the deep Russian sky, which had outlasted the tsars, which would outlast the revolution. It brought to Katya's mind not dictators past or present, not Reef's long-ago feelings, but Drew, whose presence filled the air like a melody, who would be flying into the sky and out of her life within days. She must be with him. Reef must help her.

'So many years since,' Reef said. She knew that tone. Close to self-pity, it recalled a time when he had courted her unsuccessfully with flowers and poems.

'What has Leonid said?' she asked abruptly.

He looked down at the path. 'About what?'

She stopped walking. 'Reef, please. You know what I mean.'

'There are several things you could mean.'

So there were. 'About my suspension. That's what it is, isn't it? I have been deprived of the right to finish the work I was hired to do. What had he to say about that?'

'What has he said to you?'

Reef had been working too long for the boys: he was starting to sound like them. She threw her hands into the air. 'You know the routine. "Relax. Enjoy yourself. Take some time off."'

Reef shrugged. 'What makes you think he'd tell me any more? I am not on the inside.'

'You've been with them every day.'

He took a few measured steps, cleared his throat. 'It is the same as before. Except that you are not there and Oleg has been replaced.'

'By whom?'

Reef sighed. 'Another lad with a hard face and a leather jacket. Katya, did you ask me to come out here only to listen to such questions?'

She thought of imprisoned queens and heartless *apparatchiks*, of a Russia that mistrusted its own people even more than it mistrusted foreigners. Reef kept his eyes to the ground, his hands behind his back.

Eventually she spoke: 'What of Drew? What does he say?'

'Very little. I have convinced him, I hope, of the danger of thinking he is still in America.'

'But he talks to you.'

'Well, he wants to see you. You know that.'

'I nearly came to the ministry last night. Maybe I'll come to the concert this evening.'

'Don't be foolish. You would only force Petrosian to act more severely. Right now he is prepared to let it slip away. On account of your husband, yes, but also because Oleg was ill and the full extent of your actions is not known outside the Exchange.'

'And what is the full extent?' she said fiercely. 'Go on – tell me what they know.'

Reef bobbed his head in apology. 'Please don't be angry. You wanted to know what they think. I'm telling you. You are fortunate. Let it be, and what they know won't go further. Yes, you're lucky. Leonid was himself lax in all this, chasing Larissa when he should have been watching us. The musicians will be gone soon and all will be forgotten.'

This plain statement of Drew's departure hurt her. 'Do they know he came to me?' she said.

'No. I made certain it was safe.' He sighed. 'Drew gave me no choice. He told me *he* would tell Petrosian. Would insist on seeing you.'

'He wouldn't do anything so rash.'

He fidgeted in exasperation. 'Don't you see, Katya? He won't suffer. He is returning to America.'

'Please don't keep saying that.'

'And you . . . if you drop this affair now you'll be safe.'

'Do they know I love him?'

He raised his hand in an odd, feminine way. 'They can read into your heart?'

'I must see him.'

'You saw him this morning.'

'I must be with him.'

This disturbed Reef. He blushed and quickened his step. 'We are not in Leningrad now,' he said. 'We are back in the real world.'

'The real world. Where Peter butchers his enemies and brutalizes his sister? Where love is a crime? "Bring back Koba"? Why not, Reef? Why not follow this reality to its logical conclusion?'

'Stop trying to be an ideologue. It doesn't suit you.'

'Is that what you think?'

'Please. As if I don't know what you mean. As if I agree with the prevailing viewpoint. Do you think I have given up on love?'

His eyes told of all he had hoped for and all he

had been denied, yet she sensed he would be open to doing what she asked.

'Katya, you have no idea what will happen if you pursue this.'

'I have every idea,' she said heatedly. 'Do you think I'm a fool?'

An echo reaching back fifteen years followed her outburst. He let his chin drop and assumed the hang-dog look that stabbed at her heart. She had resisted him all those years ago. Would he resist her now?

'Can you help us?' she asked.

He shook his head. 'How?'

'I need to see him. A private place.'

'A safe-house.'

'If you want to call it that.'

He took off his battered cap and smoothed his lank hair with a gloved hand. There wasn't a trace of a breeze, but snow fell from a small ash tree as they passed. The music had ceased. Ahead of them two lovers walked, hand in hand.

He sighed. 'I can make arrangements,' he said, without looking at her.

'Where?'

'In Toplistan, near the Metro station.' He gave her an address.

'When?' she asked. 'Tonight?'

'You forget he is here to do a job. The band plays every night.'

'During the day, then. Any time.'

'Tomorrow is not possible. I will try to arrange for Thursday. Phone me tonight,' he said. 'Late.'

She leaned across and kissed his bare head. 'Thank you,' she said. He glanced behind him to see who might have noticed. The path was empty. They headed for the entrance, he in deep thought, she wondering how she would endure the next two days.

In Star City an unfamiliar car sat in front of the house. It was as clean as a Kremlin staircase and carried official plates. She thought at once of the children, who were still at school, or should be. Her grandmother was with Tanya. Ilya was not scheduled to come home for another ten days, but as she let herself in at the front door his clipped tones tumbled from the living room. It sounded as if he was reciting. Below the usual gruffness she could hear a nervous, even excited pitch that caused her heart to pound as she hung her coat in the hall.

'Ilya,' she said, as she moved into the living room. He looked at her above his reading glasses. He was in full army dress, breast pocket glinting with a modest rank of ribbons and medals. Neatly centred on the coffee table was his colonel's cap. The letter he'd been reading aloud drooped in his hand, and she could see the ministry insignia at the head. A soldier stood near the window, looking out at the snow-muted landscape and shaggy firs. He did not seem to notice her. The dogs, shut into the children's bedroom, were scratching at the door.

She cleared her throat and kissed her husband on both cheeks. 'Is everything all right?' she said, but already her heart had calmed.

Ilya's eyes looked through her, focused, she could tell, on something official, grand and male. He drew away from her, removed his glasses and addressed his companion. 'Valery Ivanich,' he said. 'My wife.'

'Excuse me. Of course.' A big man, Valery crossed the room with surprising nimbleness, took Katya's hand and kissed it as he bowed. 'My pleasure. Of course.' He was like a character from Gogol, with an enormous stomach and a drinker's nose. He stepped away and crossed his hands behind his back, cocking his head. 'And may I be the first to offer on this notable day . . . ah, my most heartfelt congratulations,' he said.

Ilya beamed. 'I have been given command.'

'Command?'

His eyes creased with mild irritation at her confusion. 'The T-4,' he said curtly. 'I've been appointed flight commander.'

'It is a great honour,' Valery offered.

'Yes. Of course.' She kissed him again. Scenarios flashed through her mind, implications, variations on expectation and responsibility. 'What is the schedule?'

He waved the letter and paced the room. Valery drew back to the window, deferring again to the man of the hour. 'You have no idea. Ganichev, Benyukh – the whole team at Baikonur thinks all will take care of itself. As if by magic. The medical procedures *alone . . .*' He and Valery exchanged backroom smiles. 'And the reception, of course.' He waited for her to ask for details, which she managed between the lines of her frantic internal monologue. 'A little party they're having for me,' he said, flapping his hand, 'for the whole team, I should say. In the Kremlin. St George's Hall.'

'Where I translated for Nixon,' she murmured. He frowned. 'When is it?' she asked. 'This reception?'

Valery crossed the room and kissed Ilya on the lips with masculine sloppiness. 'Six o'clock, then, Ilya Fyodorovich.' He turned to Katya and bowed. 'Please excuse me. I am due at the ministry within the hour.'

At the door the men whispered while the dogs barked. All Katya could think of was Drew's broad chest and long fingers, his sweet, hoarse voice, his protestations and promises of for ever. For ever! Yet he was leaving in less than a week.

Ilya returned and spread his arms like a potentate. 'So. It has happened. They have seen what I am capable of. They have seen!'

'Yes, yes. When is the reception?'

'Thursday.'

'The day after tomorrow. So soon?'

'Yes. We haven't much time. Phone Mama this afternoon. She'll need a car, a hairdresser, a new frock. You can take her to the special store – I have an unlimited pass now. Tonight . . . tonight I am meeting the ministry boys at the Central. Plekhanov's kitchen remains excellent, I'm told.' He checked his watch. 'Volodya will be with me, of course, but you have the Volga. Go to Mama tonight. See what she needs and bring her into the city in the morning.' He paused, basking in self-congratulation.

She was alone with him in this vulgar room. Those letters on the wall! That photograph! She wanted to tear them down and throw them into the snowdrifts. It was not meant to be this way. She was to have this week to see Drew and work out what to do. Ilya had no business sneaking into her day unannounced.

In the silence she saw that, for the first time since her arrival, his eyes had settled on her meaningfully. His gaze was proud and possessive, flickering with expectation, and she realized, with a shudder, that he was thinking of the evening ahead: feasting with his cronies, vodka and champagne, Soviet bravado and, to top it all, sex with his younger wife on the West German bed.

She looked away. 'I'll make us tea,' she said.

But as she headed for the kitchen he grabbed her by the crook of her arm. 'You do know what this means?' he said.

'Of course.'

'It is important,' he said quietly. 'It moves us up to the next level – the top level. It means more for us all.' His touch disgusted her. He looked meaty and bloated in his tight uniform. His heavy-featured face was puffed with self-importance.

'Let me start the samovar,' she said.

From the kitchen she heard him on the phone, telling his friends, making arrangements, laughing with an unctuous confidence inspired by achievement. The appointment was the opportunity of a lifetime: it ensured professional success, an enduring reputation; it moved him to the uppermost level. No more night sweats for him. She busied herself making tea, searching within her anxiety for an excuse not to share his bed.

'Is anything wrong?' He spoke from the kitchen doorway as she set teacups on the table.

'I have no lemon,' she said. 'If I had known that today you would be – here . . .' *Home.* The word resisted articulation.

'I said, is anything wrong?'

She avoided his glance. 'Why do you ask?'

'I am now crew commander of the Soyuz T-4. They are holding a state reception for me. Brezhnev will be there. Andropov. The chief designer.'

'I offer my congratulations.'

He stretched his neck and ran a finger round his tight collar. His face was moist with perspiration. 'You seem less than happy. Unaware, perhaps, of your good fortune.'

'*My* good fortune?'

'Of course. My whole life is yours,' he said firmly. 'That was my promise.'

Promises, oaths, vows. They seemed to her like

262

so many ripples in a pond, fading out from a turbulent centre. She poured a cup of tea and handed it to him. Her hand shook so much that cup and saucer rattled. 'I must take Babushka to Nadia's this evening,' she said. 'I will stay there tonight.'

He blinked. 'To your mother's,' he said. 'This evening. And the children?'

'They will come with me.'

He set his tea on the kitchen table. 'And why must your grandmother go to Nadia's today, of all days?'

'My life must come to a stop because you appear out of nowhere? I have responsibilities, commitments of my own.'

His face reddened and swelled, as if it was being squeezed from below by his tight uniform. '"Out of nowhere". I have returned home with news of the greatest importance – for you, your grandmother, your children.'

'Do you care about them? Do you truly care? The news is of importance to *you*.'

He was stunned. Expecting joy, gratitude, deference, he had met resentment. She could see his confusion and the effort of will he made to interpret her anger. His face flushed to the roots of his thinning hair. In his narrowed eyes she saw herself as he would see her: ungrateful and irrational. In his agitation he bumped the table, knocking over his cup so that the hot tea flowed across the oilcloth. As she wiped up the mess he grabbed her again – roughly – by the arm. 'You must stay this evening.'

'While you are out getting drunk with your friends I have to stay here?'

'With my mother, if you wish. She requires your assistance.'

Katya yanked away her arm. 'I have my own mother and grandmother to look after.'

He drew himself up, gathered his dignity. He was a Soviet man, born and raised with principles as fixed as the Kremlin towers. When she had married him she had agreed to the rules. Reject them, and she was rejecting more than marriage: she was turning her back on the fundamentals of the culture, which lay beneath their days like the flagstones of Red Square. Offering such rejection, seeing him face it down with the instincts of his upbringing, she knew she had no choice but to stiffen her resolve, no matter how irrational she might appear.

'There is no discussion,' he said. 'Tomorrow you will make all necessary arrangements for Mama.'

The implied concession – that she could spend the night at her mother's – relieved but did not appease her.

With some despair she said, 'I can't do it.'

'You *must* do it!' He banged the table with his fist, and the dogs resumed their frantic barking.

'Let them out,' she said, hand to her brow. 'I can't stand the noise.'

'I will let them out when I am ready to let them out. When *I* am ready, do you understand? And when you agree to your duty.'

'I agree to nothing.'

He stood in the doorway, arms crossed. Beneath his aggression and disdain she recognized a familiar fear: the uncertainty that marked his nocturnal anxieties. He had reached, late in life, his perfect moment, and she had reminded him that, in the Soviet Union, there was no perfection. She was spoiling the finest day of his life – and she would not allow it to concern her; her own fears were overwhelming.

The impasse was resolved by the shrill buzz of the doorbell. He glared at her, then motioned her to answer. As she passed him she could feel the heat of his anger.

She opened the front door and her grandmother swept in. 'It is freezing out here,' she said, and brushed past without looking at her. Tanya's face held the usual vacancy: she would be looking forward to a cup of tea, a slice of cake, and the mindless exchange of nonsense that passed in her world for discourse. Katya raised her hand. 'Not today, Tanya. My husband is home unexpectedly and we must prepare to go out.'

Tanya peered over Katya's shoulder with troubled eyes. She didn't ask for much, and tea and cake were little enough reward for the hours she had devoted to Babushka. The dogs, now loose in the hall, were whining excitedly. 'And tomorrow?' she asked.

'Not the morning. I will phone you in the afternoon.'

'Well, let me see, now . . . Misha is coming from Zagorsk. Lunchtime. Or is it? What did he say?'

Katya all but pushed her out of the door. 'I'll phone.'

In the hallway Ilya was pulling on his overcoat while the dogs milled at his feet. Babushka stood behind him, hands clasped at her breast, small eyes alert to the tension.

'I'm going to Mama's,' he said. 'I'll take the dogs. Tell Volodya to pick me up there at seven. Tomorrow he will take you and Mama shopping at twelve.' He looked at Babushka before Katya could contradict. 'My wife seems to think that a Kremlin reception happens by itself.'

'A Kremlin reception?'

'She also seems to think that duty is a luxury, just as this house' – he swept his hand through the air – 'and all I have made available to both of you . . . is a luxury.'

He had lost the rhythm of his analogy mid-sentence and looked angrily at Babushka's uncomprehending face. With a snort, he ducked into the living room for his hat and took the dogs' leashes off the hook. Babushka stood where she was, hands frozen in their clasp, until he was gone. The door slammed, and for a minute the two women listened to the diminishing yelps of the Dalmatians.

Katya went into her bedroom and slid a suitcase from under the bed. Babushka followed her in. 'What's this? What did he mean by all that?'

'Pack a small bag, Babushka. We are going to Nadia's.'

'What are you talking about? And what of a state reception?' She shuffled over to the bed and laid a hand on Katya's arm. 'Sit for a moment, Katya. Sit and tell me.'

Her warmth was uncharacteristic and disarming. Her eyes were remarkably clear. Katya knew that her own state of mind was dangerous and that her face showed what she was feeling, but could do nothing about it. Strong feeling had the effect in her of freezing any emotion but the dominant, with joy or love or despair shaping her expression in un-ambiguous strokes, as if it were a Greek mask. Ilya had seen it, and had responded with fear and bluster.

She slumped on the edge of the bed. 'He has been awarded command.'

Babushka made a little noise – a sign of appreciation or alarm, Katya couldn't tell which.

'There is a reception for him on Thursday night in St George's Hall. Brezhnev, all the top brass, will be there.'

'It is good news. Very good.'

Katya looked her grandmother in the eye. 'Babushka, I don't want to go. I don't want to stay here. I don't want to be anywhere near Ilya.'

Babushka held her head very still. 'Where is this foolishness coming from?'

'I don't love him.'

'Of course you don't love him. Who said anything

267

about love?' She stroked Katya's arm with a ballerina's delicacy.

Katya laid her head on her grandmother's shoulder.

'Listen, Katya. There is a time to act and a time to let the world take its course. You must give him your support. He is your husband.' She held Katya's face between her hands. 'This is good news for you, of course, for the children.'

Katya was crying silently.

'There is someone else?'

Katya nodded.

'Put him aside for the moment. Soon Ilya will be in outer space.'

Katya whispered, 'That is not possible.'

Babushka straightened her *granddaughter*'s blouse and brushed hair from her eyes with compassion and curiosity. 'I'll help you,' she said. 'All will be well. Tomorrow we will go to Ariadne's, just as Ilya asked, and I will tell her what she must do. You won't have to worry about a thing, Katya. Not a thing.'

CHAPTER 22

Nadia was not happy. Scheduled to return to Ethiopia in a few days, the unannounced visit of her mother-in-law, her daughter and grandchildren forced her to retreat to her bedroom. She stuck her head out of the door every few minutes to screech instructions about who should sleep where and what food was forbidden to them. Katya had decided not to mention Ilya's promotion until the next day: her mother's anxiety was far easier to handle than her enthusiasms, so she listened to her rant and brought supper to her bedside. It was as if Nadia were the one in the midst of a crisis, not Katya.

The children, however, more in tune with their mother than Nadia could ever be, knew that something was up. On the trip into the city they had sat in the back seat of the Volga, watchful and suspicious, puzzling over the coded comments passed between their mother and great-grandmother, scratching for information.

'Mama,' Anna had said, 'are you working tomorrow?'

'No, but I have errands to run in the city. Babushka will look after you.'

'Where is Volodya?' Sasha asked.

'He is busy.'

'Why are we staying with Grandmama?'

'Stop asking questions,' Babushka said. 'I'm an old lady.'

The children had settled into stony silence. Every few minutes, Katya caught Anna's eyes in the rearview mirror, alert and accusatory. On top of everything else she was battling, she now had a gnawing sense of competition for her love. It tore her inside like an ulcer. To look after her children, she had reasoned, she must first look after herself. One problem at a time.

After midnight, when everyone was in bed, Katya called Reef at his apartment.

'Thursday,' he said. 'Eleven o'clock.'

'How long?'

'Two hours.'

'You will tell him.'

'I have already.'

'A key?'

'Knock three times. He'll be there.'

When she hung up Babushka was standing beside her. 'It is very late, Babushka, you should be asleep.'

'Late it is. Especially for a phone call.'

'A colleague. From the Exchange.'

'Ah.'

Katya stood up and crossed the room. Out of the front window she could see the darkened swimming-pool, clouds of steam rising in the moonlight. She had a date and a time. Something to live for.

'Katya.'

'Yes?'

'Be careful.'

The frozen river glistened. The Kremlin stars glowed. Never had her city looked so alien.

'Of course, Babushka.'

Nadia learned Ilya's news from Darya, who had heard it from Ludmilla, whose husband worked in the Ministry of Defence. When Katya and her grandmother returned to her mother's apartment after an intolerable day with Ariadne, Nadia met them at the door, the expression on her tanned face poised between joy and anger. Piano music tinkled behind her.

'I have cancelled my return to Addis Ababa,' she said triumphantly.

'Why?'

'Why indeed? Were you trying to keep me from the reception? I am so insignificant to you now that I must be the last to know important family news?'

Katya pushed past her into the hallway. Babushka followed, carrying a dun-coloured parcel tied with string. The bland packaging could not fool an experienced scavenger like Nadia. 'What is this? You've been shopping at the special store.'

'A dress for your daughter. She should go to the Kremlin in something old?'

Katya was afraid that her grandmother would mention Ariadne and send Nadia into an unambiguous rage.

'And what about me?' her mother said. 'What am I supposed to wear?'

Babushka stood in front of her, hands on her slender hips. She had removed her scarf as she entered and her sparse hair was swept upwards. 'Search that crammed wardrobe of yours. There are dresses in there you haven't worn twice.'

With pretended indifference, Nadia took a cigarette from a silver box on the hall table and lit it. Her foxlike features and brittle hair quivered with her excitement. 'I was ashamed, Katya. I found out from Darya. Widowed only a few weeks, poor woman, confined to that dreadful apartment on Dmitrova Street, and she knows my daughter's news before I do. I was mortified.'

She puffed furiously. Katya ignored her and went into the living room, where Anna was playing the piano and Sasha drawing rockets. They were perfectly calm even though their grandmother was howling. What must they think? She kissed them.

Babushka edged Nadia into the kitchen, and their bickering continued.

'When do we go home, Mama?' Sasha asked, without looking up.

'We must stay again tonight. Ilya has a reception at the Kremlin, and he must be alone in the flat. To prepare.'

'He has been given command,' Sasha said.

'Yes. How do you know?'

Anna's hands stopped mid-phrase. 'Grandmama told us. She said that you wouldn't tell her but she found out anyway. From her friend.'

'Well, now everyone knows.'

'Are we going to the Kremlin, Mama?'

'Of course.'

'When is the reception?'

'Tomorrow,' Katya said. 'Tomorrow night.'

Babushka came in and motioned towards the kitchen. Katya shook her head. 'Go,' Babushka said. 'You must.'

In the kitchen Nadia leaned against the sink, lighting a cigarette from the butt of the last. Dirty dishes cluttered the draining-board. Her posture betrayed a shift in her mood: within a few minutes she had passed from hysteria to self-pity to steely disapproval. Wisps of hair strayed from her temples and caught the fluorescent light of the kitchen with an artificial gleam. She ran water over the butt and tossed it into the rubbish bin. Her motions were precise, controlled. 'You were shopping with Ariadne,' she said.

Katya exhaled sharply and let her shoulders slump. 'I did my duty.'

'Isn't your duty to remain at your husband's side?'

Katya laughed. 'As you remain at Papa's?'

Nadia lifted her head, and the slack skin of her neck trembled. 'I have not loved your father for over twenty years, but I have never let him down.'

'And I am letting Ilya down.'

'You admit it?'

'I admit nothing.'

Katya was reminded of her quarrel with Ilya, and resentment rose in her. For hours she had tolerated Ariadne's oblique arrogance; she was close to losing her temper.

'I spoke to Ilya today,' Nadia said. 'Naturally, I phoned to offer my congratulations. He is puzzled. He pretends not to be, but of course I can hear it in his voice. A man arrives home from an outpost of hardship with the best news possible for his family, and his wife runs out of the door. What is he to make of that? He wonders if you will fail to attend the reception and create a scandal.'

'Oh, you had a splendid conversation, I'm sure.'

'There was nothing splendid about it.'

From the living room came Babushka's voice, lively and inspired, and the sound of the children laughing. While Katya aged, minute by minute, her grandmother seemed to grow younger and stronger.

'I made all the arrangements for his mother,' Katya said. 'I will go to the reception. I'll let that old fool Brezhnev kiss my hand if it is required. Then everyone will be happy.'

Her mother's head grew still, a fox listening for rustlings in the grass. Her eyes betrayed a dangerous curiosity.

'What is it?' Katya said.

'One of the Americans telephoned Ilya.'

'He told you this?'

'Who else has he to talk to?'

'And?'

'A man phoned from the Intourist Hotel. Looking for you.'

Katya swept crumbs from the table into her palm. Nadia stood in front of the cupboard that held the bin but wouldn't move. Katya reached round her and tossed the crumbs into the sink.

'They have taken away my job,' she said. 'I am sure my removal is confusing to men from a culture where such things don't happen.'

'So you know who has phoned. You expected the call.'

The rhetoric of the inquisition – statements and questions delivered with challenge and condescension – oppressed Katya beyond the surface meaning. The words might have changed, but she had had the same exchange with her mother for fifteen years, in several Moscow apartments, at their *dacha*, in the driving snow on Borodinsky Bridge.

'I have been working with the Americans.'

'And they telephone your home? He insisted, this musician, that he had to see you. The call was not arranged. Literally, the man picked up the telephone and dialled your number. Ilya was embarrassed, of course. How did he have the number in the first place? What business did he have in taking such a risk? Why does he insist on seeing you?' In spite of herself, Nadia was excited. Her colour was high and her eyes bright. The ash on her cigarette was so long it fell to the floor in a small heap.

With every question Katya had grown more agitated. The whole world was suffocating her. 'And what business is it of yours?'

Nadia took mock offence. 'We are concerned. Your behaviour is coarse and erratic.'

Katya went to the kitchen window and looked down into the snow-covered courtyard. She was shaking. 'My behaviour is my business.'

'So what do you propose to do? Stay here for ever? Keep the children out of school? Neglect your family responsibility?'

Katya wheeled. 'Maybe I'll divorce Ilya. Maybe I'll go to America.'

Nadia's shock was almost comic: eyes popping, she reared back and laughed. She stared at her daughter for a few moments, then closed the kitchen door. 'What are you talking about?' she said.

Katya was liberated by unreason. The swell of her anger was like music. She would show her mother what it was like to be drowned in another's hysteria. 'I have been invited.' The lie came smoothly, theatrically.

'Invited where?'

'To the United States.'

Frightened, Nadia moved close and spoke in a whisper. 'By the man who telephoned?' Katya nodded. 'He is your lover, this man?' The swiftness of her mother's discovery disarmed her. Nadia grasped Katya's arm so hard her nails cut into the skin. 'Don't be an idiot, Katya. Just when you have achieved everything. You need only to be heard saying that and you lose everything!'

'What have I achieved?'

Nadia released her arm and retreated. She shuddered and pulled her sweater tight round her shoulders. 'Everything that I have not. A good Russian home for your children. A husband whose career will improve. Protection from the filth and corruption.'

Her mother's voice, hoarse and miserable, pulled Katya back to the edge of common sense. But Nadia was a master manipulator of sentiment, a woman who could fool others because she was so good at fooling herself. Standing there in her lambswool sweater and gold jewellery, she was frightened that her daughter would bring her scandal. In her way, she was pleading for caution.

'I have told him I will go,' Katya whispered fiercely. 'They took away my job – they will not rob me of love.'

As Nadia shook her head, mouth slack, the doorbell rang. They stared at each other while Babushka answered the door and the artificial tones of Luba and Leonid filled the hallway. Nadia's face was skeletal with admonition and fear. She swallowed, glared at her daughter, and went to her guests.

'Luba, welcome,' she said, in a strained, sing-song voice. 'What a pleasure.' She kissed her friend three times. Behind them, Leonid looked uneasily from Nadia to Katya, who stood in the kitchen doorway, arms folded. Moving from wife to husband, Nadia glanced behind her briefly, a final plea to her daughter suggested by the barely lifted plucked eyebrows.

'Leonid.'

As the kissing continued, Luba spread her arms and marched towards Katya. 'Look who's here, Leonid! What a surprise!' She grasped Katya and kissed her. 'Well done, my dear. You must be very proud.'

Katya became aware of Babushka at her side, holding her elbow and urging her softly in the direction of polite acknowledgement. The standard Soviet expressions of congratulation festooned the hallway. She managed to nod and smile and make her way through the miasma of complacency to the sitting room, watched by Leonid.

'Leonid was in the ministry,' Luba said, taking off her gloves, 'and found out from one of the boys there. All hush-hush, he was told, but we just had to come over.'

'Of course I've spoken already to Ilya by telephone and offered my warmest congratulations,' Leonid said.

'He didn't tell you I was here?' Katya asked. The sound of her voice alarmed her – it squeaked, and Nadia looked at her sharply.

'He told me you were making the arrangements for his mother. And for yourself, of course.'

'Katya was at the special store this morning,' Nadia said, settling herself beside Luba on the leather sofa and lighting a cigarette. 'You don't trot along to a Kremlin reception in honour of your husband in any old frock. And as for her other responsibilities, we all know how difficult Ilya's mother can be. She's the type who believes, with admirable sincerity, of course, that Russian champagne is superior to French.'

She waved smoke from her face as Luba laughed wickedly.

Nadia's ability to disguise stress was remarkable. Her mastery of small-talk, the way she used posture and gesture as camouflage, the screen of ironic reference she erected not only around herself but also her daughter – such consummate manipulation left Katya numbed and silent. Faced with the roughshod certainties of the room's social geometry, she was helpless. She knew that her smile looked false. Her soul yearned for Drew – he was all she needed, all she wanted.

As her mind filled with his image, the chatter grew distant. She sat on an ottoman near the television, apart from the group, examining her rings. She was aware of her body, of the fullness that made her self-conscious but which Drew claimed to love. She must be with him. Suddenly Anna came and put an arm round her shoulders. Sasha, polite as ever, had put down his coloured pencils, waiting in vain to be acknowledged by Grandmama.

With her children at her side and the idle talk buzzing in the room, she recalled her kitchen hysteria. In lying to her mother she had revealed her heart's deepest desire – and recognized the impossibility of its fulfilment. She must be with him – yet what could their meeting bring but tragedy? How could she expect to escape the charade of her mother's world, the clutches of a successful husband, the corruption of the state? She clutched at her children, gazed up at her, confused.

Babushka rose from her seat. 'I'll make tea. Come, Katya. Help me.'

In the kitchen Babushka closed the door. Katya filled the samovar.

'Are you all right?'

'I'm fine, Babushka.'

'Your face shows everything, you know. It always has. You look miserable.'

'I am miserable.'

Babushka held her by the elbows and looked into her eyes. 'The trick,' she said, 'is not to dwell on sadness. In a few days we can talk about how you will move on. But for now you must not let them see into your heart. You will lose whatever advantage you might have.'

Katya went to embrace her but was surprised by a light knock at the door. Leonid entered, smiling but sharp-eyed. 'Those two!' he said, with a weary nod towards the sitting room. 'Once they get started they're like jungle birds.'

He held his cigarette, in the ceramic holder, close to his ear. His brilliantined hair and good clothes looked a touch ragged, as if he'd been on a long journey, and his face was lined and tired. When the women didn't respond, he pointed to the samovar. 'No champagne? With such cause for celebration?'

'Good Russian tea will do,' said Babushka, moving between the two and grasping their arms, as if to link them in good cheer.

'I'm surprised you're here,' Katya said to Leonid. 'I had supposed you would be preparing for this evening's performance.'

He blinked sleepily. 'There is nothing to do,' he said. 'You did everything yourself with your usual professionalism.'

'I am delighted you think so highly of my skills,' she said. 'I could be forgiven for thinking they were not appreciated.'

He puffed long and thoughtfully, then said to Babushka, 'You must be proud of your grand-daughter.'

'What is there to be proud of?' Katya interrupted. 'What have I done? I had a job I *was* proud of, which you have taken away.'

The handsome planes of Leonid's face were more defined in the white kitchen light; his eyes probed. The *apparatchik* in him had been roused.

Babushka looped an arm through Katya's and laughed. 'Katya is disappointed, of course you understand that. But she also knows her responsibility as a wife. We hope you'll be at St George's Hall tomorrow night?'

'I wouldn't miss such a glorious occasion,' Leonid said. 'We appreciate all you have done for the Exchange, Katya, but we understand that you must

281

now concentrate on other duties, pleasant as they must be to fulfil.' He bowed slowly, almost comically, but his gaze, tone, manner – every detail of his bearing – challenged her to contradict him. Squinting in the smoke, he took a last drag from his cigarette, removed it from the holder, and stubbed it in the ashtray on the table. 'Allow me to help you with the tea,' he said, smiling his most elegant smile. 'The ladies are waiting.'

CHAPTER 23

For the first time in his life, Drew was forgetting tunes. Halfway into a number, the melody would drift away from him, and he had to take refuge in safe chords and awkward silences. Marshall frowned and Salim glared, but there was nothing he could do. The notes had deserted him.

Offstage was not much better. The urge to action was like a crash of cymbals. *Do something! Act!* But another voice undermined him: *You're screwing up again. You're making things worse. Cut your losses and take off.* And it was true that, in the rare moments when he did act, his judgement faltered. Why had he phoned her house? When her husband answered, why hadn't he hung up? With dumb moves like that, how could he trust himself to make big decisions?

Yet something had to be decided.

Maybe you could come with me. As soon as he'd said those words to her, he had known it was right to pursue it. For both of them. But how? There was too much to arrange. Too little time. And too much, past and present, that got in the way.

At night, as he lay in his overheated hotel room,

puzzling over possibilities, unwelcome images visited him: his father slamming doors and shouting drunkenly in the middle of the night; his mother in Massachusetts General, her eyes saying goodbye; Jessie in the morgue, laid out on a marble slab, her thin hair sticking out, her face blue.

Big decisions? He had decided to leave Jessie – and done to her what even heroin could not.

'Where does life go? When someone dies, where does the spark fly?'

'You're asking a Soviet woman a religious question?'

He and Katya had exchanged these questions on the streets of Leningrad, in the aftermath of *The Seagull*.

'Not religious. Practical. Where does it go?'

'It goes where love goes when it is lost. The same.'

'And where is that?' he had asked.

Her arm looped through his, she had steered him towards her friends' flat, its soft sofa-bed and snow-filled windows. 'It turns into suffering.'

The fact is, Konstantin Gavrilovich has shot himself . . . The play's final words had settled on him like an unexpected chord change, calling up visions of the past, binding him with guilt. Minutes later he and Katya had been making love for the first time. Thus were love and death linked again in his sense of the world. He knew then that he would have to tell her about Jessie. And promise that he would never let her down as he had Jessie.

He must do everything he could to take her with him. Anything less would be abandonment.

On Tuesday night the band had played at the music department of Moscow State University. Reef had promised news of an assignation, and during the gig Drew could think of nothing else. He performed so poorly that Marshall approached him between tunes and asked what was wrong. 'Stomach thing. Feel like I'm going to throw up.'

The leader had looked down at him, long face shadowed with seasoned scepticism. 'Well, hang in there. We'll do the "Oleo" duo so you can take a break.'

Afterwards he had sat beside Salim in the dressing room. The university had provided a bottle of pepper vodka, squares of black bread and slices of pickle. The vodka left a hot trail in his throat and made his cigarette taste mentholated. Where was Reef? Marshall was off to the side, holding forth to a semi-circle of sombre music students.

Salim peered at Drew, hands folded across his stomach. 'What was all that about?' he had said, after a long silence.

Drew had shrugged, and Salim snorted. For several days he had been battling a head cold and was in no mood to humour someone showing all the signs of deceit. 'That's some unprofessional shit I heard out there,' he had continued.

'It's not like I'm not trying, Salim.'

'Not trying what?'

'To do my job.'

Salim smiled coldly. His stake in Drew's well-being had many strands: personal, professional, even fraternal, in an odd way. 'Your wig's somewhere else, Fish, and I don't like it.'

The door had clicked open and Reef had stepped inside, stroking his beard, his eyes searching out Drew, who knew at once he had made the necessary arrangements. Relief spread through him. He wanted to hug the man.

Salim had sensed the shift. His nostrils flared and his cheeks quivered. 'Reef,' he said, low-toned. 'Our guide.'

'Ah, gentlemen,' Reef had said hollowly. 'Excellent performance tonight. Excellent.'

'So you dug it? How 'bout our piano man? You like his playing?' He had fixed an ominous gaze on Reef, who had not been in the concert room for most of the gig. 'Of course,' Reef said. 'Very good. As always.'

Salim stood up, shook his big head and spat into his handkerchief. Reef raked at his dirty hair and looked at Drew.

'Shit,' Salim said, and left the room.

The next day he had made the foolish phone call, failing to hang up when a male voice answered.

'May I speak to Katya, please?'

Silence.

'Hello?'

'Who is speaking?' The voice deep and hesitant.

'Uh, I'm calling from the Intourist Hotel. Katya Timoshenko, please.'

'This is husband. Who is speaking?'

'Tell her the hotel called. Where the group is staying.'

Further silence. Drew hung up.

She had told him that her husband was in Kazakhstan, doing cosmonaut training and not scheduled to return to Moscow until after Drew had left the country. What was he doing home? He would see her tomorrow morning: Reef had told him where to go and what to do.

Now there was a knock at the door. It was Salim. 'What you up to?' he asked.

Drew sat heavily on the bed. 'Thinking about sleep.'

'Yeah? I was waitin' for you down in the bar.'

'That place depresses me.'

'No shit. That's the whole point.' Salim blew his nose. His eyes were bleary. 'I thought maybe we could head to the art gallery in the morning. Check out the icons.'

Drew fingered the hem of the faded bedspread. 'Reef wants me to help him with something.'

'That so?'

'Look at a piano his brother wants to buy. Something like that.'

Salim raised a hand. 'Hey, Fish, you and Reef got somethin' cookin', I could give a shit. Don't insult my intelligence. But you got a bigger problem than keepin' some half-assed story straight.'

They eyed each other. Drew breathed deeply. 'What's that?' he said.

'Marshall. You got his mind workin' overtime.'

Drew stood up and went to the window. Since yesterday he'd eaten nothing but a few Hershey bars. He felt weak. 'Overtime?'

'Suspects you might be on again.'

Drew laughed.

'Signs are there, my man. Marshall, he's thinkin': Is the white kid gonna mess it up for me? Is he gonna fuck with my band's *in-teg-ri-ty*?'

The preacher tone rang true. Drew lit a cigarette. 'Yeah? And what do you think, Salim?'

'Since when you making me play guessin' games? What kind of shit is that? Holdin' out on me.'

'I'm not holding out on anyone.'

Hands on his knees, Salim hunched forward in clear disgust. Drew stared out of the window, assessing the conversation Marshall and Salim must have had. A black man's conversation. *White kid.* There it was, out front and undisguised. Marshall was worried that Drew was back on heroin at the worst possible time.

Drew knew what this suspicion would drag up. The old jazz double standard. A white kid, the product of ruling-class privilege, a diplomat's boy, Drew had somehow managed to find his way to jazz, sure, but he had also found smack, not because he sought escape from racism or poverty but because he was too stupid to recognize his advantages and shield himself from a poison alien to his culture. Coltrane's habit Marshall could forgive, but not Drew's. It was not a defensible position for a rational man, but who could be rational all the time? Especially when Marshall's own reputation was at stake.

'The man's so off base it isn't even funny,' Drew said.

'Yeah? So talk to me, Fish. Open my eyes.'

Drew leaned over the table and turned up the radio. More Tchaikovsky, more reminders of Katya. He took a pen and paper from the desk and scrawled: *I'm in love.*

'That right?' Salim said.

The spoken words unnerved him. But writing made it easier to confess. He continued: *I want to take her back with me.*

Salim looked from the pad to Drew. He picked up the pen. *Back where?*

New York.

Salim bit his lip. 'Let's go outside,' he said.

The front door of the hotel was locked, and they were let out by an unpleasant guard wearing a new leather jacket and a Rolex. The cold was wind-less but intense. They walked up Gorky Street. The giant temperature display reported minus twenty-seven. Drew's cheeks hurt.

'Shit, Fish. This better be good.'

The frozen air made Drew light-headed. 'I'm seeing her tomorrow. Reef's set it all up.'

'You sure you want to tell me this?'

'I have to tell someone.'

'So. You're head over heels.'

'I have to take her back with me, Salim.'

'Why's that?'

'I can't stay here.'

'What you gonna do? Put her in your suitcase?'

'I don't know. Political refugee, special case, whatever.'

Salim stopped. He clutched his cloth coat and fixed Drew with eyes that filled with tears from the cold. 'You sleepin' with her?'

Drew nodded. Salim stamped his feet and faced the traffic. 'Shit.' He yanked Drew back towards the hotel. 'C'mon. We stay out here, we fixin' to *die*.'

In the bar Salim sipped straight whiskey and spoke in a low voice: 'I do *not* dislike her. I never claimed. I seen you head this way before and it was not good. Not good at that time.'

'This is different.'

'I believe you. But that does not change the basics here. You think our great government is goin' to give her a visa just because you two all goo-goo-eyed?'

The bar held the usual complement of prostitutes, opportunists and foreign businessmen. Drew had learned to recognize the KGB boys, not just the leather-clad goons but also those incognito in Levi's and Italian shoes. The bartender spoke quietly into a telephone. The nasty guy who had unlocked the front door for them strode across the lobby and whispered to an older man with a goatee.

'This isn't a fling. It's the real thing.'

'As if that makes a difference. You don't get points for sincerity.'

'Do you think I'm looking for trouble?'

'Absolutely. Think about it, Fish. Assumin' you get that far, who's goin' to be decidin' whether your ladyfriend is allowed into our great land? Be guys like those hillbillies we met first day we were here. The ones had you pegged for a junkie. You think guys like that are goin' to open the gates of paradise for Katya? Because you're in *love*? Shit.'

'Keep your voice down.'

'Those cats be lookin' to make your life a misery after the shit we gave them. They got the power stink.'

Washington. The black guy. He hadn't occurred to Drew. Salim didn't trust him, but there was a rapport there. Definitely. Get him away from his snake-eyed partner and there might be a chance. 'If I get to the right person, I can convince him.'

Salim finished his whiskey and looked askance. 'Well, *you* convinced, that's for sure.'

The goateed security man passed, stopped casually and asked: 'And how is everything this evening, gentlemen? You are enjoying yourselves, I trust?'

Salim checked him out. He was not the usual pale, suspicious assistant-manager type but a man of some authority, the voice smooth and educated, the clothes as fine as Leonid's. '*Enjoyin'* be pushin' it.' Salim nodded at the bleak bar. 'Not what you'd call a hotspot, huh?'

'No? Well, most of our guests appreciate the relaxed atmosphere. The calm ambience.' He smiled with false graciousness, fingers knitted in front of his wide silk tie.

Behind him, leaning against the glass door of the hard currency shop, the younger man smoked a cigarette and watched. There was an air of invisible menace, of trouble behind closed doors. Drew thought of Katya at home, dealing with her husband and waiting, as he was, for tomorrow. He thought of Washington. Yes, Rick Washington was the man. He had a streak of humanity. But how to get him on his own?

'If there is anything we can do to make you more comfortable,' the goateed man said, 'please let us know.'

He smiled, but Drew looked away.

CHAPTER 24

The deep cold returned. Early in the morning Katya listened to the radio weatherman plunge through the empire's temperatures – minus twenty, minus twenty-five, minus thirty. Beside her the children slept. Heating pipes clanged in the bowels of the building, and Sasha stirred. She could smell last night's cigarette smoke. Behind the heavy curtains there was no trace of light.

The day stretched before her like an ocean. She would have to phone Ilya. Flat on her back and staring into the dark, she saw that the call was unavoidable. Arrangements had to be made, details explained, rituals observed. Later, the ministry would send cars: a Zil for Ilya and herself, a Chaika for Ariadne, Babushka and the children. An assistant would brief them on their entry into the hall, how to greet various dignitaries, when to pose for photographs. In theory she had nothing to do. In practice she must provide a Soviet wife's support: unobtrusive, alert, subservient. The protocol was inevitable and insufferable. She could have asked her mother for advice – Nadia knew the routine as well as anyone, but so did Katya.

First, though, she had to construct an agenda for the day that would explain away the hours when she would be with Drew. They would have from eleven o'clock until one. Soviet habits of mind were a help: forever thinking in parallel universes, the official and the private, she was experienced in fashioning the public lie, of which all possible pitfalls branched to safe conclusions. But she could never be entirely safe: the state was too tenacious, and time was on its side.

She phoned Ilya at nine o'clock, after Babushka had taken the children out for the day. He had already breakfasted, walked the dogs and visited his mother. He didn't waste time on pleasantries. 'You are enjoying your little holiday.'

'I have been working hard, you know that. Your mother is not easy to please.'

'My mother is approaching the situation with the seriousness it deserves. And she would be far easier to please, as you put it, if her daughter-in-law were staying where she should. The situation is embarrassing for me, but I suspect that is exactly what you want.'

His words barely disguised the anxiety that came into view when he was silent. He could not attack for long: his instinct was to retreat into his narrow ego. He was most comfortable in cramped spaces – barrack-room and back office, *banya* and fishing hut. Spaces without women. His ambition was cramped, too, squeezed into the confines of materialistic pursuit as he would be wedged into spacesuit and capsule. The context of his job was infinite, yet his place in it was as claustrophobic as their marriage.

'Mama is still waiting for her corsage,' he continued.

'I will bring it out this afternoon. It will not be ready until lunchtime.'

'What florist are you using?'

'Mama's. Ponemarov, near the Belorussky station.'

Ilya snorted. 'He will charge you an arm and a leg.'

'I don't see how you can say that. Mama must watch costs far more than we.'

'*We?* I'm the only one who is watching costs in this house.'

Another pause, in which a note of deep suspicion sounded, long and meaningful over a Soviet telephone line. How she hated the familiar, muted sibilance – a white noise both animal and mechanical. It conjured men with small eyes and bad teeth, hunched over the machinery of surveillance, making it even more difficult to deceive her husband than it already was.

He broke the silence bluntly: 'You will be in Star City this morning.'

'Half past two,' she said. 'I have to get my dress taken up and my boots heeled.'

He cleared his throat. She had answered too quickly, and in the next silence she could see him tilting his head, narrowing his eyes, and running a finger beneath his collar to relieve the pressure on his windpipe. 'You know the schedule,' he said, voice wrapped in doubt.

'I do.'

'What this day means?'

'Ilya, I will be there when I say, and do what is expected.'

'I'll send Volodya.'

'I have the Volga. Now, please, I must go or I will be late. I'll see you at half past two.'

But she could not hang up. It would be like an admission of guilt. And he was a man who had had his way all his life through sheer obstinacy. He was not ashamed to appear pig-headed. In his view of the world, long-suffering was rewarded and shame could be sloughed off like dead skin.

'Volodya can take care of the frock. You tell me where and I'll have him pick it up. And the best shoemaker in Moscow is out here. Come. It is settled. He'll be there in an hour.'

'*Half past two!*' Her shrillness surprised her.

Nadia walked in, silk dressing-gown hanging loose, cigarette lifted high. Her calculated appearance gave Katya the impetus she needed to cut him off. 'I will see you then,' she said, and hung up.

Nadia bit her lower lip and waved her cigarette through the stale air. 'You have an appointment this morning?'

'Yes,' Katya said, standing up. 'I am getting my boots repaired and my dress altered, as you already know from listening to my private conversation.'

'I should be the only one listening to your calls,' she said.

'You aren't even ashamed enough to deny it, are you?'

'You talk about shame? *You?*'

From the sofa-bed Katya grabbed her makeup bag and neatly folded clothes, chosen so carefully for the morning ahead. Nadia looked at the ironing-board, the packed cases and the children's stuffed animals. Katya left the room and she followed, her face crumpled. 'I know what you're doing.'

'You don't know anything.'

'You'll ruin everything, do you understand? And not just for yourself. Are you so selfish?'

She went into her grandmother's room and locked the door behind her. Nadia banged on it with her palm and screamed,

'Forget about yourself! What about me? What about your father?'

'Leave me alone.'

'What about your children?'

'Leave me alone!'

She turned on the radio at full volume and sat on the bed until the banging stopped. The finale of Tchaikovsky's Fourth, conducted by Mravinsky, galloping, wild and glorious. Goosebumps sprang up on her arms and she was breathing rapidly. She burned for Drew, to put her cheek on his shoulder, to kiss his hands and arms. *He's always on my mind. I can't stop thinking about him.* In times past she would have read such phrases about love – perhaps used them herself – and thought them accurate. But thinking had nothing to do with it. What she experienced as she prepared herself for the morning was an incandescence that glowed from her heart to the tips of her fingers and toes. It overwhelmed her.

Abruptly Nadia stopped banging. Her bedroom door slammed. Katya turned down the radio. Nothing her mother could say or do would matter now. In less than two hours she would be with him.

She laid out her clothes on the narrow bed. Slowly, with ritualistic care, she dressed. In spite of her haste to leave Star City on Tuesday, she had packed with foresight: her silk dress, her French underwear, her best stockings. The caress of her clothing excited her. Each article she put on brought her closer to him. She dabbed perfume on her breastbone, her wrists, and above her pubis. The prospect of his touch eclipsed all else.

She fixed her hair at the back of her head with a leather clasp. She took care over her makeup, then put on jewellery and applied a touch more rouge to her cheeks. For several minutes longer she stood at the mirror, examining herself.

When she emerged it was after ten. Nadia's room was silent. She gathered the bags and set them near the front door. Babushka had taken the children, excused from school for a second day, to Katya's old nanny on the Garden Road. There, Babushka would rest while Irina took them to the Tretyakov

Gallery. Afterwards they would all have lunch and Katya would pick them up outside the National Hotel at one thirty. From there to Star City and penance.

But first Drew. She put on her fur coat, kid gloves and beret. She felt as she looked – attractive and exotic. She opened the hall door and bent to pick up the bags. Nadia's bedroom door flew open and she felt her mother tugging at her arm. 'Don't! You mustn't,' she hissed hoarsely.

'Mama, please. I have to go.'

'Liar! You dare lie to your mother?' Then Nadia's anger turned to pleading. 'Don't deny it, Katya. About these matters I have always been right. You know that.'

Katya pushed away her mother's hands and picked up the bags. 'Get dressed, Mama. I'll see you tonight.'

Nadia's weeping followed her as she crossed the hallway and waited for the lift.

Outside, the cold air took away her breath and the swimming-pool stanchions glittered in the winter sun. She put the bags into the boot of the Volga and drove towards Krimsky Bridge. The landscape – so resonant with memory – scrolled by, like the opening shot of a film. The car heater roared. Let her mother gnash and wail. In minutes she would be with Drew.

At the Toplistan apartment she knocked three times, as instructed, then waited. Drew answered the door, wearing only boxer shorts and a red T-shirt.

His legs were pale and sturdy, his arms scarred and muscular. She closed the door quickly behind her and hugged him. She could hear jazz piano music in the background. He stepped back. 'You look great,' he said.

He took her coat and hung it in the hallway. She was blushing with excitement. 'Hot in here,' he said. 'Tried to find a thermostat, but no dice.'

They faced each other, close but not touching. He stood before her as few Russian men would – casual, open, sexual, inviting her to come to him as lover and equal. She reached out, touched the front of his shorts, then stepped forward, crouched, and took him in her mouth. She had not done this for Ilya. And never would. A moan emerged from deep within him. At the critical moment he drew back his hips and lifted her. 'I want to save it for you,' he whispered.

'That *was* for me,' she said. 'This is for me. Everything we do is for me.'

She kissed him, and he led her to the bedroom. The walls were bare. The light blue curtains and bedspread were flounced with cheap extravagance but welcoming all the same. A cassette-recorder beside the single bed played the jazz she'd heard from the hall.

'The music,' she said. 'It is beautiful.'

'Bill Evans. "Waltz for Debby".'

He undressed her slowly, just as she had known he would, then kissed her in unexpected places – behind her knees, under her arms, between her

300

shoulder-blades. She took him as he was, let him do with her as he wished.

Afterwards he fetched a bottle of champagne from the kitchen.

'Where did you get this?' she asked.

'Well, I didn't find it waiting for us, I'll tell you that, honey.'

She laughed, savouring the endearment. 'Oh, I know that.'

He had also brought Finnish chocolates and American cigarettes. Only the best from the hard-currency shops, too good for ordinary Russians. They sat on the bed and smoked. After a few minutes she leaned down, hands on his thighs, and they made love again.

When they had caught their breath they talked for a long time. She told him about Ilya's promotion and the reception that evening. The Khrushchev-era apartment was of poor quality, and the walls were busy with muffled sounds: a radio or television, voices raised in anger or joy, water running and pinging pipes. The bedroom's curtained window faced the low midday sun and stained the room a pale blue. Delicately, he ran a finger from her breastbone to her pelvis.

She touched the cluster of white scars on his left arm and asked about his old habit. 'What can I say? First time you do it – whole bunch of times when you're starting off – it's like the sweetest thing. Kissed by angels.'

'Like love.'

'Well, not exactly. It's wonderful, but it's all just you. You and that cloud of bliss. Like music, maybe, or pure sex. But all you.'

'And you were alone at this time?'

'No.'

'Married?'

He was sitting on the bed, his back against the wall, one knee raised. He waited a while before answering. 'No. Never married. At the time I was with Jessie.' He lit a cigarette. 'My partner in crime. My fellow junkie.'

'You loved her?'

His eyes sought the corners of the room. 'I believe so. But, like I said, when you're high, it's just you.'

'And since then have you . . . have you seen her?'

'She was killed,' he said abruptly.

In spite of the heat in the apartment, she shivered. 'An overdose?'

'You want the details?' He looked wretched and defensive.

'Of course not,' she said. 'I understand.'

For a moment he said nothing, just stared at the bad wallpaper. She gazed at the floor and saw loose boards, mouse droppings, deep gouges, as if someone had dragged a stove or refrigerator across it.

'I was straight,' he said. 'I was off the junk. I couldn't take it any more.'

She was sorry she had asked. 'We don't have to talk about it,' she said.

'She couldn't stay clean. So I left her.' He lifted his head. 'She was dragging me down, do you understand?'

She wanted to say something, to acknowledge the pain of his confession.

'And that was it,' he said. 'I abandoned her. And she got high and did this to herself. And did this to me.'

'Did what, Drew?'

He crossed his arms. 'Threw herself in front of a train. The A Train. In Manhattan.'

He rose and went to the bathroom, closing the door. He was in there for a long time. She flipped the cassette in the player and started the other side of the tape. The first tune began with solo piano, melodic, sensitive, highly personal, almost like Debussy, but with that popular American edge. She turned up the volume, as if the sound would flush out the poison of his recollection.

He returned, his composure recovered. '"My Romance",' he said. He stood above the tape-recorder while she sat on the bed and watched him. His right hand fluttered against his leg, and he lifted his head as the melody soared. When it was over she looked at him as he had looked at her when she arrived. He fell on her with a moan.

'What will happen to us?' she cried afterwards, clutching him.

He was still gasping. 'I don't know.'

'What am I going to do?'

'I'm not leaving you. No way.'

She let go of him and lay on her back, looking at the cracked, stained ceiling. He was on all fours above her, kissing her breasts.

She grasped his head. 'You can't stay. This isn't the United States. They will force you to leave.'

'Then you come with me.'

The rawness of this offer moved her to tears.

'I love you,' he said. '*Will* love you. For ever.'

'I told you before, be careful what you promise.'

'I know what I'm promising.'

She turned her face away from him. At that moment she had all she'd ever hoped for: love as defined by the greatest writers, the pledge of eternity, the promise of escape. 'I have never been loved,' she said.

'*I* love you, Katya.'

'Ilya doesn't see me. He wants someone on his arm, someone to look after his mother and go with him to his receptions.'

'He's an idiot. He's blind. Tonight will be awful for you, but we'll be together again on Saturday. Reef has promised.'

'Hold me, Drew.'

He did. They were silent for several minutes. The clock showed twelve forty. A quarter of an hour remained. Her need now was not for his body but for his future. 'How am I to come with you?' she said.

He stood up, became brisk. 'I have an appointment this afternoon at the embassy. I think there is somebody who can help us.'

'And my children?'

The certainty in his expression juddered, and he seemed to age in an instant: his face looked more lined, darker under the eyes. 'I don't know.'

'What do you mean, you don't know?'

He walked across to the tape-recorder and un-plugged it. The blue of the curtained sunlight coloured his broad chest. He wound the cord round his fingers. Getting ready to leave.

She got up from the bed. 'Drew, answer me. What about my children?'

He dropped the cord into a box of tapes and raised his hands. 'Until I talk to the guy, I have no idea of what is and isn't possible.'

'How can I go without them?'

The sound of a television blared from next door. He picked up his trousers. 'I'll ask this afternoon at the embassy.'

She grabbed his arm. 'Is it possible they won't be allowed to come?' She was shaking. 'My heart is breaking,' she whispered. 'Take me away.'

'I will.'

'Do what you must.'

'I will.'

She drew back, held his face and kissed him. They heard footsteps in the hallway and the sound of a drunken man shouting down the stairwell. Drew stepped back and wiped tears from his cheeks. 'I love you,' he said again.

Everything would work out fine. Their love would assure it. If she trusted in love, all would be well.

It was ten to one. Reef had warned them to leave promptly, five minutes apart. They had agreed she would go first. Saturday they would meet here again, but she could not think beyond today: his meeting at the embassy, her night at the Kremlin.

They dressed quickly. The drunk was outside now, and she could tell from his shouting that he was staggering along the icy path.

They kissed. She opened the door to leave. 'Saturday will come quickly,' she said, 'and today you will go to the embassy.'

But again she was shaking violently. 'Drew,' she cried, 'save me!'

He held her as she wept. Cold air flooded through the doorway. From far away the drunk sang a popular song and a tram screeched across frozen rails. She sobbed and he held her, whispering and soothing, while over his shoulder she saw a terrified mouse scurry across the scarred floorboards.

SOME OTHER TIME

CHAPTER 25

Drew returned to the hotel, changed his clothes and left for the embassy. He walked quickly beneath a low sky that looked like wet blotting-paper. Snow threatened. The traffic was heavy and the air thick with diesel fumes. He had made elaborate excuses to avoid the day's cultural programme, and as he hurried up Gorky Street he imagined he was watched from stalled cars and high windows. His skin tingled with Katya's touch. No matter who was watching, he would take her to America.

The stars and stripes drooped above the embassy entrance. He approached the sentry box. When he peered inside he saw the easygoing MP who had ushered the band to their first meeting here so long ago.

'Hey. Musician, right?'

'Yeah.'

'How's your pal? Raiders fan.'

'Good. Even better since they won.'

The kid smiled easily, elbows on the counter. His handsome, almond-eyed face was like a map of America.

'I'm here to see someone,' Drew said. 'Rick Washington. Political officer.'

'You got an appointment, right?'

'He's expecting me.'

The MP reached for a leatherbound log from a shelf behind him, and thumbed through its wide pages. His uniform was clean and perfectly pressed, and the brass buttons shone. Drew glanced up the street, where trolleybus wires parcelled the grey air and dirty snow shadowed the kerbs.

The MP frowned. 'Washington, you say. I don't see anything here.'

'I talked to him this morning. He said come on in.'

'What time?'

'He didn't mention a time.' Drew smiled uneasily. 'Something's come up. It's pretty important.'

'Write your name for me,' the kid said. 'I'll be back in a minute.'

Across the wide boulevard a man in a fedora leaned into a doorway while he lit a cigarette. Women carrying plastic bags hurried along the cracked sidewalks, and a convoy of military vehicles passed in the direction of the river. The world appeared as through a prism, fragmented and unfamiliar.

Drew rehearsed his lines.

The MP returned, handed him a pass and showed him inside. He waited in a windowless room lined with folding chairs. Scattered on a coffee-table were the same bland diplomatic magazines he remembered from his youth, filled with turgid propaganda about the Peace Corps and photographs of smiling Africans. He needed a cigarette, but as there were no ashtrays in the room he refrained. After a long wait he was fetched by a dour, dark-suited young man and brought to a pallid office.

He waited another fifteen minutes. Confidence seeped from him like rain from eaves.

'Hey, how are you?'

It was Rick Washington, businesslike and abrupt. He closed the door and sat at the desk, a cup of coffee in one hand and a sheaf of papers in the other. His shirtsleeves were rolled to the elbow, exposing muscular forearms. A pair of reading glasses sat at the end of his nose and his tie was loose. The scholar-athlete.

'Thanks for seeing me,' Drew said.

'Hey, no problem. Can I get you some coffee? Soda?'

'No, thanks.'

Rick filed the documents in his desk drawer, took off his glasses and set a pad of paper on the desktop. His motion was smooth but urgent. His eyes revealed nothing. Drew waited for him to initiate the discussion, but he stayed silent and expressionless.

'Like I said on the phone,' Drew said, 'it's something of a sensitive nature.'

'You're playing for the ambassador on Monday,' Washington said, checking a desk calendar. 'At Spaso House, right?'

'Playing?'

'The band.'

'Yeah. Right. But what I've come here to talk about doesn't have to do with the band.'

'And you return to the States when?'

'Next day. Tuesday.'

'Mmm. Tour going well?'

'Fine, I guess.'

Washington sipped his coffee. Behind him hung a new picture of President Reagan, tanned and cocky. The white noise of office machinery hummed in the background.

Drew was desperate for a smoke. He slid his cigarettes from his shirt pocket. 'You mind?'

'We don't smoke in this office.' Washington remained passive, his face empty.

The long wait and sidelong questioning had robbed Drew of his urgency and widened the context. He was a man in love. Simply that. In love, perhaps, in a way he had never expected to be – but it was nothing special to anyone other than Katya and himself. Salim had not been impressed, and there was even less reason to expect Washington to be. The noble words he had rehearsed seemed hollow. But everything depended on this conversation.

'I'm looking for some advice. Situation I'm in.'

Washington nodded.

'I've been in touch with a woman who wants asylum. Russian woman. In the United States.' He exhaled sharply.

'Asylum?'

'Yes.'

'She's seeking safety from persecution?'

'Well, yes. Isn't everyone? Here, I mean.'

'Not legally.' Washington tapped the desktop with his finger. 'Legally, asylum can only be offered to individuals suffering from political persecution. Quite clearly defined. And it must be provable.'

'She's definitely being persecuted.'

'Definitely?'

Washington was a frustrating audience. It wasn't that he offered resistance – quite the opposite: he seemed to absorb Drew's words, render them ineffectual by soaking them into a bureaucratic blankness.

'She finds her current situation intolerable. Unacceptable. From a political and human point of view.' He gestured lamely. Now that it was out, his plea sounded weak.

'This woman's name?' Washington asked.

'Timoshenko. Dr Katya Timoshenko. Wife of a cosmonaut.'

'And your relationship with this woman? How has it come about that you're in touch with her, as you put it?'

'She works for the organization sponsoring our visit. Or was working, until they fired her. Part of the persecution.'

'But she's confided in you?'

'Well, we're involved.'

'Involved?'

'Romantically.'

Again the neutral nod, this time with his mouth down-turned. 'And what makes you think,' Washington asked, 'that her desire to come to the United States is for reasons of political asylum, rather than reasons that are, say, more personal?'

Carried into that office on a wave of passion, Drew now felt stranded beneath the other man's dispassionate gaze. He had not, it occurred to him, worked out his case in the level of detail that someone like Washington would require. He scrambled for words. 'She was practically forced into marriage. If you're a woman here, an educated woman, with ambition, what else are you going to do? And she knows what freedom is – she lived in the US as a kid.'

'How'd she manage that?'

'Her father's a diplomat. He was stationed in Washington and she went to an American school. Back in the fifties.'

Washington clicked his ballpoint and, for the first time during the session, noted something on his pad. Drew felt a stirring of hope. 'The way I look at it,' he continued, 'a defection like this would make a powerful statement. A woman of her background, her current profile, her connections. What it says is that even the privileged can't tolerate the system. And she's willing to make the move. Immediately. She's willing to appear here, at the embassy, whenever you say she should.'

Washington cleared his throat, made another note. Without looking up he said, 'What about you?'

'What about me?'

'What are your motives?'

Drew thought of her desperation two hours ago. He felt a pressure in his chest and head, an expansion of blood that almost blurred his vision. 'I love her.'

Washington raised his head sharply. 'And you don't think that—'

'I love her.'

The simplicity of this plea and the raw emotion in his voice seemed to affect the officer in a way that his previous words had not. The man's face softened. He placed his pen on the pad and rubbed his brow with the base of his palm. 'You're sure about her feelings?'

'Of course I am.'

'How do you know you haven't been watched? How do you know you aren't being compromised?'

'I know.'

Washington stood up and paced the room. He was a large man, powerful and athletic, and in moving took on a humanity that he had lacked sitting behind the desk. 'When do you see her? I take it you're not using the telephone.'

Drew blushed. 'When we were working together,' he said quickly, 'every day.'

'And every night.'

'I work at night.'

'What about since she was fired?'

'Called her a couple of times from a pay-phone, saw her once in the open air, met at a safe-house.'

'A what?'

'Safe-house.'

Washington stopped and stood still with his hands on the back of his chair, one shoulder raised, staring into space. 'What makes you think it's safe?'

'She arranged it. Listen, she has a lot more reason to fear exposure than I do, right? I can't see her taking any unnecessary risk.'

'She's in love.'

'Yeah.'

'A risk-taking frame of mind.'

In spite of the relentlessness of the interrogation, Drew chose to be hopeful. Washington was clearly assessing the case, weighing possibilities. That he was asking such questions at all proved there was hope. 'Isn't it worth meeting her?' Drew asked. 'To judge for yourself?'

'You said she'd be willing to come in here?'

'Yes. Tomorrow. Tonight, if you want.'

He shook his head. 'Too soon. Monday at the earliest. Things like this take time.'

'But you might be able to do something for her?'

Washington grimaced and stepped back from the desk. 'I'm not saying anything.'

'But there's a chance?'

'Just leave it with me.'

'And her children? She has two kids.'

Washington waved his hands in front of his face. 'Whoa. Slow down. One step at a time. She has kids, that's a whole separate issue.'

Drew rose from his chair. His desperation had risen to a pitch where it could only be expressed physically, but Washington was not the type to welcome intimacy. 'But you can help her?' Drew said. 'Her, at least.'

'When are you seeing her next?'

'We're meeting Saturday.'

'At the safe-house?'

'Yes.'

'What time?'

'I'll be told tomorrow.'

'Right. Meet her as usual. Keep her calm, keep yourself calm. Tell her to be ready. Maybe, just maybe, we can get something in motion.'

Drew wiped sweat from his face. Being told what to do was hugely welcome. 'I can't thank you enough.'

'I'm not making any promises.' Washington looked away, flexed his forearms. 'Call me on Monday. Early. I'll see what I can do.'

Washington saw him out. They slid through the bland buzz of the embassy offices, surrounded by the smell of administrative America: carpet fibres, pencil shavings, the burnt-dust odour of new lamp-shades. The smell of Drew's youth. He thought of his father, who would have been appalled by his appeal. But what did his father know about love?

In the lobby Washington took him aside. He allowed a certain sympathy to temper his tone: 'Look, if the situation is as you say, there's a chance we can do something. But you can't say a word to anyone. Not even to your friends in the band. No phone calls, no meetings, nothing out of the ordinary. See her on Saturday and call me on Monday morning. And keep your own counsel.'

Drew nodded. He had done right to come here. He had found hope.

When he left the embassy it was snowing heavily. The sentry box was empty. A big American sedan with darkened windows stood at the kerb, hazard lights flashing. He was overcome by the sharp change in scene: from the pristine, hard-edged embassy interior to an infinite and ill-defined landscape of crepuscular buildings and imperial sky. The daylight was centreless and diffuse. He turned his face towards the void and let the flakes melt on his face. Under such a sky the impulses of ordinary men like him seemed scarcely relevant. But he had done what he could. He had acted. And received instructions.

Trust in Washington. What else was possible?

Hands in his pockets, head bowed, he headed towards the Metro station. Extending ahead were fresh footprints, black and glistening in the virgin snow. The left print was oddly angled, as if the walker, nearby but invisible, was limping into the blizzard. He took his baseball cap from his pocket, pulled it low over his eyes and followed the quickly disappearing trail.

CHAPTER 26

On the way to the reception, Katya sat well apart from her husband in the back seat of the Zil. He fussed with his uniform, peered out through the back curtain and checked his watch repeatedly. His physique seemed contaminated by anxiety: he sweated heavily and his breath was hard as kerosene. He spoke little, and when he did he was distant and impersonal. For him, she was part of the background, indistinguishable from their driver or the traffic police who, recognizing the Kremlin plates, raised their batons deferentially as the limousine sailed past.

His distraction suited her. She was immersed in the memory of Drew's touch, the odd curve of his leg, the feel of his neck beneath her hand. She had not showered, the better to sense his trace on her skin.

They used the special lanes all the way into the city centre, past old Moscow doorways, courtyards, ironwork, deepsashed windows from where citizens watched the Zil swoosh along, as their counterparts in centuries past had observed the bear-drawn sleighs of Peter the Great and the ornate carriages of the Romanovs. She remembered lines from Lermontov: 'Every stone on every tower sacred lore from age to age passed on.' Her Moscow. The same streets she had ridden through with her parents twenty years ago, when Khrushchev had tousled her blonde curls with his big paw.

But now the rusted pylons and ugly tower blocks of Toplistan floated in her imagination like the invisible city of Russian folklore, magical and iridescent, and the lights of the Kremlin seemed mundane and depressing. And just as well, perhaps, as all that surrounded her would soon be lost: the personal history and patterned association, the ghosts on street corners she had crossed a thousand times, the layers of myth and experience that made up a Russian life. All lost, to be replaced by Drew, his earthy smell and expert hands, and whatever landscape he would lead them to in the days ahead.

At the Grand Kremlin Palace they left their coats in the hands of anonymous attendants and were led up the Parade Staircase to St George's Hall. Katya held her husband's arm, as she knew she must. Ariadne, Babushka, Sasha and Anna trailed after them. Greeted by applauding well-wishers, Ilya nodded and harrumphed, caught between embarrassment and the sense that being honoured in this grand venue, with its air of gelid power and medallioned achievement, was no less than he deserved.

'Good man!'

'Ilya Fyodorovich!'

'Old sport, you've done it!'

His friends swarmed around him, a montage of nasal hair and simian grimace. Adolescent platitudes and giddy gestures flashed beneath the bronze chandeliers. Men at the centre of things, charged with the aura of power. Ilya first, chosen, blessed, to be followed by the big boys, Brezhnev, Andropov and Bubnov, the chief designer. Within the imperial shine of the famous room, men slapped his shoulder and chattered, eyes straying to the big oak doors as they waited for the leaders of the empire to appear.

Katya slipped away and found the children. They stood to the side with Babushka, poised and well behaved. They kissed her and pointed at the long tables laden with canapés, caviar and dark bread, vodka, champagne and Pepsi Cola.

'A magic tablecloth,' Babushka said.

'Yes. Is my mother here?'

'I haven't seen her.'

'Mama?'

'Yes, Anna?'

'Will you sit with us?'

Katya avoided her daughter's eye. 'No, darling, I have to sit with Ilya, of course.'

'Why can't you stay with us?'

'I'll come to you after dinner.'

'Why, Mama? Why can't you sit with us?'

'Shush,' her grandmother said. 'Leave your mother alone. Later she will be all yours.'

Katya felt a pain beneath her breastbone and gasped.

'Are you all right?' Babushka said.

'Yes. Take care of the children, Babushka.'

She thought of Drew. Not a thousand metres from where she stood, he lay on a rumpled bed in a grey hotel room or drank whiskey in a badly lit bar. That he knew something about their future which she did not was unbearable.

Ilya caught her eye and she flushed, as if he had read her thoughts. He motioned her over. 'You must stay with me,' he said. 'The General Secretary will be here at any minute.'

At his side, she stared straight ahead, blinkered by displaced passion and the fear that she would crack under the pressure of her role. Images from midday played in her head and her face warmed. Oh, let it be over! Let her be with Drew again, in Toplistan, New York or wherever Fate took them. Ilya hitched at his uniform jacket, whispered his anxieties, and waited for his moment of glory.

'Colonel Timoshenko, this way, please. It is time.' A small, neatly groomed man with an Errol Flynn moustache led them out to the receiving line, roped off with velvet and flanked by attractive young women with arms full of flowers. He placed Ilya at the line's end, straightened his medals and showed him how to hold his hat. He handled Katya like a piece of furniture, positioning her at her husband's elbow and pinning a carnation to her dress.

As they faced the entrance, waiting for the VIPs,

Nadia arrived, accompanied by Luba and Leonid, unflustered by her latecoming. She looked splendid. The gaunt savagery of that morning was gone and she tripped lightly along the red carpet, ahead of her friends, aware of the lights and the photographers, animated by the theatricality of the occasion. As she congratulated Ilya at length, ignoring her daughter, a commotion bloomed at the hall entrance. Brezhnev and his entourage had arrived. At the key moment it was Nadia whose hand lay on Ilya's forearm, Nadia who stared at the General Secretary like a deer in headlights, Nadia who had to be led gently by the small, moustachioed man to her place inside the room.

It was seven years since Katya had last translated at the highest levels, working in this hall on Nixon's second visit in 1974. She remembered how tired and pale the American president had looked, just months before his resignation, while Brezhnev had been sanguine and lively, secure on his throne. Burly, beetle-browed, gregarious, he had drunk vodka steadily without effect and chain-smoked Philip Morris Multifilters, drawing them from a silver case one after another with oddly feminine fingers. But tonight his appearance shocked her. Followed by Andropov, he tottered through the high doors, supported by his aides, his face bloated and masklike, his once broad chest lost beneath a loose dinner jacket that sagged with medals. He barely acknowledged the dignitaries lined up to meet him, and by the time he reached Ilya he looked about to collapse. But the aides, conscious of protocol and the waiting photographers, brought him to a halt.

'Colonel Ilya Timoshenko,' one said to him, in a stage whisper. 'Cosmonaut and Hero of the Soviet Union.'

Ilya saluted briskly and Brezhnev raised a limp hand halfway to his brow. The cameras snapped. Katya had a vision of looking back on this moment from far into the future and remembering not the desiccated sarcophagus before her but Drew's warm body and musky smell. In this glimpse of herself to come she was old yet alert, in an alien surrounding but happy about all she had sacrificed for the man she loved.

The old man moved on and Andropov shook Ilya's hand, his quick, intelligent eyes taking in Katya with, she thought, a knowing glance. Then the procession was over, and Ilya searched out not his wife but his mother, his face stretched taut in a leer of self-congratulation.

At dinner she was seated between Ilya and Bubnov. He was gracious and old world, well-spoken and well-read, with a small mouth and a becoming lisp. He did not allow evidence of his great technical ability to seep into their conversation and at moments even dared to poke fun at the event with a subtle lift of his white eyebrows. And he flirted.

'Your husband seems preoccupied,' he remarked.

'The nature of the event,' she replied.

His big hand lay on the white tablecloth, close to her own. 'He should pay less attention to empty praise and more to his beautiful wife.'

She smiled as Soviet wives do when admired by important men, allowing him to graze her hand with his own, falling back on habit to still the desperation in her soul. Because although her future life had continued to take shape within her, something was wrong. In sailing through this vision she had emerged at the landfall of a distant time, Drew at her side, the past long gone and irrelevant. So why the despair?

Her children were not there.

She scanned the room. They sat with Babushka, waving to her and giggling soundlessly. She summoned the energy to smile and wag a finger, a sign of mock irritation and their cue to whisper conspiratorially and glance at her with mischievous eyes.

'Your children?' Bubnov said.

'Yes.'

'Charming.'

Anna lifted a bottle of Pepsi Cola, forbidden at home, and held it high. Teasing her mother, she put it to her lips. *Stop me*, her expression said. *Just try*.

'Are you all right?' Bubnov asked.

She nodded, unable to speak. His face loomed before her with a surfeit of physical detail: a tracery of fine blood vessels, bags like damsons beneath his eyes, one incisor folded over the other in his crowded mouth. He took a handkerchief from his pocket and offered it to her. Puzzled, she gazed at him.

'You're weeping,' he said.

She wiped away the tears and returned the hand-kerchief. To her right she heard Ilya say to one of Brezhnev's aides: 'You know, you're right. The sturgeon *is* off.'

Brezhnev and Andropov left before dessert, and everyone in the hall rose in tribute. Everyone except Katya. Ilya had to pull her to her feet, and she knocked over his glass of wine. Across the hall Nadia was watching, cigarette by her ear, eyes sharp. The men were getting drunk: their voices boomed and cackled. The toasts began, ritualistic, male, interminable.

The vodka flowed, Katya's head ached. Again she wept, and Bubnov examined her with grave concern. Nadia appeared behind her. 'Katya,' she whispered. With Bubnov she helped Katya to her feet and guided her away from the table and to the women's lavatory. Ilya didn't notice.

'Now, Katya, there there.' She led her to a stool, an arm round her shoulders. Katya could smell the familiar blend of perfume and cigarette smoke. The party echoed behind the closed door.

'Mama!'

'Ssh, Katya. I'm here.'

She looked up and, for a moment, did not recognize her image in the mirror – tear-streaked, dishevelled, wild-eyed. Beside her slender mother she looked heavy and unattractive.

Nadia patted her arm. 'Everything will be all right. It is an emotional occasion. A proud moment.'

Katya wiped her eyes. 'No,' she said. 'It is not a proud moment. Not yet.'

She stood up and washed her face while Nadia lit a cigarette. 'What do you mean, *not yet?*'

'It will be proud when I walk out.'

'You wouldn't dare.'

'No?'

Yes, it was that easy. She would walk out. What could they do to her? It was as if Drew had appeared in the palace and beckoned her to him. She freshened her lipstick and combed her hair.

Nadia bit her bright nails and blew smoke at the mirror. 'I will tell Ilya,' she said.

'Go ahead.'

'They won't allow you. They won't.'

'Let them try to stop me.'

'The children. You will leave them?'

She looked levelly at her mother, as if from another dimension. 'Babushka will care for them.'

She walked calmly out of the lavatory and down the Parade Staircase. Nadia followed, evidently not daring to speak her mind amid the throng of aides and soldiers. At the palace entrance Katya collected her fur, allowing the attendant to come out from his post and assist her into it, all the while thinking of Drew. It was simple. She would go to him. She would go where she belonged.

'Katya.'

She settled into the fur and walked to the entrance, putting on her hat and gloves.

'*Katya!*'

The doorman opened the door and the bracing air enveloped her. As she set forth Nadia grabbed her. Now, in the cold air, her mother looked shrivelled and brittle. Nadia displayed no hysteria, but when her twisted mouth opened to speak nothing emerged.

Katya pulled away her arm and, without looking back, walked into the tended frigidity of the Kremlin grounds. Past Assumption Cathedral, the Tsar's cannon and the great cracked bell. Across flagstones scrubbed clean of the blood of patriot, traitor and martyr. Out through Spassky Gate and along Red Square, where she could see the drab lines of the Intourist Hotel, windows lit at random. Drew was behind one. She ran through the pedestrian subway and emerged on Gorky Street. Traffic streamed past. The cold was bitter. She walked quickly, to a music in her soul as expansive as the night sky.

After the splendour of the Kremlin the stippled concrete canopy of the hotel was coarse and ugly. She was back in the ordinary Soviet world, and her certainties wavered. Carefully she walked up the chipped steps. The glass doors were locked, and she pressed the bell.

After a few minutes a young man in a leather jacket appeared and stared at her through the glass, smoking slowly and making her uncomfortable. His dark hair was slicked back and he wore an expensive watch. A security expert, a state thug, a contemporary version of a type that had been part of Russian history for centuries.

She gestured at the handle. Slowly he unlocked the door. '*Da?*'

'I'm here to meet a guest,' she said in English. She had done her best to summon her institute voice, but the words faltered.

'Passport.'

'I don't have it with me. I work for the ministry. I am here to make arrangements for the American musicians.'

He dropped his cigarette to the floor and crushed it with his shoe. His experienced ear would have caught her desperation, her involuntary ingratiation. He had been picked for this role not only because he could resist the pleas of the unauthorized but because he enjoyed the petty power of resistance. 'What ministry might that be?' he said in Russian.

'The Foreign Ministry.'

'Papers.'

She knew now that she was not going to get in, but the thought of turning away from Drew and back into the cold was too much to bear.

'Papers,' he repeated, eyes hard, foot braced against the door-frame.

'It is cold out here. Let me in and I can explain everything.'

She pulled her fur close and flashed her kid gloves, the better to emphasize her privilege. But he was unimpressed. He started to close the door. She put her hand into the gap and inadvertently touched his jacket.

'Don't be foolish,' he snarled. 'Go home or you will be in trouble.'

'I must see him. You must let me in.'

He pushed away her wrist and made it clear that he would hurt her if necessary. Hysteria shot through her like an electric shock. She put her palms on the glass as he locked the door.

'Please!' she said.

He lit another cigarette and watched her, mockingly. She banged on the glass with her palms. He blew smoke at her and turned away. She banged harder. Soon she was hitting the glass with frenzy, sobbing and calling Drew's name. The tears on her cheeks had begun to freeze. The suffocating cold pressed in on her. She reeled back from the door, slipped and fell on the rough concrete, hurting her knee. She got up, weeping hysterically, and stumbled to the footpath. 'Drew!' she screamed.

She craned her neck and looked up at the bleak building, blurred by her tears. Tonight she had a right to see him. It was unbearable that she should be denied. '*Drew!*'

But the sky swallowed his name.

At the door the security guard returned with a tall man in a blue sports jacket. He pointed at her. She limped away, staring at the ground, her cheeks stinging from the frost and her blood thudding in her ears.

CHAPTER 27

During the bad times there were nights when the shape of Drew's feeling was determined by hidden variables, when his appetites were deranged, when he lost all interest in what truly gave pleasure. On these nights any acceptable version of himself was out of reach; music and love ceased to exist. On these nights only smack could protect him from the darkness.

On Friday, as the day closed, the tension of waiting reminded him of those times. He would almost have welcomed the release of heroin.

At seven o'clock Marshall appeared at his door. 'You got the message?'

'The dinner?'

'The dinner.'

'I'm not hungry.'

'Neither am I, but I'm going. And so are you.' He walked in. The clothes were as sharp as ever but his face was pale and lined. He didn't look well.

'You OK?' Drew asked.

'Food poisoning.' He stared at Drew. 'How are *you* doing?'

Drew weighed the possible responses. He didn't have the will to go where Marshall wanted. 'I've been better.'

'Yeah? Well, so have I. Get your shoes on.'

They ate at Slavyansky Bazaar – the band members, Reef, and Dmitri, their new KGB minder. In his late fifties, Dmitri had a long neck, a thin face framed by metal-rimmed glasses, and a shock of grey hair that rose from his brow like the bristles of a broom. He liked to talk as much as Oleg liked silence.

'You do not enjoy our food, Mr Fisher?'

Possession was always plural for Dmitri. Our food. Our music. Our architecture. And Drew had never felt more singular. 'It's fine.'

'Please. *Bon appetit.*'

But Drew's food went untouched. Across from him, Reef nibbled from his plate and avoided eye-contact. He had yet to confirm the details of tomorrow's assignation.

A couple of vodkas had taken off the edge, but Drew was still distant from reality. He couldn't imagine Katya. Couldn't believe that tomorrow he would meet her and make love to her. Couldn't imagine how he could stand the wait, first for her, then for Washington's news on Monday.

The talk around the table held the peripheral hiss of despair. Leonid and Yoshi were in hushed discussion at one end of the long table, Salim and Marshall at the other. Dmitri sat at the centre, the better to monitor multiple conversations. He chain-smoked untipped Russian cigarettes, which had yellowed his fingers and left a permanent snowfall of ash on the narrow lapels of his suit jacket. Something cruel in his expression kept Drew looking into the corners of the room.

In front of the table, dancers in gypsy costumes flared their skirts to the sounds of clarinets and balalaikas. Dmitri ate pickled herring and boiled potatoes, and smoked at the same time. At the end of the tune he applauded stiffly, cigarette between his lips, spectacles glinting. 'You like our cultural dances?' he asked.

When Drew didn't answer, Salim said, 'The real McCoy Tyner.'

Dmitri looked at Marshall. 'Very professional troupe,' Marshall said grudgingly. He didn't like Dmitri: that was no secret.

'A famous Moscow restaurant and hotel,' Dmitri said, sweeping his arm through the air. 'In life and in the classics. One of our most famous literary scenes happens in this building, in the apartments directly above where we sit.' He pointed at the ceiling with a crooked finger, leaving his arm extended so long a waiter thought he was being summoned. '*Dama s Sobachka*,' he said to Reef. His English was excellent, but to show that he was in control he made Reef translate a stray phrase once in a while.

'*Lady with Lapdog*,' Reef said warily. 'By Chekhov.'

'Yes. In the climax of this most famous story, a man and his mistress meet here illicitly and discover how they are trapped by their bourgeois attitudes like birds in a cage.'

'That is one interpretation,' Reef said.

'It is the correct interpretation,' Dmitri said.

Marshall had a sudden severe coughing fit. He took a handkerchief from his pocket, covered his mouth and stepped away from the table. When Yoshi handed him a glass of water he waved it away. 'I have to use the bathroom,' he said. 'Please excuse me.' He searched out a waiter and allowed himself to be led away, looking uncharacteristically frail.

Dmitri fretted.

'Don't worry,' Salim said. 'Marshall's a big boy.'

But Dmitri wasn't listening. He snapped his fingers, and when a waiter appeared he issued instructions in aggressive Russian.

Beyond these unambiguous pronouncements, Drew was beginning to hear Washington's voice, moderate in comparison, strained by circumstance and the desire to do right. How could Katya be left behind, to be preyed upon by men like Dmitri, Oleg, and her husband? Washington would come through for her. Washington would deliver.

The music glided into an extended passage of improvisation, the clarinets weaving sinuously beneath the frenetic strumming of the balalaikas. Drew and Yoshi smiled at each other, and Salim tapped a drum roll with his fingers.

Dmitri continued: 'We were speaking, I believe, of *Lady with Lapdog*. A tale of bourgeois hypocrisy.'

He waited for Reef to take the bait. Reef finished chewing what was in his mouth and laid his napkin on the table. 'Secrecy,' he said.

'I beg your pardon?'

'The story is about secrecy, Dmitri. About double lives. And I don't believe the bourgeoisie has a monopoly on that.'

Dmitri gave him a withering stare. Reef looked into the distance and recited, as if reading from a hidden screen: ' "He had two lives: an open one, seen and known by all who needed to know it, full of conventional truth and conventional lies, exactly like the lives of all his friends, and another life that was completely secret." ' He smiled wistfully. 'The translation does not do justice to Chekhov's prose, I am afraid, but I offer you a humble version of my favourite passage in our literature. Our *Russian* literature.' He bowed his head professorially.

'Why, thank you, Reef,' Salim said.

As Dmitri was about to respond, one of the clarinet players broke away from the group and came over to their table. He must have known who they were and that they liked the music, because he cut loose. When he had finished they applauded, and Yoshi cut loose with a two-fingered whistle. Dmitri leaned away from the display of emotion.

'Cat swings like a motherfucker,' Salim said. He looked at Dmitri. '*Motherfucker*. Reef, you want to translate for Mr D? He ain't been round us long enough to know the groove.'

'No need to translate. Bad enough we must hear this vulgarity in English.'

'Sometimes vulgarity is the only language to say what needs be said.'

Marshall reappeared and touched Reef's shoulder. 'You'll have to excuse me. I'm not feeling well. I have to go back to the hotel.'

'What is this?' Dmitri said, twisting in his seat. 'Go back? You cannot return now. Dinner is just beginning.'

'I'm sorry. I don't think I can eat. Reef, get Maxim.'

There was a sharp exchange in Russian. Reef spread his hands and tilted his head towards Marshall. Dmitri pushed back his chair and stood up. The maître d' bustled over, hands clasped in concern. Recovering his composure, Dmitri said to him in English, 'Our guest is ill. Please get his coat and call for his car. Reef, you will accompany Mr Powell to the hotel. Then you will return.'

Drew gave them enough time to gather their coats. He leaned across and whispered to Salim, 'I'm going with them.'

'Fish – don't do this to me.'

'Got to. Explain later.'

He stood up quickly, went to the cloakroom and retrieved his jacket without looking back. Outside he caught the Volga as it was moving off and climbed into the back seat beside Reef. Neither Reef nor Marshall registered his arrival – they sat perfectly still, looking at the falling snow. Wheels spinning, Maxim pulled on to the slippery road. 'Turn the heater off, Maxim,' Marshall said, with his eyes closed. 'It's not too cold.'

Maxim turned the heater up, not off, and Reef corrected the misunderstanding. They drove in silence. Drew watched the snow fall, thinned by now to a slow sprinkle.

'Drew,' Marshall said.

'Yeah?'

'You should have stayed.'

'Maybe.'

Marshall turned in his seat, his long face ashen, his eyes yellow. 'Where are you going?'

'I'm going to bed. I'm tired.'

Marshall nodded, and this small gesture of trust revived hope in Drew. He was away from Dmitri and ready for Reef to give him the word. Tomorrow held its promise of intimacy, like a dream deferred. One more chance at love, and then on to the next step. What would happen? Would Washington get her out? What about the meantime? He feared that forces larger than love, aided by separation, would alter feeling. Like the silences in a Monk solo, distance might push their relationship in unexpected directions. And in this instance he wanted not the squinting rhythms of bebop but the reassurance of a more traditional form. A happy ending in waltz time, on the beat and unsyncopated.

Washington would come through for them – Drew felt it in the reassuring hand at his elbow, in the disguised sympathy, the serious face. He was not the type of guy who would mislead.

In the meantime they had each other. Even while they were apart. The movement of the car was like a caress, and the dry, large-flaked snow, which she, too, would be watching from her sterile house in the cosmonaut complex, continued its silent descent. While he thought of her he knew she was thinking of him. Yes, Washington would come through for him. There was no other option.

At the hotel Marshall eschewed help and went in through the front door, clutching his abdomen. Maxim sheltered beneath the concrete canopy and, with a crisp motion that said he would not be denied a break, lit a cigarette. Drew and Reef stood side by side in the snow, gazing at the sluggish traffic, its stream of tail-lights moistly luminous. This spot and posture had, in the short time he'd been in Moscow, become stamped on his consciousness in way he knew he would never forget.

'He will be all right?' Reef said.

'Marshall?'

'Yes.'

'Marshall's tough. He'll be fine by the time he has to play. Which isn't till Monday.'

Snowploughs churned up Gorky Street, chained wheels clanking. Reef was tense and vulnerable, hunched in on himself like a tightened fist. All along he had endangered himself on Drew's behalf; now Drew had raised the stakes and couldn't tell him.

But discretion was imperative and, besides, he could do nothing to imperil the final meeting with Katya.

'So,' Drew said, 'about tomorrow.'

'About tomorrow. Yes.' Reef glanced at Maxim, ensured he was out of earshot. 'As before. But two o'clock this time.'

'How long we got?'

'The same. Two hours.'

'Two hours.'

Reef stroked his thin beard. His glasses were streaked with moisture and his magnified eyes were gentle and tired. 'Whatever you must say you must say tomorrow. Phoning her will be impossible. But she knows this as well as you and I.' His hands made a subtle but unmistakable gesture of fatalism. He sighed. His weariness could not be accounted for simply by the strain of acting as go-between, dangerous as the role was. Some deeper regret was pressing in on him. 'Katya is someone for whom I have always had the greatest respect,' he said. 'She is . . . she is a close friend.'

Drew raised his hand. Reef, he suspected, was warming up for confession and he no more wanted to hear it than to voice his own. They had reached the limits of speech. 'What about the key?'

Reef reached into his inside coat pocket and pulled out an envelope. Maxim had returned to the car. Its lights were on and exhaust puffed into the gloom. Drew took the envelope. 'And Dmitri?'

Reef's head bobbed with impatience. This was one question too many. 'What of him?'

'He's dogged. How am I going to shake him?'

Reef took a dirty handkerchief from his coat pocket and blew his nose.

After Tuesday where would Reef's life proceed? Drew wondered. Back to where it came from, of course, though with a few stories that could not be told and another stratum of melancholy to his trek between the Cultural Exchange and his thirty-square-metre apartment. But, as Drew saw it, the whole world would change, come Tuesday.

'Don't worry about Dmitri. Just go to Toplistan. It is all arranged.'

Suppressing a request for one last reassurance, Drew turned towards the hotel entrance.

Reef stopped him. 'Drew.' Mournful and hesitant, the small man gripped his jacket as if he were trying to escape. 'Tomorrow. Please be careful.'

'I will, Reef.'

'I mean, be careful what you say.'

Drew nodded and went to the hotel door. While the guard checked his passport he looked back and saw the Volga fishtail on to Gorky Street, Reef's meek silhouette filling the passenger-side window like a wraith.

CHAPTER 28

Katya stared out of the bay window, searching, in the muted shapes of snowdrift and fir, for words that might relieve, or at least explain. Words for herself and for her children. Beside her, Anna played the theme from Tchaikovsky's first piano concerto. Sasha lay on the carpet, leafing through a catalogue of American cars.

Her attention kept drifting to the telephone. She willed it to ring. Reef had promised to call before ten. Babushka was in her room and Ilya was out. Katya had removed his photograph from the wall and put it into the drawer that held his socks and underwear. 'Sasha, it is time to get ready for bed.'

Without looking up from his catalogue he said, 'Anna's still up.'

'Both of you. Time for bed.'

'Tomorrow's Saturday, Mama.'

When she was feeling good, her children reflected her best qualities. Distraught, as she was tonight, she saw only the worst in herself that she had bequeathed them: impatience, stubbornness, lack of consideration. For dinner she had made them pancakes with raspberry jam and allowed them each a bottle of Pepsi. They ate and drank silently, showing no gratitude.

Or had fear kept them silent? All day she had been nerve-racked and irrational, quick to shout. As she watched them eat she had resolved to speak to them, slowly and clearly, before they left the table. If she did not, she would collapse in desperation. But she had not spoken, and had not yet collapsed.

Her knee was swollen and sore. Last night, after she had fallen in front of the hotel, she had limped to a public phone and called Volodya. He had come at once, driven her to Star City, and somehow managed to get a message to Babushka, who arrived with the children at around eleven. The late hours were confused, strained and exhausting. Fortunately Ilya stayed away all night. The next day had been a steady battle to stave off hysteria and avoid explanations – for Ilya, who had appeared, sanguine and hung-over, and stayed an awful couple of hours; for Nadia and Leonid, who had telephoned; for Babushka, who had eventually fled to her room.

But words had to be found for the children.

The music stopped and Anna said, 'Can I get you anything, Mama?'

The offer brought her close to tears. She couldn't speak. Sasha looked up from the floor. 'Would you like the ice pack?'

They were not inconsiderate at all: it was she who had failed them.

She wept. Sasha joined his sister and Katya took their hands. 'I love you both,' she said. 'You know that, don't you?'

They watched her, resisting the impulse to look at each other for guidance.

'I'll get Babushka,' Anna said.

'No. Let her sleep. She is very tired.'

'Where is Ilya?' Sasha asked.

'I love you, Sasha.'

'Yes, Mama. But where is Ilya?'

The air in the overheated house was dry and oppressive. Her throat felt raw.

She let go of their hands and coughed. 'Let me tell you a story,' she said.

The children relaxed. Perhaps their mother was not going mad after all.

'In Moscow there lived a woman who was beautiful and gifted. A dancer.'

'Like Babushka,' Anna said.

'Yes. This woman had studied with Nijinsky and performed in the finest theatres in Russia. She was beautiful and elegant. She had a young son who was everything to her, and a husband who loved her.'

'What was her name?'

'Let's call her Sofia. Anyway, Sofia's fate was to be bound into slavery and sent to the east, without her family. For over two years she was treated like an animal. She was fed only *kasha* and stale bread. In the most bitter cold and under the terrible summer sun she was forced to pull wagons full of timber. A woman with delicate ankles and a face like a flower. A dancer, as I said.'

'What had she done wrong?'

'Nothing, Anna.'

Anna's head was tilted, her eyes shiny with tears.

'In her third winter a convoy of male slaves arrived at the camp. Men who, like Sofia, had once been accomplished and respected – professors, writers, musicians – but now they had been in solitary confinement in the far north for over a year and were thin and filthy, with long beards and eyes like death. Sofia, of course, had lost her own beauty and dignity. Half of her teeth were gone. She weighed less than thirty kilos and was dressed in rags. The slave-drivers put the men in a compound next to the women's, separated by a row of barbed wire.'

The skin around Katya's thumbnails was torn and bloody. She clasped her hands as if in prayer. 'What do you think happened?'

'Tell us, Mama.'

'The night of the men's arrival, after the guards had gone to their warm bunks, the women came out to the fence. The snow was up to their knees and the temperature was minus twenty. They called for the men, who also left their huts and lined up along the barbed wire. Nothing was said. The men and women stared at each other in the moonlight. Some reached through the wire and touched fingers.'

Katya stood and went to the window. 'And in this way, immediately, Sofia fell in love.'

'Ah,' Anna said.

'Love at first sight. With a musician from Kiev, though of course she knew nothing about him then. Just the look in his eyes and the shape of his suffering.'

'What about her husband,' Sasha said, 'and her son?'

'Unknown to her, her husband was already dead. Murdered by the slave-owners. Her son survived.'

Anna came to the window and grasped her mother's hand. 'What about Sofia, Mama? Did she survive?'

Katya couldn't look at her.

The phone rang. She ran across the room. 'Hello, yes?'

'Katya.'

'Reef!' she cried. 'Tell me what to do!'

CHAPTER 29

Drew set out for the safe-house a second time. Again he took the Metro from Sverdlova Square, counting out the eleven stops to Toplistan. Again he walked three hundred metres west, looking for the apartment block with two sledges hanging from the highest balcony. Again he tapped in the door code and took the elevator to the seventh floor. But although the route was the same, the skies this time were clouded.

He wanted her to leave him feeling loved and optimistic. He wanted to say the right things – to be careful, as Reef had warned – and lend her the strength to face the time ahead. He could not raise her hopes unfairly, but he needed to let her know that everything possible was in motion. They were there to make love, but he also had a job to do. And it made him nervous.

At the flat door he took a deep breath and slid the key into its slot. Skin to skin the doubts would fall away, if only for those few blissful moments, moments like music. He must trust in love. He had no choice.

As he entered the flat he smelt cigarette smoke. 'Reef?' he called. 'Reef, is that you?'

'In kitchen.'

He was at the door before he remembered that Reef did not smoke. A large man with a bulldog face and a bushy moustache was sitting at the wooden table. Drew's first thought was for Katya – she would arrive in less than ten minutes and had to be warned. He turned back towards the front door and saw a second, even bigger man step in front of it, arms folded, chin thrust out. 'Mr Fisher. Please. Sit down.'

The man in the kitchen pulled a second chair out from the table and gestured towards it politely. On the tabletop were a cut-glass ashtray, a brass lighter, and English cigarettes in an oblong package. Drew glanced back at the thug at the door, then sat.

'Your jacket, Mr Fisher. You have permission to remove. Moscow apartments very hot.'

'I'm fine.'

The man shrugged. 'As you wish. Not for me to make you uncomfortable.'

In spite of his burly appearance he had a soft voice, and his speech was marked by the steady click of his tongue against the roof of his mouth. The corners of his eyes drooped, as if in imitation of his moustache, and his dark hair was greased in a careful, old-fashioned way.

'Cigarette, perhaps?' He offered the pack.

Drew reached into his jacket pocket and took out his own. 'I'll have one of these.'

'As you wish.'

Already Drew knew that the repetitious, formal phrasing and solicitous eyes were going to get on his nerves – were supposed to – and he concentrated on staying calm. If Katya was at risk it was up to him to find out what he could to protect her. The man extended him a light. As he leaned towards it he noticed closely bitten nails and, on the hairy wrist, a scar the size of a dime.

'Stove, I am afraid, is not working or I would offer tea. No gas supply. Or perhaps you remember from last visit?' He smiled, showing a gold tooth.

Drew unzipped his jacket and put his hat on the floor, distracting himself from the man's menacing politesse and probing gaze. 'I didn't use the stove,' he said.

'No, suppose not.' The man took a long drag from his Dunhill and made brief eye-contact with his associate. Drew heard the front door open and close but did not turn round. He had concluded that Katya was not coming. His stomach churned. He smoked quickly. The man smiled inanely.

'Look,' Drew said, 'if I'm being held here against my will, I want to call the embassy. The US Embassy.'

'You know, funny thing. I don't think telephone works either. Of course, I send Igor with message if you wish.'

'Why don't we just get on with it?'

'What get on with?'

'With whatever it is you brought me here for.'

348

The man pushed back his chair from the table and stood up. He walked to the kitchen window and looked through the cracked glass at the streets below. Sweat trickled from Drew's temple. He took off his jacket and hung it over the back of the chair.

'You brought yourself here, Mr Fisher.' The man spoke while he was staring out the window. 'Or you forget? Maybe is you should tell me the whatever-it-is. Yes?' He turned and smiled, hands behind his back.

Drew sensed a carefully segmented plan with distinct objectives. The first segment had concluded when the man stood up. They were into a new phase. The smile was tougher and the air in the flat a little more stifling. 'I came here to meet a friend.'

'Ah. A friend.'

'A colleague, I guess I should say.'

'Colleague rather.'

'Yes.'

'And this meeting was on agenda?'

The tone of the man's responses was ambiguous: he might have been looking for information, he might have been mocking him. The formality, the irritating repetitions, the click of his tongue and the flatness of his smile – these tics distanced meaning and threw responsibility for the conversation back at Drew. The man knew everything – he must – but he wasn't going to reveal anything until he was ready.

'I think you know what's been on my agenda. Isn't that your job?'

The man sat. He leaned on the table, lowered his head, and spread his thick legs. His eyes had watered since Drew's arrival and glittered like mica. 'You wish to know my job?'

'I'd like to know what this meeting is about. I am an American citizen being held illegally. I believe I'm owed an explanation.'

The man pushed out his lower lip and turned his hands so that the palms faced up. 'Who is held? To speak of illegal, you come illegally to Soviet house. I ask why only. No one is held.'

Drew didn't move. The heat of the flat and the man's clicking phrases were getting to him. The voices in his head were starting up. He worried about Katya. About Reef. About how all this would look to Washington if it emerged. He needed the conversation to pick up pace, and if he waited for this guy he'd be waiting all day.

So he said, 'I came here to speak to my friend about a visa application. She has been invited to the United States.'

'She?'

'She and her children.'

'You invite them?

'I am inviting them and the US Embassy will issue the visas.'

The man seemed to consider Drew's words. He offered another cigarette. When Drew shook his head he lit one for himself. Growing dizzy, Drew gripped the edge of the table.

'So you have diplomatic meeting in Toplistan.

In flat with no gas supply.' His eyes glimmered. Evidently he was enjoying himself. 'Rick knows about meeting, yes?'

'Who?'

Cigarette between his fingers, the man waved his hand through the air, leaving trails of smoke. 'Rick Washington. My good friend.'

Drew looked at his own hands, folded in front him, resting on the table. The long fingers that could play 'Waltz for Debby' with great tenderness and passion looked unfamiliar, the hands of a stranger.

'Rick say to me, "Slava," he say, "we understand each other. We both know hardness of diplomatic life."' He had livened up, into another phase.

Drew scrambled to interpret the information and the manner of its revelation. It was approaching three o'clock and the flat was darker. He peered at the man through the gloom. 'Is that what you are? A diplomat?'

'All of us diplomats, yes? Even you, Mr Fisher, are diplomat, trying to bring *refusenik* wife of cosmonaut to USA.' His gold tooth caught the diminishing light.

From behind the drifting smoke came a flash of hope, the bare suggestion of an illuminating possibility. Was this episode part of an American process? Was Slava on the team? 'Well, I *am* trying. I think it's the right thing to do.'

'Right thing? For you is moral issue?'

What was the right answer? How was he to play his part?

'You work with Rick Washington?'

The man laughed at the change of subject. 'As I say, Rick my good friend. Yesterday, in afternoon, telephone rings. Is Rick. "Slava," he say, "I have problem." If Rick have problem and call me, I have problem. So I listen. I say, "Rick, no worry. I will go." Because you see, Mr Fisher, not first time we have spoken of you and Dr Timoshenko.' He tapped the table with the edges of his hands, as if squaring away a sheaf of papers.

Drew watched his body language, its confident swivels and *basso profundo* gestures. 'So you and Rick are working on this together?'

Slava's face hardened into a grimace that broadened his moustache and furrowed his brow. Drew breathed slowly, watched and listened.

'We have system,' Slava said. 'Rick knows system, of course, but also detail in this case. We have reports from all Soviet citizens in contact with foreigners. Dr Timoshenko – her reports worthless, of course, but others tell truth. Leonid Petrovich. Reef Nikolayich.'

'Reef?'

'But of course.'

'Intelligence reports . . . what, for Rick? They're all working for the US – is that how it goes?'

Slava cleared his throat and spat on the floor disdainfully. 'You are not stupid man, Mr Fisher, but you are fool. I am KGB. True KGB, not low-level like Oleg or Dmitri. Rick know I stop foolishness before you make scandal.' He lifted his eyebrows and tilted his head, like a salesman who had just clinched a big deal.

All hope drained away. Drew felt weakness move from his knees to his bowels. So they had known all along. Both sides. And Rick Washington had set him up. But Reef would not have participated, not willingly. 'What did you do to him?' he asked.

'Who?'

'Reef.'

Slava scoffed. 'What? You think he is your friend? Reef, he come to us. He tell us of inappropriate behaviour.'

'I don't believe you.'

Slava stood up. It was time for bluster. 'First, you believe, you don't believe – no difference. Reef is nobody. Translator. Failed man. He knows information will get him new Lada or bigger apartment closer to city centre. Second, we know everything. Please understand. *Everything*. I say Rick your foolish behaviour two weeks ago. We wait. Expect foolishness stop. But no. More foolishness. So we allow you to have private flat. Everything we record, we photograph. You understand?' His voice boomed in the thinly furnished apartment.

'Yeah,' Drew said. 'I understand.'

'You think we cannot control everything?'

'You can't control feelings. How Katya feels about me.'

Slava nodded. 'Is true,' he said. 'We cannot.' He walked to the door, looked back. 'Not yet.'

He left the room, and Drew heard him speaking

softly at the front door. Frightened and trembling, he sweated profusely. What was he going to do about Katya? What could he do? But when he tried to reason out a plan, even a next step, he found himself thinking of how Washington had calmed and reassured him. Washington and Slava were enemies? He and Katya were the enemies. *Love* was the enemy. And Reef. Reef of all people. He didn't believe Slava. They must have had something on him to make him turn.

Well, he would not give in. He would not leave. He would create an international incident. They would have to put him in a straitjacket to get him on the plane. And if they did that, he would go to the press: he would spill his story to the *New York Times* and get her out of this horrible place, no matter what it took. He channelled his fear into anger. If they thought they could scare him off they were mistaken.

Slava returned and casually tossed a wrinkled paper bag on to the table. 'Look. Please.'

'I'm looking.'

'Inside.'

Drew poked the bag with his finger. He had a premonition of trouble and folded his hands. 'You want me to see what's inside, you're going to have to show me yourself.'

Slava ripped open the bag and a plastic sachet of white powder fell out. Drew didn't have to guess what it was. 'I have to use the bathroom,' he said.

Slava stroked his moustache. 'All right. Use.'

Bent double, he made his way to the toilet. Through the open bedroom door he saw the same flounced curtains and floral bedspread that had draped his morning with Katya two days ago. *My heart is breaking*, she had whispered. *Take me away.* And he had promised he would. And every word had been recorded. Was it his promise that had moved them to blackmail? Or was this visit Washington's idea? Whatever prompted the grey men, they now had him by the balls. Why? Because love was the enemy. His bowels emptied violently, and he gasped as he gripped his gut and stared at the dirty tiles. He thought he'd been scared? *This* was scared. What were they going to do to him? Worse, what would they do – had they done – to Katya?

Back in the kitchen, he said, 'Is Katya all right?'

'I think no.'

'What have you done to her?'

'No, Mr Fisher – what have *you* done? What will you do?'

His mouth was dry. He spoke slowly. 'What do you want me to do?'

Slava pulled his shoulders together and nodded like a satisfied schoolteacher. 'Now you understand. You see, very unpleasant if I must say I find in your pocket.' He lifted the sachet by a corner and tossed it to the side. 'Yes. Now. To be clear. Dr Timoshenko will go to psychiatric hospital. You understand?'

Drew grew agitated and Slava raised his hand. '*If.*'

'If what?'

'If you not do what I say.'

'What's that?'

'No. Listen first. She will go to hospital. Children will go to father's family.'

'He's not their father.'

Slava shrugged. 'No difference. They will go. We tell them whatever necessary. In such hospitals KGB are directors. Doctors deputy only. We give necessary drugs and so on. You understand?'

'Yeah.'

'Very unpleasant. Is like life sentence with no trial. Think of privileged lady like Dr Timoshenko. Now live in Star City in fine Soviet *dacha*. Husband Hero of Soviet Union. Has certificate-roubles for shopping in special stores. How you think for such lady in psychiatric hospital? What is better for her?'

'I think it's a pretty shitty deal, no matter which way you cut it.'

'Choice is yours.'

'How so?'

Slava pushed aside the full ashtray and leaned across the table so that his face was inches from Drew's. He smelt of hair oil and cologne. His lined face showed the confidence of a man smart enough to recognize all contingencies and thorough enough to prepare carefully for each of them.

'Tomorrow, twelve o'clock, Dr Timoshenko alone in Star City. Husband and children away. You telephone. Will telephone.'

'At twelve. Twelve noon.'

'She expects. KGB listening, of course. You will say her you do not love her.'

'That's impossible.'

'I think no. I think you will say. Then Dr Timoshenko has good Soviet life and not hospital.' He leaned back. His posture made clear that he was not negotiating.

'What makes you think she won't do something drastic?'

'For example?'

'Harm herself.'

'She is Russian. She will accept fate. If harm herself, is because she think you still love her. You must convince.'

'Is that right? What am I supposed to say?'

'Is your job, Mr Fisher.' He looked at his watch. 'Twenty-four hours for preparation. Like music rehearsal, yes? You practise well, you play well.'

The big guy at the door trotted into the kitchen. Slava spoke to him in rapid Russian.

'You say well,' Slava said to Drew, 'then she accept. She no accept, then hospital. And for you . . .' He lifted the bag of powder and let it drop on to the tabletop.

He felt trapped. As he had at his mother's deathbed. As he had when they had brought him to the morgue and lifted the rubber sheet from Jessie's face.

Slava stood up and allowed the guard to help him

into a long blue topcoat. He put on an expensive fur hat. 'Igor bring you to hotel,' he said.

'I don't want to go to the hotel.'

'What you want make no difference now, Mr Fisher. You are in Soviet Union.'

He left the flat. Drew waited for the door to close, then fetched his cap from the floor and put on his jacket. Hands behind his back, Igor tapped his foot on the scarred floor. Drew wanted nothing so much as to punch his emotionless face, but he followed Igor down to the street. A familiar-looking black Volga waited at the kerb, cigarette smoke drifting from the driver's window. Maxim sat behind the wheel, and Drew wondered how he'd ever believed that he wasn't being watched.

He climbed into the back, Igor beside him. Maxim did not start the car, did not even move – just stared straight ahead, occasionally puffing his cigarette. There was a tap at the window. It was Slava. 'You understand everything, Mr Fisher?'

The back of Maxim's head somehow suggested that he had heard nothing, would remember nothing, and Drew was suddenly awash with loneliness. 'Not much to understand,' he said, 'is there?'

'No. Not much. Very simple.'

Slava put his hand on the roof of the car and peered in. The quills of his sable hat were dense and iridescent. Beneath the dense cologne Drew could smell his metallic smoker's breath.

'You will be success,' Slava said. 'I know it. You will convince.'

'What makes you so sure?'

'Because you wish to save her.' He leaned even closer. The gold tooth sparkled. 'Because you promised.'

He moved back from the window and hit the car roof softly with a gloved hand. Maxim floored it.

CHAPTER 30

He bought a bottle of whiskey in the hard-currency shop and went to his room. After four or five shots he phoned the hotel operator. 'I want to call the United States. Missoula, Montana. A Mr John Davis Fisher.'

'Who is telephoning? Name, please.'

'This is Drew Fisher. I want to call my father in Missoula, Montana, USA.'

'Telephone number?'

He gave it, and she said she would call back shortly.

He had another drink and stared at the telephone. It rang, startling him.

'Your call is arranged,' the operator said. 'Monday at midnight.'

'Monday? But today's Saturday.'

'Monday at midnight. Please be ready for call.'

'But I have to talk to him now.'

She had hung up. He looked at the green glow of the radio dial and crossed the room. He leaned his forehead against the window, and his breath misted the glass. The flow of traffic boxed Red Square in rectangles of cold light.

He pushed himself away from the pane and closed the curtains. 'Fuck it,' he said. He dialled her number.

'*Slushyat.*' It was her husband's voice. He imagined he heard a note of triumph in the dolorous greeting. Drew said nothing, and nothing was said in return. It was as if the two men were staring at each other across ramparts, the silence combed by a susurrus of voices, crossed lines. But it was those he could not hear who were to be feared. Beginning with the man at the other end, alert and suspicious, too canny to say another word.

This time Drew hung up. He put on his baseball cap and went to the bar. Everyone he met along the way seemed to size him up: the floor matron, the cloakroom girl, the dull-eyed man in a maroon jacket who emptied the ashtrays. All agents by virtue of their employment, noting movements and times, withholding smiles, and looking beyond him with self-preserving blankness.

In the bar he drank a couple more whiskeys and felt the unwelcome clutch of drunkenness. It offered no escape. He drank to stun the obvious questions. He drank so he did not have to reason. But his random thoughts were dark and burdensome. If only his father were here, to soothe him with rants and tell him what to do.

A woman sat beside him at the plastic table and offered him the day's first smile. She was a poor actress. Her eyes were pale with boredom and avarice. 'I am Katya,' she said.

He jerked back. A joke or a set-up? He could not admit coincidence.

On the table her hand lay between them like a dropped handkerchief. 'Where are you from?' she asked.

He pulled his cap low. 'Not today,' he said.

She took a cigarette out of her bag, then looked for a light, displaying the low cut of her dress. A sob leaped from him. 'No,' he shouted. '*No.*'

The bartender glanced his way, but otherwise his outburst was ignored.

'Another drink,' she said. 'Whiskey, yes?'

He left her and took refuge at the bar. Two stools down from him was the bearded pimp of his first night, wearing the same sunglasses and flipping a beer-mat as if it were a coin. The bartender poured Drew another shot and nodded at the Russian. 'No,' Drew said. 'Not for me.'

But the drink was in front of him. The man stopped flipping the mat and placed it carefully beneath his glass. Ivan, that was his name.

He slid into the seat beside Drew. 'You not like Soviet hospitality? Not like Katya?'

Again the name unnerved him. The evening was shaping into nightmare, its details tangential to reality, its flow condensed and disturbing. 'What do you want from me?' Drew said.

'Question is, what *you* want.' He smiled, his moustache clinging moistly to the corners of his mouth. Drew caught a whiff of his dill-scented breath. 'To be left alone.'

'Is that so? You are sure?'

Ivan's offer of two weeks ago, made quietly while Don and Salim gibed over steel and politics, came back to Drew. *I have the real good stuff. From Afghani mountains.* Through the screen of his drunkenness a tantalizing contentment beckoned, an oasis rising from the dunes of his despair. 'Maybe I am interested,' he said.

'Ah. Man with taste. Man who knows importance of pleasure.'

The bar was filling up, a Saturday-night crowd of businessmen and tourists, women of the night. Russian folk music drizzled from ceiling speakers. But for Drew the physical surroundings had receded: he sat in a landscape of temptation, glittering and fresh. It would be so easy to drift away from all that crowded these parched moments. 'When can you get it?' he said.

'Get it?' Ivan leaned forward. 'Katya? Or others? What you like?'

'The real stuff. The real Afghani.'

Ivan's shoulders lifted, and his shaded face contracted.

Drew took off his cap. 'How much is it?' he said. 'How many dollars you looking for?'

'You know,' Ivan said softly, 'I think maybe you misunderstand. Katya, Olga, Oksanna, they are ready for you. All arrangements can be made.'

The thought of smack and the blissful release it would bring had quickened Drew's pulse and dried his mouth. His need was not to be denied.

'No, I understand exactly. I don't want Katya. I want heroin.'

Ivan took off his sunglasses. His eyes were cold and knowing. The cartoonish face acquired a depth of field in which Drew's error was not absorbed but reflected. And it was too late to stop now.

'How much?'

'Is not possible.'

'You offered. Before. You told me.'

'Is not possible.' They sat, eyeball to eyeball, aware that Drew's desperation had grown dangerous.

'God*damn* it. You *said*!' Drew banged the counter with an open hand, knocking over his whiskey.

This time the bar went quiet. Ivan stood up and pushed back his stool. The bartender mopped up the mess.

Drew was waving his cap in the air. 'Coming in here with your bullshit pimping and dealing! Well, I'm buying, pal. Good American money. Hard cash. What the fuck you going to do about it?'

He was grasped from behind, quickly and firmly. He struggled, cursing and crying out.

'That's enough, Drew.' It was Marshall, holding him in a bear-hug. Drew's wriggling brought them face to face. 'He tried to sell me skag,' he whispered. 'Tried to get me hooked again.'

Marshall tightened his grip. 'Who?'

Ivan had disappeared.

'Cat beside me. Sunglasses. Here a minute ago.'

Marshall took the scene in with a frown. The boys in leather jackets, discreetly angled but on high alert, and the goateed man in a tailored suit were ranged behind the potted plants that marked the edge of the bar. 'Let's get you out of here.'

Upstairs Marshall removed Drew's shoes and helped him into bed. He ordered tea and unplugged the radio.

'What did you do that for?' Drew asked.

'You haven't learned that trick by now? Stops them listening.'

When the tea arrived, Drew sat up in bed and drank it slowly. Marshall picked up the half-empty bottle of J & B, tilted it deliberately, and poured himself a glass.

'They're watching me,' Drew said.

Marshall grimaced. 'You should be watching yourself.' He drank the whiskey in a single swallow. The skin on his neck was loose and wrinkled. In the weak light of the overheated room, he looked tired and old. 'What was going on down there?'

Drew set the empty teacup on the floor. 'I was provoked.'

'That right?'

He lay so that he faced the wall. He could hear Marshall pour himself another drink. 'It's not what you think, Marshall.'

'What do I think?'

'He did offer me heroin. Our first night here. Salim was right – they set traps for you. Both sides.'

'Keep your integrity and you won't go wrong.'

Marshall's judgement pressed on Drew's back like

the heat of the sun. 'It doesn't matter what you do,' Drew said. 'It's rigged from the beginning. One big set-up.'

Behind the walls the hotel machinery groaned.

'So you're not down there trying to score?'

Drew's answer was like a last breath. 'No.'

Marshall cleared his throat. 'But something else is going on, right?'

'Right.'

The fragile limits of the tawdry room – thin curtains, noisy vents, scarred walls – seemed incapable of containing the loneliness that expanded in Drew.

Eventually Marshall asked, 'Are you going to be able to play on Monday?'

'Is that what you're worried about?'

'It's you I'm worried about.'

Drew wept silently, his body heaving. The floorboards creaked as Marshall crossed the room and gripped his shoulder. 'Call me if you need to. Or come on up. I'm not going anywhere.' He stood there for a few minutes, breathing heavily. When he left he closed the door softly behind him.

He called her from his room at the stroke of noon. She answered in English after a single ring.

'It's me,' he said.

'Drew!' She was breathless with expectation, and his heart seized.

'Who told you I'd call?' he said flatly.

She paused, and the telephone line sang with

static. Try as he might, he could not forget who was listening in.

'You know who told me,' she said. 'The same.'

He had rehearsed his lines carefully but wasn't prepared for the pain of her breathing, the shape of her need. 'Reef,' he said.

'Be careful. Please. What information do you have?'

Her shorthand speech was fraught with all it could not express. He saw her at the phone, lips parted, free hand at her breastbone.

'I don't have to be careful,' he said.

'We must always.'

'No.'

She gasped. Or was it his imagination?

'Please tell me the time,' she said.

'There is no time.'

'What do you mean?'

Staring at the floor, he saw a bit of dried fruit crushed into the carpet. He squeezed his eyes shut. 'It's over.'

'Over?' she said. 'What is over?'

'I'm going home on Tuesday. That's it.'

'Drew!' Her cry whistled down the wire. 'Tell me when we shall meet. Tell me!'

Her desperation caused him to hold the receiver away from his ear. Shaking, he summoned the worst of visions: Katya straitjacketed, drugged, and terrified in a distant institution, never to see her children again. He took a deep breath and said: 'It would never work. I don't love you.'

'Drew – no. *No!*'

'I don't love you. I never loved you.'

She cried out, instinctive and animalistic. As it was uttered he knew the sound would haunt him for the rest of his life.

'Listen carefully,' he said. 'I was wrong. I misled you. I never loved you. I am going home on Tuesday and we will never speak after this call. Never.'

Again the cry, scraping his nerves.

'Goodbye, Katya.'

'My heart is broken!'

He put the receiver back in its cradle. In his mind's eye he saw her in the Star City flat, shattered and alone. His own life stretched away from this moment, a chain of mangled opportunities and ceaseless loss. Outside, the red stars of the Kremlin towers glowed inexorably.

SONG FOR KATYA

CHAPTER 31

For years afterwards, Drew's final days in Moscow were hard to reconstruct. His last conversation with Katya endured; the gig at Spaso House on Monday night was clear; the time between was hazy.

For most of those long hours he lay in bed, staring at the striped wallpaper and allowing self-pity its haphazard ebb and flow. He did not eat. The last of the whiskey stayed in the bottle. At times he felt absorbed into the underground life of the building, part of the pipework and wiring. He rose only to smoke and stare out the window.

But there were spikes of unavoidable activity. Later he recalled these scenes, compressed, dream-like, arranged in a warped chronology. He might as well have been high for all the sense he was able to make of those days, but faces had appeared, tasks were carried out, the minutes sifted. At some point he sat in the rear of a Lincoln Town Car, watching the dark streets unfurl. Visited Spaso House. Was measured for a tuxedo by a small Italian tailor. Went over the charts for the gig with the band. Salim hulked in the background, acting as if he knew the whole story. Had Drew told him, or had he gleaned the truth from Drew's despair?

His dreams were vivid, with a weight and clarity missing from his waking hours. In them he was falling, fording rivers, being pursued. They took place in past landscapes far more detailed than the pale forms of daytime memory. Running along Rattlesnake Creek, lungs burning, a white moon hanging above grey hills. Driving back roads in his dad's old pickup. Splashing along the creek's sedge-lined curves up to the pine-shadowed meadow above the town. Always moving. Always chased, anxious, in trouble. Always waking to a deep lone-liness that linked his current torment to the path-ways of his youth and the limitless Montana sky.

Katya was absent from these dreams. When he woke he wondered if he had excised her from his unconscious, and he pushed the bedclothes off his sweating body in distracted self-reproach. It was just as she had predicted. Love did turn to suffering. A cold, lonely, unredemptive anguish that crossed the borders of night and day.

Yet somewhere in that time of crisis the song had come to him, the notes blooming from an uncorrupted corner of his soul.

He remembered being propped between Marshall and Salim in the back seat of the embassy Town Car. Marshall whistled, while Drew looked out at the massed buildings, the piles of snow, the trundling Muscovites wrapped against the cold. The back of the driver's head was oiled and gleaming.

The ambassador's wife met them in the lobby of Spaso House. Mrs Wheelock was a tall, stately woman with iron-grey hair pulled up at the back and turquoise earrings that glittered when she moved her head. She stood beside a glass case that housed a stuffed bald eagle. In the lobby corner was a cigar-store Indian, which Salim eyed disdainfully. She shook their hands and led them at once to the ballroom.

'Mr Spinelli is waiting for you in the library,' she said, 'but I thought you might first like to see where you'll be playing tomorrow night. I want you to *approve*.' She inclined her head towards them and smiled with delicate irony. She reminded Drew of his mother, and into his soul's emptiness flowed another sadness. Poor Clare. What would she have told him now? That love was too much to hope for from this world? That music would have to suffice as consolation? But how could it compensate for total loss? Music that would not come to him anyway, entombed as he was in hopelessness.

In the domed ballroom a Steinway grand, polished to a brilliant sheen, sat beneath a gold and crystal chandelier. Mrs Wheelock said, 'Now, which of you plays the piano?'

Something, too, of Katya in her bearing and her intelligent eyes. Drew was too disturbed to answer. He was back in Mayakovsky Hall, on the day when she had played the Tchaikovsky rondo and he had begun to fall in love with her.

'That would be Fish,' Salim said. When she

373

raised her eyebrows Marshall introduced the band members, finishing with Drew.

'Please, try it out,' she urged. 'Tell me that the scandalous amount I paid to get it refurbished was well spent.'

He had no choice but to seat himself. He took off his jacket, adjusted the stool, wiped his hands on his trousers. An expectant silence filled the room. *Help me*, he thought, without the vaguest notion of where the words were aimed. *Help me, please*. His fingers rested on the keys. He had no will to move them, no ability to recall even the most familiar tune.

They all waited. The silence became an embarrassment, and Salim shifted from foot to foot. Then Drew's right hand played a new melody, a simple figure that seemed to well from everything he had lost: a father's confidence, a mother's guidance, a lover's trust. Jessie and Clare and now, most cruelly, Katya. He repeated the line, found the accompanying chords for his left hand. It had the definition of a finished composition. Something Bill Evans might have written. It would need work, but it was a real tune. He finished and bowed his head, saying nothing.

The final chord echoed in the dome above them. Salim stood still. 'Lovely,' Mrs Wheelock murmured.

The song got him through the tuxedo fitting. Mr Spinelli's small hands and fussy manner, Salim's fuming discontent, the sight of Marshall's surprisingly spindly legs below a dinner jacket. He worked the tune over in his head, adding voicings, filling in the bass line. He was eager to write it down. The winds of loss howled, but now he had something small to grasp, something to distract him from the pain. It was in waltz time, with a melody that descended gently and climbed back to the upper registers *in diminuendo* before blending into silence like smoke on a windless day.

Afterwards Mrs Wheelock led them to the dining room, where they were served tea and sandwiches. Wistful and relaxed, she spoke of her four years in Moscow and her friendship with Jimmy Carter. She asked them each about their background and interests. Drew answered in monosyllables, his right hand thrumming desperately against his thigh. He was relieved when Marshall stood up, thanked her, and led them to the car.

The hotel foyer was jammed with Japanese tourists checking in. The leather jackets were out in force. Marshall disappeared and Yoshi paused to watch his compatriots, his face lit with amusement. Before Drew could join Marshall in the elevator, Salim held him back.

'You OK?' Salim said.

'I want to go upstairs.'

'That tune. Where'd it come from?'

'It's mine.'

'Since when you writin' and not showin' me?'

A tiny confused couple in green slickers asked Yoshi for assistance. He pointed at the front desk.

Drew squeezed his forehead with his fingers. 'It came to me there. At the piano.'

'Don't be shittin' me.'

'I'm not.'

'Got to put that on the playlist, you know what I'm sayin'?'

Drew didn't respond.

'Shit,' Salim said, and Drew knew from his tone that his attention had turned elsewhere. He looked up and saw Reef lurching drunkenly towards them. He held his fur hat in front of him, like a blind man holding out his stick. Salim went to him, his own arm extended to help, but Reef pushed him aside and came to a swaying stop before Drew.

'So here you are,' Reef said. His glasses had slipped to the end of his nose and his eyes were watery and unfocused. On his neck was a triple stripe of welts, as if someone had clawed him. 'Here you are, preparing to leave.'

'We're not goin' anywhere,' Salim said. 'Not yet.'

Reef ignored him. He pointed at Drew with his hat. 'You make danger for us all. You come from your free country and act as if we also are free, and you make danger. And then you leave.'

'Fuck you, Reef.'

'Hey, now,' Salim said.

Reef's head swivelled with a drunk's careful imprecision. 'Say what you say. Make harsh comments. What do you know about Russian character? About Russian ways?'

Drew moved close enough to smell the liquor

on his breath. 'I know you were informing on us,' he said, his voice low. 'I know that while you were pretending to help you were screwing us, you son-of-a-bitch.'

'Us, what is this *us*?'

'Katya and me. You turned us in, and now you've ruined her life.'

The security boys stared across at them, and Salim moved to block their view.

'No. It is you,' Reef said. '*You* ruined her life.'

Drew hit him in the chest, more of a slap than a punch, but enough to send Reef sprawling on the polished floor. He lay there, legs thrust out at odd angles, his hat like a dead rabbit six feet away. Drew was shaking with anger and shame. Images of Benny Parsons on the subway platform, Jessie in the morgue, Lenin in his tomb flashed through his mind.

'Goddamn it, Drew,' Salim said. 'What the fuck you doin'?' He bent down and helped Reef to sit up. Reef was weeping. Drew knelt beside him. 'I'm sorry,' he whispered. 'I shouldn't have.'

'Do you believe everything you are told?' Reef said.

'I believed you. And look what happened.'

'You don't know anything. You don't know.'

'What's not to know? You told them.'

Reef's face twisted, his lip curled above discoloured teeth. 'You would prefer the alternative? For me *and* for her?'

'I would prefer the truth.'

Resolutely, savagely, Reef said, 'The truth? I loved her. That is the truth. I *do* love her.'

Drew stood, walked to the lift, punched the button, returned. 'Don't talk about love,' he said. 'If you loved her, why did you betray her?'

'I ask you the same. The very same.'

'Well, who does *she* love?'

But Drew's question was hollow. What did it matter now whom she loved? He *had* betrayed her. To save her, perhaps, but betrayed her all the same. As Reef had betrayed him. It was all over.

He and Salim helped Reef to his feet. He was weeping uncontrollably. 'Don't cry, Reef. Please don't cry.'

Salim had one hand on Reef's shoulder and the other on Drew's. To a security man peering at them he shouted: 'What the fuck you lookin' at?' The man took a drag from his cigarette and wandered off.

Hunched and limp, Reef would not stop crying. Drew took him into his arms as if he were a child. 'Please, Reef. It's okay.'

'I love her,' Reef said. 'I would never hurt her.'

'Ssh. Don't say anything. Please.'

Drew hummed softly, partly to soothe Reef, partly to block out the sounds of distress. From the reception desk the Japanese tourists headed for the lift, cameras around their necks, expensive overcoats hanging from slumped shoulders. Dragging giant suitcases on tiny wheels, they flowed around those in their way, one or two glancing curiously at the big black man in a *dashiki* and two white men in an odd embrace.

For several minutes Drew rocked Reef and hummed his calming song. It was the tune he had been working on all afternoon.

CHAPTER 32

Entering the ballroom in Spaso House on Monday night was like walking into a funeral parlour. Neat rows of Hitchcock chairs faced a crêpe-fringed bandstand. Sprays of yellow flowers, freshly watered, spilled from Oriental vases like those his mother had collected. The lighting was dim and the air dense with the smells of furniture polish and pot-pourri. Guests murmured in the lobby while the bleak emanations of a fractured day loosed themselves from Drew's skin and spiralled into the room's high dome. Lid propped high, the Steinway gaped like an open coffin. He took a deep breath and sat at the stool.

With the other musicians he checked the sound. The piano's action was superb, but the notes his fingers played were like dead leaves. He heard Mrs Wheelock telling the new arrivals how she had acquired the John Singer Sargent hanging in the hall. There was vague laughter, American somehow in its controlled joviality and Philistine tone. He waited for a curious head to poke itself through the door, but the band was left alone. He rolled up the sleeves of his tuxedo, then played some chords and limp scales. Salim frowned. A few resonant notes from Yoshi brought a fit of tears, but he recovered and did what was required of him. At least, for the moment, he didn't have to talk. Playing was tough, but facing the stuffed shirts before the gig would be tougher.

After a while they were tuned and loose and could delay no longer. They joined the reception in what was called the Blue Room, actually painted green. Salim put on his sunglasses before he went in and laughed at Yoshi's bow-tie, which was upside-down. White-coated waiters trudged about with trays of champagne and canapés. The guests – mostly service personnel from the Western embassies, with a sprinkling of friendly Soviets from the world of the arts – kept their distance.

A silver-haired man with a dentured smile and wire-framed glasses approached, hand extended. 'You must be Drew Fisher. I want to show you something.' He swivelled adroitly, in a way that suggested he was used to being followed. He pulled a book from a huge walnut case, flipped it open to a photograph at the centre, and handed it to Drew. Four men in tweed jackets and thin ties stood beneath an oak in full bloom; behind them Ivy League brickwork and mullioned windows. 'Spitting image. Knew as soon as I saw you.'

Drew's father stared out from the picture, confident, youthful, brash. A clump of tangled hair rose from his broad forehead. His hand lay on the shoulder of the young man next to him, a young man who had aged into the well-fed mandarin now at Drew's side.

'Harvard Square,' Drew said.

'Summer of 'thirty-nine,' the man said. 'Your dad was just back from China and I was running a special institute in Cambridge – think-tank, I guess you'd call it now. International relations. Cream of the cream were there but he was the man. What an intellect. Rest of us could barely keep up. Super-intelligent *and* street smart. The whole package.'

His dad was full of hard confidence and compressed ambition. The photographic context – academic pose, throwback black-and-white – deepened the intensity of the face.

Drew turned the book over and read the spine: *A Time of Passion*, by Robert H. Wheelock. He was the ambassador. An old friend of his dad. Hope flared. This guy had some power. 'You're the ambassador.'

'Bob Wheelock. You know, I had no idea until I saw you. What a kick. How's the old bastard doing anyway?'

The old bastard. Gazing up at his son from forty years ago, the rage in his face incipient but clear. What endings did he glimpse in the camera lens? Or was it all *becoming* at that point, kinetic energy and infinite appetite? Young John couldn't have known. Wouldn't have dreamed it. East Coast urbanite, man of the world, adviser to warlords, he was destined to close his days in a mountain lodge, embittered and alone.

And Drew was headed for the same place. Unless . . .

'I've been on the road,' Drew said, 'but he's doing okay, I guess.'

'He still in Montana?'

'Yeah.'

'When was the last time you talked to him?'

'Before I left. He didn't think it was a good idea for me to come here.'

Wheelock barked a laugh and slapped his thigh like an old-time comedian. 'I'll bet he didn't. Always favoured the Chinese, did old John. Did he ever tell you about the time we hosted the Soviet consul at the Hasty Pudding Club? A Stalin henchman if ever there was one, face like Vyshinsky, smug but vicious. Your old man screwed him to the wall, he did, had the guy wriggling, pinned by his own contradictions.' He shook his head with admiration. 'Guy could argue, let me tell you.'

'I know.'

The ambassador patted a generous belly and smoothed the ruffles of his dress shirt. He went quiet. Something in his mood had tilted.

'Mr Wheelock, can I ask you something? A favour?'

But the ambassador hadn't heard. His eyes were misty, focused on something well beyond the room, the moment. 'And Clare,' he said. He set a hand on Drew's arm. 'Oh, I know the news. Old news now, of course, but I'm sorry. Your mother was . . . exceptional.' He stroked his chin. 'Well, a lovely woman. A good woman.'

He glanced over at his wife, and Drew sensed a secret he would never know. That no one would ever know except Bob Wheelock. No one living, anyway. But what Drew did know was that he would not be asking for any eleventh-hour favours. That some secrets were destined.

Wheelock cleared his throat. 'Looking forward to hearing you guys. Our swan song tonight, I guess you know that. Reagan guy coming in next week and, let me tell you, I don't think you'll be hearing any jazz in Spaso House as long as *he*'s here.' He slapped Drew's shoulder and moved off.

Drew was conscious of intersecting worlds, cold stars, and infinite spaces where not even music could be heard.

A waiter in a red coat walked through the room ringing a bell. Showtime. Salim strode purposefully towards the door. Yoshi was cracking his knuckles. Marshall glanced at Drew, eyes and chin raised slightly: *You ready?* And if he wasn't? No bailing out on a gig, one of the unwritten rules. Anxiety seeped through him. His nerves were naked, and he had no sense of his ability to perform. Against all he was required to do, his tattered will seemed scarcely adequate. Knees quivering, he went to his post. Beneath the stool lay his music sheets, cigarettes, a folded towel. He sat on his hands to stop them shaking and faced the darkness.

The gig started poorly. Marshall had trouble finding his lungs; his sound was thin and costive. Salim roared out of the traps as usual and, in the absence of microphones, overwhelmed the other instruments. The sheathed women and overfed men in the front row leaned back at the percussive blast. The band whipped through 'Cherokee' and 'Confirmation'. Drew found it hard to keep up. To settle things down Marshall followed with his canned speech on 'the music we like to call jazz'. The audience, breathless and relieved, applauded the rhetoric. Drew stared at the keys as Marshall introduced the band. When his name was announced he nodded at the audience, catching sight of the Wheelocks, Bob's pink cheeks and glinting glasses, his wife's round, intelligent face.

They slowed it down with one of Marshall's compositions, a minor blues, followed by 'Bye Bye Blackbird'. Distracted by images of flight and distress, Drew played stiffly, and the music came to his ears as if he had no hand in its making. He was not listening to the songs as a musician should, to the chord changes, the instrumental interplay and harmonic possibilities, but with maudlin reference to personal events. He was going. She was gone. Ahead lay a dark road lined by familiar ghosts, beckoning him towards the ultimate absence.

At the next pause he lit a cigarette and moved the sheets from under the stool to the stand. In spite of the rocky start, something was beginning to happen onstage. Marshall had sorted out his sound. Yoshi was in a groove. And Salim had settled into his usual magnificence, explosive and swinging, tight with intense effort and fierce dedication. The purity of his commitment was physically revealed: sweaty face grimacing, arms swirling, body heaving as he grunted for joy.

So, gradually, as Salim laid down the beat and Marshall's improvising formed towering, oblique geometries in their heads, Drew's own efforts lifted, and he started playing for the sake of the song. They did a Coltrane set: 'India', 'Naima' and 'A Love Supreme'. Marshall's rough, bluesy tone kept them tethered to the earthly as they navigated the ethereal striving of the compositions. Drew yielded to instinct and soon found he was playing purely, intuitively. The audience had also made a leap. Maybe it was Salim's energy, maybe Marshall's musical authority, but they caught the mood and swung with the band, cheering and shouting as the sequence finished. The Wheelocks led the charge.

'Thank you,' Marshall said, 'thank you very much.' He allowed the audience to calm itself, then named the songs. 'We would like to continue now with another original composition, this one by our piano player, Drew Fisher. From Missoula, Montana, by way of New York, New York.' Catcalls and whistles. Marshall looked down at Drew, his face golden in the light. 'Drew has a new tune for us, brand new tune, which I believe he calls "Song for Katya".'

Marshall pulled his music stand close and moistened his reed. They had rehearsed the song only twice. Never before had he allowed a new composition – much less one that required him to put on his reading glasses – to be added mid-tour.

Yoshi did not need to read: he had memorized the chart. He and Drew began together, bass and piano chiming the cadenced, waltzing opening. The melody fell naturally, as if the notes had always existed in this configuration, and a shiver descended from Drew's hairline through his back and arms. This blissful rush was free of ego – the song and its arrangement had come to him so effortlessly that he could no more take credit for them than he could his love for Katya. As they restated the theme, Salim joined in, delicately glazing the cymbals with his brushes to create a sound like trees rustling in the wind. In whispering tones, Marshall played *obbligato* behind the melody, and the audience, raucous only moments before, was spellbound. As Drew began his solo he was in complete control of the room and his listeners.

A profound peace washed over him. The song wrapped itself around this time and place, suspending its particulars so that the moment became the centre of his life, with all its minutes, hours, days, weeks and years rippling out from the phrases of his solo. Past and present blended; all joy and sorrow were encompassed by the story the music told. As it had on the night at the Moscow Hotel when he first met her and she danced with Reef to 'Some Day My Prince Will Come', time slowed, then appeared to stop altogether. A swirling stillness reigned. His improvisation orbited the band, the audience, the people of his past. Behind it all, sustaining his vision, were the languor of Salim's brushwork, the singing of Yoshi's bass, and the breathy murmuring of Marshall's tenor. A single voice, expressing what he had written alone and interpreted now with the help of his friends. His family.

And in this waltz she was with him. Would always be with him. Their heartbreak was framed and presented by the tune, released from the clench of circumstance and the choke of pity. Their suffering, though not lessened, was given contrast and scope by the beauty of the music, and their isolation acquired the cold brilliance of stars. In this constellation he also saw his mother, Jessie, Bill Evans. But most of all he saw Katya, shining down upon her song as he played, and the audience held its breath and the notes ascended into the dome above them.

This song would always be. The underground life of his music had opened to include his secret love – a secret most painful because she would not share it. And though no one would understand his love but himself, it would keep growing in his heart like a song, endlessly improvised, endlessly beautiful. And when he was gone, and

Katya, too, like the others he had loved, the song would still be there, stretching into the future like the evening sky, its violet expanse arching over worn hills and fragrant firs, its star-flecked brilliance reflected in shadowed rivers flowing towards a mineral sea.